OTHER TITLES BY PETER TEMPLE

An Iron Rose
Shooting Star
In the Evil Day
The Broken Shore

THE JACK IRISH NOVELS
Bad Debts
Black Tide
White Dog

PETER TEMPLE
DEAD POINT

TEXT PUBLISHING
Melbourne Australia

The Text Publishing Company
Swann House
22 William Street
Melbourne Victoria 3000
Australia

Copyright © Peter Temple 2000
First published in Australia by Bantam 2000
This edition published by the Text Publishing Company 2006, reprinted 2007

Design by Chong Weng-ho
Typeset in 10.8/14 Baskerville MT by Midland Typsetters
Printed and bound by Griffin Press

National Library of Australia
Cataloguing-in-Publication data:

Temple, Peter, 1946- .
Dead Point.

ISBN 978 1 921145 00 1

1. Crime - Australia - Fiction. I. Title.
A823.3

For Gerhard and Karin,
dear friends, for all the good times:
Kom dans, Klaradyn.

On a grey, whipped Wednesday in early winter, men in long coats came out and shot Renoir where he stood, noble, unbalanced, a foreleg hanging. In the terminating jolt of the bolt, many dreams died.

Later, in the car, Cameron Delray sat behind the wheel, looked straight ahead and made no move to get going. Harry Strang, head deep in his old racing overcoat, held his knuckles to his forehead. After a while, he said, 'Act of God, no bloody insurance for that.'

I was in shock, rubbing my hands together, trying to comfort myself. Most of them you can lose easily and there are fifty reasons why. This was the one we couldn't lose. If the ground was firm. If the horse didn't miss the start, and this horse was not going to miss the start, it was the best-schooled horse in the world, if it didn't miss the start, it could street the small field by at least six lengths, probably ten.

And nobody knew that except us.

The ground was firm. It didn't miss the start.

All Renoir had to do was run 1000 metres. On lazy days, not pushed, we had clocked him doing that in around 57 seconds. Only one horse running against him had come close to such a time. Afterwards, that creature swabbed positive for Melazanine and hadn't run under 65 since.

So that didn't count. Drug-assisted times don't count.

The day before, Harry Strang, walking next to Kathy Gale, big hand holding her elbow, said, 'Can't win with you up, he can't win. Just mind you get him out with em, keep him away from em, don't touch him, he'll do the rest.'

All Kathy had to do was get the horse to jump cleanly out of gate number six, just urge him on, one bend, it didn't matter about looking for the short path, being out wide meant nothing, he could beat them if he ran on the grand-stand rail, the horse was ten lengths better than any of the competition. Just go for the judge.

Renoir, black as the grave, stood in the stall with the patient air of a Clydesdale, no sign of nerves. The VE 4000 showed me a calm, intelligent eye and Kathy Gale's face, her mouth, the upper teeth resting on the plumped pillow of the lower lip, the tooth next to the canine that jutted slightly, that broke the rank of her seagull-white choppers.

I saw Kathy put out a hand and rub Renoir under his left ear. It twitched. He liked that; she had done it to him hundreds of times. They stood in the gate, a horse and a small rider, at their ease, friends, together greatly superior to the men and animals on either side of them. And when she urged him, he would respond with a great thrust of dark and gleaming thighs.

The race caller said, 'Three to come in, very serious plunge on Renoir for a horse with one place from nine starts, never run this distance. He's shrunk from 30–1 to outright favourite, 4–5 on, pressure of the money, started as a trickle. Not just the bookmakers either. TAB pool is astonishing for a pretty ordinary autumn race.'

A pool swollen by our money, ours and the money of all the price-watchers who got on with us in the last moments before betting closed.

'Last one goes in, that's Redzone,' said the caller, 'the line's good, light flashing…'

The moment.

The gates opened and they came out together, eight abreast, but only for a moment because Renoir needed no more than half-a-dozen strides to draw away, a length, two, three. Then Kathy settled him, didn't let him bolt, used what she knew about sitting on horses to manage him. Just before the bend, she looked over her shoulder, just a jerk of the head, saw the inadequate herd well behind her, and she took the horse over to the rail. In the straight, Renoir's dominance was complete. With three hundred to go, he was six lengths clear and Kathy was riding him hands and heels, copybook riding, and drawing further ahead with each stride.

'Well, isn't this easy,' said the caller. 'Renoir's thrashing this field, drilling the bookies who got caught early, he's in another league altogether and Kathy Gale isn't even…'

I had Kathy and Renoir in perfect focus, all grace and power, an unbidden smile on my face, and then I saw her head drop and her arms in their silken sleeves go forward to clutch the lovely black neck and I saw shining horse and rider falling, falling, falling, all gainliness gone, all grace and power departed in a split second of agony.

They fell and she lay still and he, the proud and lovely creature, struggled to stand and the field had plenty of space in which to part and ride around them so that some undeserving twosome could be declared winners.

Now, in the car, Harry took his hands from his face and fastened his seatbelt. 'Home,' he said, 'have a bit of Bolly, thank the stars the Lord didn't taketh away the girl.'

On the way, on the hideous tollway, in post-adrenalin shock, I was thinking about life, the brevity, the silliness, my life in particular, the fragility of life, how unfair it was that the huge burden should be carried on such slender and brittle supports, when Cam said, driving with two fingers in a suicidal rush of trucks and boofheads, petrolheads, 'The giveth is we got average fifteen with the books, just on ten on the tote.'

I sat up, heart pumping as if from a dream of flight, enraged and irrational. 'You put money on that?' I said. 'A fucking thing not fit to lick Renoir's boots, shoes, whatever, hooves, bloody hooves…'

Harry had his head back, against the headrest. 'Jack,' he said, sadly, 'they don't have races with only one horse.'

I slumped in my seat, a child gently chastised. How often do you have to be told some things?

Lyn, the fourth Mrs Harry Strang, opened a French door at the side of the mellow red-brick house as we came up the gravel path from the carriage-house. She had the sexy look of someone who'd been running, followed by a hot shower and a rough towelling. Her right hand came up, fell. She knew. She was once a trainer's wife, she knew.

'Had better days,' said Harry without being asked anything. 'Might have the bubbly in the study, love.'

In the awesome room, we stood with our backs to the five-metre-high wall of books that held everything ever published on horses and horse racing and looked out across the terrace and the lawn and the yew hedges to the naked maples moving like things possessed.

There was a knock. Cam opened the door in the library wall and Mrs Aldridge came in with a tray. I saw the delicacies, salivated. I'd had them before and they featured in my dreams. Ethereal capsules, a shell of champagne batter just puffed in hot oil. Inside, the teeth would meet a fresh oyster wrapped in tissue-thin smoked salmon.

Lyn Strang followed, three flutes on a silver tray, a bottle of Bollinger, uncorked, stoppered with a sterling silver device.

Harry looked at his two women. 'What would I do?' he said, head to one side. I had never seen him like that.

'Stuff yourself with all the wrong things,' said Mrs Aldridge, sharply. She left the room.

Harry looked at Lyn. 'Glass short,' he said.

'No,' said Lyn. 'Can't bear racing post-mortems.'

She touched his cheek, smiled, a brisk nurse smile, and left.

Harry poured. Cam and I waited for the toast, Harry always proposed a toast to the next time. It didn't come. He sipped, and we sipped. My eyes met Cam's.

'Well,' Harry said, putting his glass down on the tray, looking out at his garden, 'I'm thinkin of givin it away.'

I didn't want to hear this. It had been in my mind from the moment he said, 'What would I do?'

'An act of God,' said Cam. He was holding his flute to the light, studying the minute bubbles. 'Whoever that is. There'll be better days.'

'Not today's stuff,' said Harry, still not looking at us. 'That's the business. The punt's the punt, can't cop it, drop it. The commissioner, that's what makes me think it's time to shut the shop.'

'We'll fix the Cynthia thing,' said Cam. 'We're workin on that.'

I wanted to second Cam's statements but I didn't believe them and I couldn't find a quick reassuring lie.

Harry picked up his glass, had a generous sip, shook his head, pretended to cheer up. 'Got to be good for ya, don't ya reckon?' he said.

'We'll fix the Cynthia thing,' repeated Cam.

Cynthia had been the commission agent for four big plunges, marshalling teams of old-age pensioners, young-age pensioners, the bored, a retired bank manager, two strippers gone to flab, an ageing hooker relishing undemanding vertical work.

The most recent plunge had been a simple matter involving a nightclub owner who believed, correctly, that a non-performing horse he secretly owned through his sister-in-law's cousin would show unexpected ability in a feature race at Flemington.

Afterwards, Cynthia had collected the large sum her platoon of punters had taken off the bookies. She was in her old Mazda, driving to meet Cam, cruising down a narrow Yarraville street, when a four-wheel drive forced her to the kerb. Two men got out, asked for the money. She said she didn't think that was on, and, in full view of an old man on sticks and a woman on a bicycle, one of the men punched her in the face six or seven times, held her by the hair, turned her head and broke her jaw and her nose and impacted her cheekbones. When they were gone, she got Cam on her mobile, speaking thickly through the blood and the crushed cartilage, then lost consciousness.

Cam more or less drove across country to reach her, ignoring traffic lights and stop signs and other vehicles, took her to Footscray General. The number the woman on the bicycle had written down belonged to a vehicle stolen less than an hour earlier. It was found in the city, in Latrobe Street, just after 6 p.m.

Cynthia now had less than forty per cent sight in one eye. We weren't going to be able to fix Cynthia. And the Cynthia thing wasn't any easier.

'Can't get over that,' said Harry. 'Not a thing used to happen. Bash a woman like that, bastards'd do anythin.'

I knew what he was thinking. He was thinking about his women: his wife, thirty years his junior, the final fling, and his housekeeper of thirty-five years, a person who left England for him, left home and kin to look after a broken-bodied jockey. He was thinking about Lyn and Mrs Aldridge because he loved them and he was fearful for them. Not for himself, not for Harry Strang, the champion jockey of whom an English racing writer once wrote, 'In his presence, agitated English horses become calm and calm English jockeys lose their composure.'

Cam knew too. He finished his glass, poured for us, for himself. 'Just run-through boys,' he said, his face expressionless. 'Too clever for banks, too lazy for drugs. Somebody told em about Cyn, one of her troops would be right. We'll get there, sort it out.'

We wouldn't. Cam and I had already been over Cynthia's troops. All we found was that one had gone to Queensland suddenly. So did we. We joined the woman at her ailing aunt's bedside. She was so shocked and showed so little evidence of new-found riches that Cam slipped her two $100 notes when we left.

'Won't make any quick decision,' said Harry. 'Nothin comin up, sleep on it for a bit.'

We finished the bottle and didn't move on to the customary second one. Harry came to the front gate with us, out in the blustery night, trees thrashing, held me back, fingers like a bulldog clip on my left bicep.

'Two knocks in a row, Jack,' he said, 'you'll be hurtin. Not a write-off, though. Get twenty-five, thirty cents in the dollar back, thereabouts.'

'Can't drop it, cop it,' I said. 'Isn't that right?'

He squeezed my arm, more pain. 'Remember the Bank of Strang, cash advances for the creditworthy. Also, a little legal matter, need some consultin. Next week suit?'

'Day and night,' I said.

'Cam'll make a time.'

He let go. We looked at each other. 'Harry,' I said, no mental activity preceding what followed, pure emotion. 'Cynthia. We'll take care of that.'

The front door of the house opened. Over Ha[rry?]
I saw Lyn Strang, short, strong, warm peach-colou[r]
on her hair and shoulders, a carpet of peach laid aroun[d]
shadow on the broad verandah. 'I wanted to say goodb[ye,]
I was upstairs,' she said, something in her tone, not relief but
something like that.

In the street, beyond the high red-brick wall, Cam
started the transport we'd come in, a much-modified vehicle
apparently known to some as an eight-bore streetslut. It
made a feline noise, the sort of sound a prehistoric giant
sabre-toothed tiger might have made.

I raised my hand at Lyn. She waved back.

'We'll fix it,' I said to Harry, repeating the stupid, unful-
fillable promise.

'Wouldn't surprise me,' Harry said, no confidence in his
voice. 'Pair of bright fellas like yerselves.'

Cam drove me to my place of residence, the old boot
factory in North Fitzroy, early Saturday night traffic. Lots
of taxis, sober people going out for a good time. He double-
parked outside, turned down Bryan Ferry on the eight-bore's
many speakers.

'The big man's a worry,' he said. He lit a Gitane with his
Zippo, rolled down his window. 'Seen it comin for a while.'

Cold air and the pungent Gallic smoke sent a tremor
of craving through me. 'There's nowhere else to go on
Cynthia,' I said.

'Cyril,' said Cam. 'Come at it from Cyril's end.'

We dealt with Cynthia through Cyril Wootton, professional middleman, dead-end and cut-out, collector of
non-enforceable debts, finder of witnesses, skips, shoot-
throughs and no-shows, and my occasional employer.

'Cyril's deeply shonky,' I said, 'but this, no.'

9

'Can't leave him out,' he said. 'Can't
turned his head and looked at me,
hing, wanting me to agree to the

talk to him tomorrow.'

...ing out when Cam said, 'Jack, this trot, it'll end,
don't be shy.'

He too was offering to lend me money.

'Thanks,' I said. 'Could come to that.'

I watched him drive away, slowly in the quiet street, the
deep, feral sound of eight cylinders entering the blood-
stream, agitating it.

There wasn't anything else to do but light the fire in a clean grate, prepared on a nervous race-day morning with scrunched paper, kindling, a few sticks of bone-dry wood, cut and split and chopped and delivered by Harry Strang's man in Avoca. He was the owner of a calm grey mare called Breckinridge, a horse now burdened only by the weight of children. It had been four lengths clear when it won the Ballarat Cup at 30–1, and from then on some people got their wood free and I got mine at a discount.

There was a time when I thought I'd never go back to the boot factory. Having your home blown up by people who want to kill you can have that effect. But when the time came to decide, I couldn't let an explosion rob me of the place I'd shared with someone I loved beyond the telling of it. I packed my bags and left the converted stable I'd been living in, grown used to, and went back to where I'd kissed Isabel goodbye on the day a mad client of mine murdered her in a carpark. I walked up the stairs, unlocked the front door, went down the passage to the big, empty living room, looked around, opened a window, and I was home.

Ignite the fire, watch that Avoca kindling go up like a cypress hedge. Now, to the kitchen. What follows Bollinger and oysters in champagne batter? Perhaps a slice of sirloin, a thick slice, moist and ruddy in the centre, served with a cream, mustard and finely-chopped caper sauce, some small vegetables on the side. Yes, but the kitchen wasn't going to run to that. Next. Open the fridge. There was a piece of corned beef. A corned-beef, cheddar and pickle sandwich and a glass, glasses, of Heathcote shiraz, that was what it was going to run to.

How old can corned beef get before it kills you? I sniffed and pondered, studied the iridescent surface of the chunk of meat and, sadly, decided that risk outweighed reward. Now it was cheddar and pickle, mature cheddar, not mature when bought but now most certainly. And then it flashed through my mind that it was bread that made the Earl of Sandwich's innovation possible, you needed bread. Next.

I thought briefly about getting out the Studebaker Lark, agonised, then rang Lester at the Vietnamese takeaway in St Georges Road. Lester answered, a non-committal sound with which I was familiar. He was a client. I'd sorted out a small matter that troubled him. For an immoderate fee, in cash, a woman lawyer in Richmond had done the paperwork needed to bring his aged mother into the country. Then a man came around and told Lester that it would cost $150 a week, also in cash, to keep his mother from being sent back. The money would be passed on to a corrupt official in Canberra.

Lester had been paying for three years when he consulted me, referred by someone he wouldn't name. I made some inquiries, then spoke to the Richmond solicitor on the telephone. She had no idea what I was talking about, she said, highly offended and haughty. I didn't say anything for a while, then I said I'd appreciate a bank cheque for $23,400 payable to Lester, delivered to me by hand inside the hour.

She laughed, a series of starter-motor sounds. 'Or what?' she said.

'Or you can practise law in Sierra Leone,' I said. 'How's that for an or?'

A silence. 'Your name again?'

'Irish, Jack Irish.'

Another silence. 'Are you the one who killed that ex-cop and the other guy?'

My turn to be silent, then I said, 'I wasn't charged with anything.'

The cheque arrived inside an hour. I took it around to the takeaway and gave it to Lester's wife.

A few days later, Lester knocked on my office door. He was carrying a sports bag and he didn't appear overjoyed. 'How much?' he said. 'You?'

I wrote out a bill for $120. He studied it, looked at me, studied it again. Then he unzipped his bag and put wads of notes on my table, fifties, twenties, perhaps five or six thousand dollars, more, in used notes.

Temptation had run its scarlet fingernails down my scrotum. What did it matter? A success fee, that's all it was. Merchant bankers took success fees. But I wasn't a merchant banker. People like that grabbed what they could within the law. In my insignificant way, I represented the law. I was a sworn officer of the court. I was a thread in an ancient fabric that made social existence possible.

I *was* the law.

Sufficiently psyched up by these thoughts, I leaned across the tailor's table, plucked two soiled fifties and a twenty, pushed the rest back his way.

'Lester,' I said, 'not all lawyers are the same.'

Now I said, 'Lester, it's Jack. Any chance of Bruce dropping off some food?'

'How many?'

'One.'

'Fifteen minutes,' he said. 'Jack, you want prawns?'

'Lester, I need prawns.'

A glass later, the buzzer sounded and I went downstairs and opened the door to bright-eyed Bruce, the elder of Lester's two teenage sons. He'd come on his bike, cardboard box on the carrier. I tried to give him some gold coins but he was under instructions. 'No thanks,' he said. 'My dad says no-one's allowed to take money from you.'

Virtue may be its own reward, but there are other possible spin-offs.

I said, 'I wish that were a universal principle, Bruce.'

He smiled, he got it. No shonky lawyer was ever going to get fat on this new Australian.

Upstairs, the phone rang. I made haste up the old, squeaking stairs, both hands on the food box. Lyall had been known to ring on a Wednesday night, Thursday night, any night, from any time zone, usually from some troubled place, satellite phone borrowed from the CNN person or a UN person or, once, from the head of the Chechen mafia.

'Irish,' I said, winded. It was a handy name, you could say it as a sigh, one syllable, a longer surname would have had to become double-barrelled.

'Jack, Jack,' said Cyril Wootton, his resigned voice. 'Whatever became of obligation, of sense of duty?'

My breath came back in a reasonable time. Recently I'd been running around Edinburgh Gardens in the early morning, going up Falconer Street and down Delbridge to Queen's Parade, running and walking, limping really, streets empty, sometimes a dero lying on the pavement, clenched like a fist against the cold, the occasional pale young man with dark eye sockets and a stiff-legged walk, and always the three women at the tram stop, head-scarves, smoking and talking quietly, perhaps the last sweatshop workers to live in the gentrified suburb.

'Got no idea, Cyril,' I said. 'I don't follow the greyhounds. Never bet on anything that's trying to catch something else, that's the principle. Good names, though.'

In the moment before he spoke again, I heard the sounds of his midweek haunt, a pub in Kew he stopped off at to slake the thirst he developed after leaving the Windsor in Spring Street.

It was a raffish spot for Kew: two financial advisers had once fought to tears in the toilet, and the legend was that three pairs of women's underpants were found in the beer garden after a local real-estate agency's Christmas party in 1986.

Wootton expelled breath. 'There is considerable anxiety,' he said. 'I am under pressure to produce results. And you cannot be contacted.'

I felt some contrition. I hadn't done any serious looking for Robbie Colburne, occasional barman.

'Feelers are out, Cyril,' I said.

'What feelers?'

'He's not using his vehicle, that narrows things.'

'Narrows? There was no belief in Cyril's voice. 'Are you saying he hasn't gone anywhere?'

'Within limits.'

The trawl through the airlines hadn't produced the name but that meant nothing. You could give any name if you paid cash to fly or you could travel by bus or taxi or a friend could give you a lift or you could ride your bicycle out of town, rollerblade, run, walk, limp.

'Quite,' he said in his assumed Coldstream Guards officer's voice. 'Is he spending?'

'He's a part-time barman. What would he have to spend?'

'So you've got nothing to show for three days?'

'Cyril,' I said, 'I'm probably being over sensitive, but, at this moment, my inclination is to say bugger off, get someone else. Silly, but that's my state of mind.'

While Wootton weighed up his options, I listened to a surf of witty real-estate and financial-advice banter, the women shrieking, the men baying like hounds, randy hounds.

'Jack,' he said, 'it's serious.'

Even against that background of happy parasites at play, I recognised a Wootton plea.

'Tomorrow,' I said. 'My total attention to this matter.'

He caught my tone, knew that I was in earnest. 'Yes. Give me a ring, old chap.' I'd be giving him more than a ring. I'd be paying him a visit, and the thought gave me no pleasure.

By ten, I was in bed, betwixt fresh linen sheets, steaming Milo on the bedside table, classical FM on the radio. In my hands, I held a novel about young Americans undergoing rites of passage in Venezuela.

All alone at the end of the day. Lyall no doubt in some godforsaken country.

Outside, a cold rain was falling on the city. I didn't need to go out to know that. I could feel it in my heart.

I woke before daylight without need of an alarm, splashed my face, put on the saggy old grey tracksuit and went shuffling through the park, around the streets. In Delbridge Street, an insane Jack Russell terrier threw himself against his front gate with a hideous bark-shriek, catching me by heart-stopping surprise for the fiftieth time. The dog would have to die. There was no other way.

Back home, I lay in the huge cast-iron bath for an hour, drinking tea, tapping off cold water, running in hot, reading the *Age*, ruminating on creeping flab and aching knees and other matters of the corpus. Then I dressed in sober business clothing and drove to Meaker's in Brunswick Street for breakfast. Meaker's had been the writing on the wall for working-class Brunswick Street when it opened in the late 1970s, serving breakfast at all hours to people with vague artistic leanings who didn't know what time it was and couldn't afford to eat at home because of the infrastructure required. Now the whole street provided that service and lots, lots more.

'The look I like,' said Carmel, the newest waiter. Despite having the appearance of a 14-year-old waif, she had been married twice and now, sensibly, had retired from dud men, any men, and was the companion of a sleek home-wares buyer for a shop called Noir. I knew this because she had told me, unbidden and unencouraged, when we met by chance early one evening soon after her debut at Meaker's. Much has been learned, not all of it life-affirming, at the Brunswick

Street laundromat. Something about the place—its tropical warmth, the sullen chugging of the machines, the way the newly cleansed garments swirl and flirt and twine in the perforated stainless-steel drums—encourages intimate revelations.

Down there on the left bank of the river Brunswick, Carmel spoke freely about her life and aspirations. Then her companion arrived to fetch her, a severely edited person, nothing more could be subtracted from her dress or manner or speech without her being rendered partially unclothed or immobile or incomprehensible.

'Good tie that,' said Carmel now.

I said thank you.

'My first only ever used his ties to tie me up,' said Carmel. 'Mind you, they were school ties, greasy, ballpoint marks and bits of food on them. He went to Wesley.'

'That's really the only use for old Wesley ties,' I said. 'Melbourne Grammar boys sometimes tie theirs around their waists when they're naked or use them to commit suicide.'

Carmel nodded. 'Or for scarfing,' she said. 'Like that singer. What can I get you?'

'Just toast and tea,' I said. 'Italian breakfast tea.'

'One latte,' she said.

Afterwards, I caught a tram into the city, stood all the way to Collins Street with the barely awake and the glowing pre-dawn joggers, the perfectly made up and the bloodily shaven, the hanging out and the merely hungry.

Offloaded, I took myself up the stairs of the stone building to face Mrs Davenport. I found the bureau chief to Cyril Wootton, CEO of Belvedere Investments, in her usual rigid position behind a desk in the firm's panelled reception room.

'Corporal Wootton fronted yet?' I asked. I'd known the man when he was a redistributor of military stores, an illegal wholesaler of Vegemite and Tim Tams and Tooheys beer, a saboteur of the war effort in Vietnam.

The silver-haired exemplar drew breath and it pinched her nostrils. Nothing else ever moved. There was no knowing her age; she had mummified her face through discipline. 'I'm afraid Mr Wootton's engaged,' she said. 'Would you like to wait indefinitely or make an appointment?'

Mrs Davenport knew precisely how dubious Wootton was, how thin and swaying was the rope he walked, and yet she had no difficulty in presenting herself as if she were Moralist-in-Residence at the Centre for Applied Ethics.

'The former,' I said, 'I'll just sit down and look at you and puzzle over how a person so coldly beautiful can also be so warm and caring.'

She left the room, came back inside ten seconds and said, 'Mr Wootton will see you.'

Wootton was behind his big oak desk, palms on the top, every centimetre the bank manager of the 1950s, essence of jovial probity, careful with the bank's money but decent and understanding, a man who never failed to count that air shot on the golf course that no-one saw. He pointed to the client's chair.

'Early for you. Reforming your habits?'

I didn't sit down. I went close to the desk, loomed over him.

'Cynthia.'

He frowned. 'Yes?'

'Cam thinks you might be the one.'

Wootton's hand went to his collar, fingers inserted above the tie knot, four fingers, not much room there.

'Fuck, Jack,' he said, 'are you…?'

I didn't say anything, just kept looking into the brown eyes of Corporal Wootton, a corporal of stores. There wasn't much to see.

'Jesus,' he said, emotion in his voice, 'he can't be bloody serious. Jesus, Jack, he's not serious? Don't tell me Harry…'

'Cyril,' I said, 'if you are the one, say so now. I'll give you two hours to arrange to give the money back, plus a hundred and fifty grand for Cynthia's pain and suffering. And that's letting you off lightly. You then disappear. Forever. I'll try to keep Cam from coming after you. Try, that's all I can do.'

He looked at me in despair, mouth opening and closing. 'No, Jack,' he said, 'no, no, no. You can kill me but no, never, I don't know anything about it, she's a friend of mine. I would never…Cam's mad, I'd never ever do anything…'

He tailed off, closed his eyes, squeezed them tight, shook his head like a dog with a grass seed in an ear.

'Say so now, Cyril. You don't want to wait for other circumstances. Hanged through the Achilles tendon from a meat hook, those circumstances.'

'I swear. I swear. No. Jesus, no.'

I sat down. 'I'll take your word on that,' I said. 'I hope that's not a foolish thing to do.'

Cyril opened his eyes, blinked rapidly, straightened his pin-striped shoulders, regained some composure. 'Don't take my word,' he said. 'I don't want you to take my word. Tell Cam to check me out, every last thing.'

'I'll tell him I believe you when you say you had nothing to do with it.'

Cyril looked away, stroked his tie, a regimental tie, though certainly not the tie of his regiment. 'Do you?' he said.

'For the moment.'

His head turned. 'I should bloody well hope so,' he said in a cub-lion growling tone, recovering rapidly. 'This your idea of fun?'

'Of kindness, more,' I said. 'It was me or Cam. Or worse. Both. But I'd be lying if I said I didn't enjoy your snivelling.'

'Christ,' he said, sniffed, 'threatening me, you're supposed to be a lawyer.'

'Things not always incompatible. I'm going to tell Cam I don't think you need shaking. That's an act of faith. If I'm wrong, Cyril, I'll be there to see you dropped into that compactor in Hopper's Crossing. They say it makes a noise like a dog chewing chicken bones.'

'Jack.' He cocked his head in pain.

'Moving on then. I can't look for this Colburne prick on what you've given me. What's the story?'

Cyril composed himself in an instant. 'In that matter, your services are no longer required.'

I shook my head. 'What's this, revenge? Don't be petulant, Cyril.'

He pointed to a copy of the *Herald Sun* on his desk. 'Page five,' he said, an expression of distaste on his face.

I opened the paper at the page. The first item in a single-column collection of briefs had the headline: *Body in garage*.

The story said: *A man was yesterday found dead in a car in a garage in Rintail Street, Abbotsford. Police identified him as Robert Gregory Colburne, 26, a casual barman.*

The story went on to say that police were treating the death as accidental but were keen to talk to anyone who had seen Colburne recently.

'There endeth the lesson,' said Wootton, cold as the widow's lips. 'Now, if you'll excuse me, I have matters to attend to. People depend upon my understanding the concept of urgency.'

I saw no reason to prolong this encounter or to say goodbye. Time would heal. Or not. At the door, turning the big fluted brass knob, I heard Wootton clear his throat.

'In his own vehicle,' he said, 'in his own garage.'

I continued on my way. As I passed Mrs Davenport in the anteroom, her nostrils contracted fractionally. 'This has been prepared for you, Mr Irish,' she said.

I stopped. She held out a hand, pearl-coloured nails, perfect ovals, and young hands, hands far too young. What secrets had this woman learned during her long stint in the pay of a specialist in sexually-transmitted diseases? I shuddered inwardly, took the envelope she was offering and left the premises.

On the tram, enjoying the presence of a few teenage drug dealers heading for Fitzroy, I opened Mrs Davenport's envelope: a cheque for three days' work at the usual rate.

Out loud, I said, 'Cyril, oh Cyril.'

One of the adolescent drugporteurs not on his mobile heard my utterance, misunderstood completely, turned, made the selling signal.

I gave him the look and the continental flicking fuck-off sign. Although he was probably untravelled, he got the message.

As I had received Cyril Wootton's message. That he behaved honourably even when I did not.

Detective Sergeant Warren Bowman had the good-humoured manner of a man in sales, not any old sales, specialised sales, motor spares or plumbing supplies or bearings, some secure line of work where the pros know stock numbers off by heart and the customers expect them to say things like 'Almost got me there, mate' and 'We have the technology'.

'They're sayin it's an ordinary OD,' he said.

We were sitting in the Studebaker Lark just off St Kilda Road, the day turned irritable, periods of sunshine, sudden snarls of rain. Detective Sergeant Bowman was speaking to me courtesy of another policeman, Senior Sergeant Barry Tregear, someone I'd known since I was a boy sent to fight abroad for my country. At the request of some other country, the way it had always been for Australia.

'Family doesn't want to know that,' I said, lying.

Warren turned his long head and appraised me. He had bushy black eyebrows that he brought together and parted: quick, slow, slow, quick, an eyebrow Morse code.

'Yeah, well, not always your best judge,' he said, dot, dot, dash. 'The family.'

'No. Funny place to OD.'

Dot, dash. 'Well, they don't set out to OD.'

'Shooting up in his garage? Be more comfortable in his unit.'

Dash, dot. 'No knowin. It's like suicide. Go a long way, some of em. Mountains, some, they like to go to high places.

But there's others want to creep away. Toppin's a bit like hide and seek, know what I mean? Some kids always go for the wardrobe.'

Expertise in dark matters. Warren knew these stock numbers.

A couple walked by, young, handsome in black clothing, arguing, heads flicking, spurts of words. He stopped, she stopped, he raised a hand, inquiring. She knocked it away in contempt, walked. The man waited for a few seconds, turned and came back towards us, jaw moving, small chewing movements.

'He's bin screwin around,' said Warren. 'Some blokes got no idea when they're lucky.' There was a stain of resentment on his tone.

'So Robbie went into his garage, locked the door, got into his car, shot up, that's it?'

He nodded.

'The fit's there?'

A nod.

'Tracks?'

'Yeah. User.'

'User ODs alone in his Porsche parked in his garage. That would be unusual, wouldn't it?'

Warren shifted in his seat, looked at me, dash, dot, dash, took his lower lip between thumb and forefinger, gave it a tug. 'I'm in the box here, am I?'

You forget that people are doing you a favour, at some risk to their careers.

'Sorry,' I said. 'Get carried away.'

He kept looking at me, a long dash.

The angry young woman in black was coming back, in a hurry, full of regret, hoping to catch the man. Her calf-length coat was unbuttoned and it flapped open at every stride, long legs flashing, pale legs.

'Jesus, women,' said Warren, tone pure resentment now. 'Fucking looks, all the bastard's got is looks.'

'For some things,' I said, 'all you need is looks. The key to the garage, he have that on him?'

He said nothing.

I looked upon the empty winter street, trees pen-and-ink lines against the sky, first hint of closure now, the imperceptible dimming of the light that some part of the cortex recognises.

Nothing more to be gained from this encounter. I said my thanks. Warren didn't seem eager to leave the comfort of the old, squat American V-8 beast.

I said, 'Warren, Robbie, any form?'

He shook his head.

'A person of interest?'

He didn't congratulate me on my intelligence, opened his door. 'Thought you'd never ask,' he said. 'As I understand it, definitely. The car that attended, they called in, next thing two drug squad heavies are there, the uniform boys are back on the road.'

I said, 'I'm not cross-examining here but are you still saying they actually believe this bloke's an OD?'

Warren turned to me, a shrug, his eyebrows went dot, dash, dot, dash above the friendly salesman's eyes. 'Believe?' he said. 'I dunno what they believe. Believe in a Big Mac and large fries. They *say* there's nothin says anythin else. What they *believe* I haven't got a clue, mate.'

'Any chance of a snap of the bloke?' Cyril didn't have one.

He sighed. 'I'll see. Duty calls. Cheers.'

I watched him go. He crossed the street, walked down some distance, crossed back and went to his car. He didn't drive off immediately, waited a while. A cautious man. Still, there was every reason to be cautious if the drug squad was involved in the matter of Robbie Colburne.

The Prince of Prussia was busy for a Thursday evening, any evening, at least twelve customers. To the left of the street door, a table of young people in black and shades of grey lowered the average age of the patrons by about 25 years. As I came in the person nearest to me, a cropped-haired blonde, said, 'I mean, he's too *exhausted* for sex and then I get up to pee, it's like 2.30 a.m., he's on the net perving at this bondage porn. Extreme bondage. It's his net-pal in Canada tied up like a salami. How gross is that?'

'Well, the net's essentially a passive medium,' said the woman next to her.

'This was active,' said the blonde. 'He was interacting. I know interacting when I see it.'

I didn't move, looked around the room. The Fitzroy Youth Club were in position at the far end of the bar, within easy reach of the door marked GENTS.

At the black and grey table, a shaven-headed man, scalp the colour of the underside of an old tortoise, said, 'I can tell you guys worse.'

I couldn't go without knowing worse, couldn't move.

'I had this partner,' said the man, fat finger pushing at his round dark glasses, 'he comes home, he's faceless, right, he's with this Arab taxi driver and he goes: "Meet Ahmed or whatever, he's your co-driver for the night."'

A thin woman with a beaky nose leaned forward, shook her head and made a contemptuous sound. 'Worse? Jesus, grow up, I'll give you worse.'

Conquering my desire to hear baldy's poignant tale eclipsed by some other speakable act of sexual unmannerliness, I moved to join the three men at the end of the battered bar. They were not young, not shaven-headed, not in black or fashionable shades of grey. They were ancient and in colours from the chewing tobacco, snuff and washed-out old mauve cardigan end of the spectrum. Of depravity, they could know a great deal: more than 230 years of experience sat in this brown corner.

'So, Jack,' said Norm O'Neill, nodding at my reflection in the speckled mirror we faced, 'deignin to grace us with your presence.'

I said, 'I don't have anywhere else to go.'

'Had to take a taxi,' said Eric Tanner, the man next to him. 'Bloody fortune. Extortionists.'

'I was up north,' I said.

It was expected that the Lark would convey the men to St Kilda games, with a stop on the way to place a few bets. Once it had been to Fitzroy games but we didn't have Fitzroy anymore, Fitzroy didn't suit the national league's plans, so they took the club around the back and drilled it between the eyes. Now we supported St Kilda, my idea, a misguided attempt to cheer up the lads, give them something new to argue about, something to do on weekends.

'Up *where*?' said Norm, as though I'd invented a new compass point. He adjusted the fit of the spectacles on his promethean nose.

'Queensland,' I said. 'Went to see my daughter.'

The heads turned to me. 'Daughter?' said the wizened Wilbur Ong. 'Since when've you had a daughter?'

'A while,' I said. 'She's twenty-one.' Somehow the subject

of my daughter hadn't come up in years of talking football and horses.

'Well, this is bloody news to me,' said Norm, aggrieved. He stared at me. 'Now you've got a girl. And the young fella playin for Fremantle that's the bloody spit of Bill? Wouldn't know anythin about that, would ya?'

'Not a thing,' I said. 'I swear.'

Bill Irish, my father, dead these many years, was a Fitzroy Football Club hero of the late 1940s, a patron of this pub. He had undoubtedly at some time stood where I was standing, resting his stonemason's boot on the same brass rail. And his father's workman's boot had probably been there before his. Daniel Irish was also a Fitzroy player, career cut off in its prime by a Collingwood hoon jumping on his arm accidentally. Twice. Given these male genes, old Fitzroy supporters didn't understand why I hadn't played football, didn't understand and didn't forgive.

'Played shockin, your team,' said Eric. 'The fellas got problems findin the general direction of goal.'

'Not to mention what bloody happens when they do,' said Norm. 'That bugger looks like he's outta Pentridge on day release, he misses four, couldn't reliably piss inta the sea.'

Wilbur nodded. 'Dunno about this coach either. Five goals behind, he lets the flower girls give up, talks to em all kind and gentle. Decent coach'd give em the red-hot poker up the backside.' He paused. 'Disgrace, I reckon, this team of yours.'

The trio's eyes were on me, unblinking bird eyes, the eyes of eagle fledglings, ruthless, demanding. Even in the closing stages, Julius Caesar faced a friendlier looking audience. Better looking too, I had no doubt.

'So now it's *my* team?' I said. 'Well, so be it. That's that then. I'll stick with my team. You lot can go back to not having a team. Or go for the Brisbane Lions. No, go for Collingwood, that's a nice team, run by television money.'

The bird eyes all flicked away. Then Norm's came back.

'Steady on,' he said. 'Man's entitled to give his team a bit of a buttocking.'

'A man who's got a team, yes. Men who don't have a team can't.' Out of the corner of my eye, I saw Stan the publican gliding across from serving the shaven-headed man.

'Jack, my boy.' His smug mood was upon him.

'Stanley. What've you done to your hair?'

Stan ran five pork sausages over his scalp. He'd had the sparse pubic springs shorn to a uniform height. 'Today's look,' he said. 'Got to keep up.'

'Very fetching look,' I said. 'It was big in the Gulag archipelago.'

'The what?'

'Nothing. I see the clientele's going upmarket.'

Stan gave his conspiratorial nod, leaned across the bar. 'Drink vodka,' he said, winked at me. 'Stolly. They're in new technology. The IT crowd.'

'Who?' said Norm O'Neill. 'Eyeties? All in Carlton, the eyetalians. Accident of history. Coulda settled in Fitzroy. Makes you think, don't it? We'da had Serge Silvagni, lotta grit that bloke, then his young fella, always rated that Steven high, I have.'

'Barassi, he's an eyetalian,' said Wilbur Ong. 'Go back a bit, them Barassis, though. Not convicts but a fair way back.' He sighed. 'We coulda had Barass.'

'Barassi come from Castlemaine,' said Eric Tanner. 'Jeez, there's a lotta ignorance around here.'

Stan looked at the Youth Club and shook his head. 'IT.

Information technology. You blokes think the flush dunny's new technology.' He turned back to me, coughed a polite cough. 'Word's gettin around,' he said. 'These people, they're on the cyberfrontier. On the other hand, they like a bit of tradition. Well, you want a bit of tradition, the Prince's the place.'

'Tradition?' I said. 'Really? Tradition of beer tasting like soap? Tradition of toasted cheese sandwiches that fight with your teeth? Tradition of needing gumboots to go to the toilet? That's what they're after, is it? Well, Stanley, you're in the pound seats.'

Stan shrugged. 'Jack, too critical, always bin your problem. Take the world as you find it, my old man always said.'

'Morris never in his life said anything like that,' I said. 'Morris can't stand the world as he finds it. And what's this past tense? Either Morris is alive or he's been phoning me every day from the afterlife.'

Stan's father owned the Prince and five small commercial properties around the suburbs. I acted for him in his endlessly problematic dealings with his tenants and he sent me instructions daily from his retirement villa in Queensland.

'On that subject,' said Stan. He leaned his head closer. 'Listen, Jack, the wife's talkin to someone the other day, he reckons I could get power of attorney for the old bloke, no problem. Eighty-eight, infirm of mind, that sort of thing.'

'Could we get a round here?' I said. 'The old technology crowd. Soapy beer will be fine.'

Stan didn't move. 'Course you'd still do the legal stuff, don't worry about that.'

I put my face within five centimetres of his. 'Stanley,

when I detect any signs of mental infirmity in Morris, you'll be the first to know. As things stand, the message is more likely to go in the other direction.'

Stan worked this out, sighed, went to get the beer. I settled down to a serious discussion with the repentant Youth Club of the Saints' chances against West Coast on Friday night. Perfect hatred of the non-Victorians drove out any fears about the ability of our side to orientate themselves towards goal.

I drove home through a cold drizzle, the Lark's erratic wipers smearing the lights. It was just after seven, the truce time, day people retreating, night people not ready to advance. At the Queen's Parade lights, I punched the radio, got a boring man talking about tax reform, punched again, got a silly pair of teenagers talking about bad exam experiences, punched.

A voice said: *Should the new government have scrapped its predecessor's granting of a licence for a privately run ski resort and casino at Cannon Ridge? Let's hear your views on 1300 3333, that's 1300 3333. I'm Linda Hillier, talking with you on 3KB, Melbourne's station for the new century.*

It was a voice I hadn't heard for a long time. Drivers behind me began to hoot. I came back to the present and got the Lark moving, turned left. Outside the boot factory, parked under a dripping elm, I listened to Linda Hillier and her callers. She had the talkback touch: silk and steel, kiss them and kick them. Touch had always been her strong point. Early in our relationship, we'd sat in this car at this spot, glued at the mouth, hands going about their business, the business hands want to go about.

But that was long ago.

I killed the radio and lugged the shopping bags upstairs.

Each year, the eventide falls faster and only sound and activity can hold the gate. I lit the fire, put on some Mahler, loud, got busy cooking, rang Cyril Wootton's numbers, all of them. I found him in the last refuge of the scoundrel: home.

'My God,' he said, 'where are you, what's that ghastly noise?'

I turned down the volume. 'The person. There's room for speculation here.'

'Matter's closed. You've been remunerated.' The clipped military tone was blurred by a long day of duplicity and substance abuse.

'Time on the meter, as you well know. Tell the client your information is that the official explanation doesn't hold up.'

I could hear him suck his teeth.

'Get back to you, old fruit,' he said.

Back was five minutes. 'The client would like a meeting. Maximum discretion is required.'

'And who,' I said, 'is better equipped to provide that?'

Then I rang Cam's latest number. A woman answered, light voice, not a voice I knew. 'I'll see if Mr Delray is in the mood for callers,' she said.

Cam came on. 'Jack.' He'd been close enough to hear my voice. What did that mean? Silly question.

'I'd cross Cyril off the list,' I said. 'There are things you can't fake.'

'Glad to hear it. Monday morning, free early? Eight-fifteen? We could eat.'

'What meal is that, your time?'

'Too soon to know yet. Pick you up where?'

'Charlie's. He's away. I've been slacking. Bring something.'

I ate in front of the television, watching the first part of a

33

British drama about a middle-aged artist with an unsympathetic wife, a doctor. The man hit the singing sauce closer to breakfast than lunch, rooted the nanny in the mid-afternoon lull and, before dinner, wine glass in hand, delivered a withering attack on bureaucrats, multinationals, cultural imperialists, and people he didn't like much.

I identified strongly. Not much later, I went to bed and succumbed to the arms of Milo. One day these crumbly grains will be a listed substance, prescription only, traded on cold streets, the price floating on the surging sea of supply and demand.

'Do you know who I am?' the man in the perfect dark suit asked.

I nodded. My inclination on seeing him had been to leave and, later, to chastise Wootton severely for not warning me. 'What would you like me to call you?'

He hesitated for an instant. 'Colin will be fine.'

The waiter arrived, a plump young woman in black, not fully alert yet. In that condition, we were companions.

'Weak latte for me, please,' said Mr Justice Colin Loder.

'Short black.'

The judge was short and trim. His curly dark hair was razor-cut, parted at the left with the aid of a ruler. He looked as if he'd gone to sleep before 9 p.m. the night before, and come to our meeting fresh from swimming five kilometres followed by a full-body massage. I envied that in a man.

We were sitting at the window table in a cafe called Zanouff's in Kensington, in Bellair Street, across the road from the station. You could see the trains taking the condemned into the city.

'Don't judges have flunkeys they send out on business like this?'

'Good flunkeys are hard to find these days,' he said.

Colin Loder put his elbows on the table, put his fingertips together. Steepling they called it in the body-language trade. 'You have something to tell me about Robert's death.'

'I don't think it was an accidental overdose.'

A deadpan look. 'Why would you know better than the police?'

I gave him a dose of steepling. He noticed. 'It's hard to know what the police know,' I said. 'You can't find out from what they say.'

He unsteepled, moved his mouth, almost a smile. 'Like politicians. What do *you* know?'

'I don't like the proposition that someone doesn't come home for days and when he does, he accidentally overdoses in his garage.'

Colin Loder's black eyes were on me. 'But it's possible, isn't it?'

I said, 'Yesterday I was told that the police were interested in Robbie before his death.'

He touched his chin with a finger, brushed the blue cleft. 'Told by?'

I looked at him, letting him know I wasn't going to answer, my expression telling him, you're not in your court now, Mr Justice Loder.

He held my gaze and then his mouth moved, a tiny twitch of the ruby lips. He'd got it.

'What does interested mean?' he said. 'Exactly?'

'It's an inexact term.'

'Here we go,' said the plump serving person, striving to be cheerful. 'Weak latte and a short.'

We watched a train leave the station.

Colin Loder sipped, put his cup down. He wasn't going to lift it again. He wasn't meeting me for coffee, probably didn't drink coffee, for health and fitness reasons.

I tried mine. Terrible. 'Would you know about police interest in Robbie?'

He raised an eyebrow. 'No, I wouldn't know about that.'

Spots of rain on the tarmac outside. I wanted to end this encounter, drive to Meaker's and there drink decent coffee and dwell on more interesting matters. For example, the form for Cranbourne.

'Well, I thought I should express my doubts to you,' I said. 'I've done that. And the coroner will probably agree with the police.'

I stood up. He didn't.

'It's Jack Irish?'

'Yes.' He knew that.

'Someone said he couldn't understand how you kept your practising certificate.'

'Someone?'

'I mentioned your name to someone.'

'Tell someone I'm of a lovable disposition and my legal clients don't complain,' I said. 'That's how I keep my practising certificate. Nice meeting you.'

He held up a placatory hand, a pink-palmed soft hand. 'Sit down, Jack.'

Reluctantly, I did.

'I'm sorry,' the judge said. 'That was impertinent of me. And I'm sure your doubts are well founded.'

I didn't want an apology. I wanted a reason to leave.

'Well, obviously we need to know more,' he said.

'I don't think there's anything more I can do.'

He looked down. 'I'd deem it a kindness.'

Pleading is hard to bear, even a judge's pleading. 'It would save lots of money if someone gave me Robbie's history,' I said.

'This may sound strange, but I don't know anything about him. Just that he came from Sydney and was a casual barman at The Green Hill.'

'I'll tell you what I know about Robbie,' I said. 'He lived alone in a one-bedroom unit. The neighbours liked him. He put in a light bulb for the old lady downstairs, took her garbage out a few times. He wasn't seen often but he came and went without any noise. That's it.'

Loder nodded. 'Did he have a drug habit?'

'Hard to tell. Not one that left marks on him. Can I be impertinent and ask why you wanted him found if you don't know anything about him?'

He sighed. 'He's related to someone. The person turned to me for help. People think…people in my position can reverse gravity, change the orbit of the earth.'

'So this relative could tell you or me about him?'

'No. The person hadn't been in touch with Robert for a long time. Then she met him again, briefly, and then she lost touch. And so she came to me and I contacted Cyril Wootton.'

'May I ask why you didn't consult the police? My under-standing is that they come when people in your position call.'

'I chose to hire someone to find Robert.' A pause. 'Which brings us to where we are now.'

I looked at the street. A man in a raincoat was approaching, something on a string leading him. It looked like a hairy loaf of bread.

We had a short time of not speaking. The rain was getting harder. I heard him run his hands over his temples, the faintest sound of palms over freshly shorn hair, an electric hiss.

'This could turn out to be a complete waste of money,' I said. 'It probably will.'

'If the police won't consider other possibilities, then we must.' He looked at his watch. His wrists were hairy, wiry hairs peeping out under the Rolex. 'I must run,' he said. 'Enjoy your coffee.'

He dropped a note on the counter, didn't wait for change. I watched him walk briskly in the direction of Macaulay Road.

The green hill was once in the worst part of South Melbourne. Now there was no worst part: the whole area was a pulsating real-estate opportunity. Even the most charmless flat-roofed 1950s yellow-brick sign-writer's shop could be transformed into a minimalist open-plan dwelling suitable for thrusting young e-people.

In defiance of the weather, many of these people were sitting at tables outside The Green Hill, a three-storey Victorian pile. Perhaps the telephone reception was bad inside: at least half of them were talking on mobiles so small that they appeared to be speaking to their fists. As I approached, a short-haired and skeletal waiter wearing a long black apron came out and served coffees to two men, both on the phone. I got to him at the glass double doors.

'The bar,' I said. 'How do I find the bar?'

He tilted his head, eyed me. His skin had a shiny water-resistant look. 'Bar X? Che's Bar? Or Down the Pub?'

Too much choice. 'I need to talk to someone about a casual barman who worked here.'

'Human Resources.' He pointed. 'In there, up the stairs, door's straight ahead.'

Economical.

I went into a lobby, an empty room with a marble-tiled floor, dark wood-panelled walls, a single painting lit by a spotlight: it was an early Tucker, an angry painting, a political painting, from the heart. At least they hadn't hung it in Bar X. Doors to the left and right were unlabelled. The staircase was to the right, a splendid thing of hand-carved steam-bent cedar and barley sugar turnings. I ascended.

The door opposite was open. I knocked anyway.

'In, in,' said a male voice.

He was at a long table, a stainless-steel top on black metal trestles, fingers on a keyboard, monitors, printers and other hardware on his flanks.

'Gerald,' he said, smiling, a round-headed man around thirty, balding, olive-skinned, in a collarless white shirt.

'Me or you?'

'You're not Gerald?'

'No.'

His smile went. 'We're currently only hiring in kitchen. And if your CV shines.'

'Glitters,' I said, 'but not currently in the market. You employed a casual barman called Robert Colburne.'

He sat back. 'Police? You've been here.'

'No. I represent his family.'

Represent is a good word. It suggests.

'I'll tell you what I told the cops. Colburne worked here for five weeks, three shifts a week. A few times we called him in to fill a hole. He was fine, he was tidy, people liked him. But nobody here knows him, knew him. Outside work, that is.' He held up his palms.

'He had another job, did he?'

He shrugged. 'Don't know.' Pause. 'How come his family don't know?'

'Drifted apart, lost touch.'

'The cops wanted to find the next of kin. Has the family been in touch?'

'I presume so. Did Robbie come with references?'

'References only mean anything for kitchen staff in this

business. He said he'd worked all over the place. Queensland. We gave him a one-hour trial. He knew what he was doing.'

'Anyone around who worked with him? Just so that I can tell the family I talked to a colleague.'

There was a slight unease about him, something more than having his time wasted. He cleared his throat, picked up a slim telephone handset. 'I'll see.'

He tapped three numbers. 'Janice, call up Robbie Colburne's last three shifts, see if anyone on them's here now.'

We waited. He didn't look at me, looked at the computer screen on his right. Figures in columns, a payroll possibly.

'Okay, thanks.' He put the handset down. 'Down the Pub. Ask for Dieter.'

'Thanks. I appreciate your help.'

He didn't say anything, didn't smile, just nodded, looked at the screen again.

You couldn't get into Down the Pub from the street. Entry was through a heavy studded door in a narrow lane separating The Green Hill from its neighbour. No need for passing trade here. Beyond the door was a vestibule and then you passed through small-paned glass doors into a long room where lamps in mirrored wall niches cast a warm and calm yellow light. The walls were wood panelled to the ceiling, there were booths and tables with leather chairs, and the oak bar with brass fittings was like an altar to drink.

The place was almost empty: two couples in a booth, three men at a table, two lingering male drinkers at the bar. I stood at the counter as far from them as possible. The barman stopped polishing a glass and was in front of me in an instant.

'Sir,' he said. He was tall with wavy dark hair and a neat beard.

'I'm looking for Dieter.'

'I am Dieter.' A German accent.

'Jack Irish,' I said. We shook hands. 'You knew Robbie Colburne?'

'Not too well, a colleague for a short time,' he said. 'It's very sad. Are you family?'

'He lost contact with his family.'

Dieter recognised the evasion. 'So you're not family?'

'No. I'm acting for the family.' I was, at a small remove.

'Acting? I don't…'

'I'm a lawyer.'

'Legal business?'

'Sort of, yes. There's an estate involved.' There had to be.

He nodded. 'I saw him here only. A friendly person, a person easy to work with. Yes. Not like some.'

'Friends?'

'Friends?'

'Barmen have friends. They make friends.'

'Oh, friends? I don't know. He was friendly to everyone. But that's part of the job.'

'So he didn't have any personal friends come in?'

'Excuse me, sir.' Alerted by something, he left me to pour a glass of red from an open bottle. I glimpsed the label: a Burgundy, a Pommard. Dieter took the drink over to the florid man at the opposite end of the bar and came back.

'Robbie's friends,' I said.

'Yes. No. Not here at work.'

A voice behind me said, 'Now Dieter, the guest hasn't got a drink, what's goin on?'

It was an Irish voice, a lovely purring, lilting Irish voice.

The owner was a man in a tweed suit, a pale, handsome man in his mid-thirties with dense black curly hair, red lips and perfect teeth. He had his hand out to me and he was smiling.

'Xavier Doyle,' he said. 'I'm the publican here and I don't know your face and I want to do somethin about that.'

'Jack Irish,' I said.

'Irish? There's a name to make a man sing. What'll you be drinkin? First one's on the house, first and a few too many in the middle says the accountant. Got no heart, these counters of beans.'

He was a man you could like without thinking about it.

'A beer,' I said.

'Not just a beer in this establishment.' He waved. 'Dieter, my fine Teutonic friend, a couple of pints of the Shamrock, there's a good lad.'

'Sir.' Dieter slid off.

Doyle leaned his back against the bar, patted my arm. 'Now Jack, the feller upstairs says you're askin about young Robbie. There's a tragedy for you. Why would a young feller like that get into the drugs? We'll never know, that's the answer, isn't it ?'

'Someone who knew him well might know.'

'I can't say that I did, Jack. I wish I could. You'd like to know all your staff well, wouldn't you? But there's near sixty work here and they're comin and goin, grass's always greener, and the competition always out to poach em.' He paused, a sad look. 'So, no, I can't say I knew Robbie well. But an excellent worker, top of the class, we'd a put him on permanent at the drop.'

The beers came, silver tankards topped with two fingers of foam.

'Let's get in front of some of this Irish gold,' said Doyle. He had a way of holding your eyes, as if looking into them gave him great pleasure.

We drank. It wasn't bad stuff. I wiped off my foam moustache. 'Robbie didn't want a full-time job?'

'Bernie asked him but he said he had other commitments.'

'Another job?'

'Entirely possible. How'd you like this beer?'

'I like it.' I drank some more. He drank, wiped his lips with a red handkerchief drawn from his top pocket.

'Next time you come we'll be drinkin The Green Hill pinot noir. We're takin delivery of vintage number one in a coupla days. From our own little estate out there on the Mornington. Nectar, I tell you, a drop fit for a crowned head.'

He waved at the barman.

'Some of them pecan nuts, Dieter lad. Now Jack, you're in the legal line the boyo says. That's the solicitorin, is it? Or are you one of them fellers wears a ferret on his head?'

'Solicitor.'

Dieter positioned a silver bowl of pecan nuts.

'Good few of your kind drop in here,' said Doyle. 'Corporate, a lot of em, the Lord knows what they do. How'd you get involved in this unfortunate affair?'

I chewed a nut. 'His relatives,' I said. 'Lost touch with him, now they want to know a bit more about his life.'

Doyle nodded. 'Perfectly understandable.' He flashed a cuff, looked at his watch. 'Day's flyin away from me. Jack, it's a pleasure to meet you. We'll be seein more of you now? Promise me that.'

'Promise,' I said. 'Xavier.'

45

'Call me Ex,' he says. 'It's what they call me.' He turned his head to Dieter. 'Fix this feller in your mind,' he said, 'and take proper care of him.'

He was at the inside door when he turned and came back. 'Next week we're launchin this little cookbook we've knocked out, Jack. *The Green Hill Food* it's called. Lots of the legal brotherhood comin. And the sisterhood, mind you. Your presence is required. Got a card on you?'

On the way out, I waved goodbye to Dieter. He was standing at a hatch talking to a young woman on the other side. They were both looking at me. He waved back, a polite wave.

Outside, in the rain, the meter had long expired and the Stud had a note under the driver's wiper. It read: 'If you ever consider selling this, ring me.' There was a name and a number and, after it, in parentheses, the words Traffic Inspector. Such is luck.

'Kashboli?' I said, studying the menu. 'What does Kashboli mean?'

'Where have you been, Jack?' asked Andrew Greer, my former law partner and friend since law school. 'Kashmiri plus Bolivian. Two interesting cuisines.'

I loosened my tie. 'With absolutely fuck-all in common.'

'Exactly. Until united by fusion cuisine.'

We were sitting in the window of Kashboli, an eating and drinking place on lower Lygon Street whose premises had previously housed a famous Carlton drycleaning establishment. Where a bar with a mosaic top now stood, garments were once handed over, precious garments, mainly Italian men's items handed over by Italian women—dinner jackets the men had proposed in, wedding suits, good linen trousers, dark single-vent jackets, many let out a bit at the seams by the skilled fingers of loved ones. It had been my drycleaner when I was a five-suit man practising criminal law with Andrew in nearby Drummond Street.

'Hello, young lovers, wherever you are.'

A seriously big man, big and fat man, in loose white garments, shaven skull, no neck, head like a nipple with features, had appeared behind the bar, sang the line in a singing pose, chin raised, hands up, palms outwards.

Andrew gave him a wave. So did all the other patrons, late-working trade unionists from headquarters down the road by the grim and dedicated look of them.

'Our host, Ronnie Krumm,' said Drew.

'Is that Kashmiri Ronnie Krumm or Bolivian Ronnie Krumm?'

'Neither. Ronnie's from Perth, travelled widely in search of the new. I understand the family's in hardware, very big in the hardware.'

'Hardware, software, Ronnie's big all over. What's the fat content of Kashboli tucker?'

Drew was intent on the menu. 'Excessive but only good fats. Premium, I'm told. No finer fats available. Well, what's your fancy or will you be guided?'

'Be my trained labrador.'

Drew ordered what appeared to be a form of fish stew. It came in minutes, a minefield of a dish. You chewed uneventfully and then you bit on anti-personnel chillies and your eyes lit up from behind. Fortunately, it came with a glass of a sweet off-white substance, a neutralising agent, possibly crushed antacid tablets in a sugar solution.

'Interesting,' I said, recovering. 'Fusion brings electrocution. Tell me about The Green Hill.'

Drew was savouring the Kashboli fish and chilli stew with no sign of strain, no resort to the pale liquid.

'The Green Hill? He raised his glass of Bolivian cabernet to the light, his eyes narrowed, the long face took on a stained-glass religious look. 'Not your kind of place. Very few geriatrics arguing about football at The Green.'

'Tell me,' I said.

'Thinking of taking someone? A date, is it?'

'With destiny. It's for a Wootton client. And I've been there. This afternoon.'

'Shit. Boring. How is the love life?'

'She's taking pictures in Europe. Not enough time between assignments.'

'To do what?'

'Fly home for twenty-whatever hours and go back the next week.'

'Serious concern?'

'I suppose.'

'Extremely fetching person. In a mildly intimidating sort of way. Not talkative exactly,' said Drew.

'No. Well, she can be. Depends.'

'Yes. All life depends. It's pendant.'

'The Green Hill?'

'Testimony to one man's dream,' Drew said. 'Xavier Doyle, heard of him?'

'I met him. Very affable. He shouted me a pint of Shamrock, told me to call him Ex.'

'Radiates charm, Mr Doyle. Gave character for a bloke of mine, waiter at The Green, stark naked outside the National Gallery on New Year's Eve, pointed his bum at a cop. By the time Doyle was finished, I thought the mago was going to award the lad compensation.'

Ronnie Krumm was coming our way, a white tent with a large shining head where the flagpole should be, hipping his was through the tables.

'Everything all right?'' he said. 'Not too hot for you?'

'Was this a hot one?' said Drew. 'Ronnie Krumm, Jack Irish. Jack used to be my law partner.'

I shook Ronnie's fleshy hand.

'And you eat together,' said Ronnie. 'Amaazing. I'm still trying to kill my ex-partner.'

'I never heard you say that,' said Drew. 'Call me when you succeed, I'll see what I can do.'

Ronnie winked and moved on to one of the tables of trade unionists.

'Yes,' said Drew. 'Xavier Doyle, the boy's a dreamer and a doer. Cook from Dublin, guitar player, he sees the huge old place, used to be a temperance pub, falling down. So he finds the money to buy it, plus megabucks for renovations.'

'How do you do that?' I tried to defuse a bite of stew with a big swig of the Bolivian.

'I don't know exactly. They say he won over Mike Cundall. And Mrs Cundall, no doubt. And now he's in with little Sam Cundall and the Sydney sharks, tendering for ski resorts and casinos.'

The Cundall family were in commercial property, carparks, mortgage lending, internet dream factories, many other things. They also gave away large sums and, by all accounts, turned on a good party.

'Cannon Ridge. How do you know he's in that?'

Drew was looking into his glass. 'Because I know things. So what's the interest in The Green?'

'Someone called Robbie Colburne was a casual barman there. Dead of an overdose.'

He drank, rolled the wine in his mouth, squinted. 'Bolivian,' he said in wonder. 'Excellent. Half the price of an equivalent local drop. And made by Aussie mercenaries. What happened to loyalty? Patriotism?'

'You sound like Cyril.'

'Now there's a patriot. Fought abroad for his country.'

'Which broad was that?'

He gave me the Greer frown. 'Very weak, Jack. It's all that buggering around with carpentry. You don't do enough law. Keeps the mind alert. So what's the problem with a dead waiter? The more the merrier, I say. Did he have a ponytail?'

'A barman. I'm told the cops were interested in him.'

'Always interested in barmen, the cops. Source of free

drinks. I ran into your sister the other day.' His eyes were not on me; they were on something behind me.

'It's usually the other way around,' I said. 'Did she mention that she's uninsurable?'

'At lunch with my friends the Pratchetts.'

Dick Pratchett QC was the doyen of the criminal bar, a huge bearded man who cross-examined in a hoarse whisper and sometimes waited for answers with his eyes closed. Juries loved him and so did many murderers and lesser criminals roaming free.

I said, 'Ah. The trophy bride. Rosa's friend.'

Pratchett had recently married my sister Rosa's doubles partner, a woman a good 20 years his junior. Strike three.

'An attractive person,' said Drew, still not looking at me. 'Intelligent to boot.'

'If you like booting. Her predecessor's IQ just topped her chest size. Considerable for a chest but only for a chest.'

'Rosa, I'm talking about your sister.' Drew met my eyes, looked uneasy. 'We're having lunch on Sunday.'

'My sister. That's an entirely different matter.'

Rosa was rich, spoilt beyond redemption. But it wasn't the money that did it. It was being the focus of three adults' lives. My maternal grandparents' money had all gone to her and she used it to do nothing. Unless shopping, playing tennis, having brief affairs with unsuitable men and agonising over life constituted doing something.

I let Drew wait. Then I said, 'She usually lunches with young men. Spunks. Studs. Studs in their ears, studs elsewhere.'

He still wasn't too keen to hold my gaze, looked over my shoulder again. 'More of a meeting of minds, this. No objection is there?'

I studied him, shook my head. 'Really, Drew, you can look at me when you raise matters like this.'

He looked at me. 'Well?'

'It's your life.'

'What's that mean? Of course it's my fucking life. Don't you approve?'

'Approval doesn't come into it.'

'So you don't approve?'

'Forget this approval stuff. You're not asking for my permission, are you?

'Well, no. Yes, I suppose I am.'

'Don't. I don't give permissions.'

A long silence. I thought he was going to get up and leave, let me pay for the explosive fish stew.

'So,' he said. 'Not a good idea, you think.'

We fingered our glasses.

'Fucking awful idea,' I said. 'From my point of view.'

Drew filled our glasses. 'Exactly why is that?'

I'd never been called upon to do something like this. Since her mid-teens, Rosa had always had two photographs beside her bed: a photograph of Bill Irish, the father she never knew, and one of me, in tennis clothes, the older brother to whom she told everything, whether he wanted to hear it or not.

In short, I knew too much.

'The risk is,' I said, 'the risk is that between the two of you you'll end up creating some fucking vast, treeless, mined no-go area. For me.'

'For you?'

'For me. This is about me. You're asking me.'

'What about me?'

'How can I say this? You're a divorced prick looking for

love and affection. Rosa, on the other hand, is only looking for romance. Do I have to say more?'

Drew considered this statement, looking at me. Then he said, 'No, your honour.' He emptied his glass. 'Let's get the other half.'

Over at the trade union table, an argument had broken out between a short-haired woman with thick-lensed glasses and a man with a wispy beard. 'The question isn't whether it's a women's issue,' said the man, 'it's whether it's a union issue.'

The woman looked at the ceiling and said through tight lips, 'This is so fucking unbelievably eighties, it makes me want to puke.'

'A lot to be said for the eighties,' Drew said, signalling to a waiter. 'Bernie Quinlan kicked 116 in '83.'

'That was '84.'

'No, he only kicked 105 in '84.'

There was a moment of non-recognition, then the old woman said, 'Mr Irish, yeah, wait on.'

I heard the boards complain as she went back down the passage. Through the crack in the door came a smell of cat pee, pine-scented disinfectant, paint and food cooked to disintegration.

The old planks signalled Mrs Nugent's return. She opened the door, revealing that she was wearing a yellow plastic raincoat. 'Paintin,' she said. 'The kitchen. Here.' She offered me a suitcase. 'Good clothes, mind you give em to the boy's rellies.'

'Have no fear,' I said. 'It was the landlord, was it?'

I'd left my card with Robbie Colburne's neighbour and she'd been on the answering machine when I got back from The Green Hill.

'Yeah. Come round yesterdee. Give me $20 to clean up the place. Take anythin I liked, give the rest to the Salvos, throw it away.' She hesitated. 'Money's money.' A further hesitation. 'The towels and that, the kitchen stuff. Kept that.'

'Right thing to do,' I said. 'Didn't find anything with an address on it? Letter, anything?'

She shook her head. 'Them others coulda taken anythin like that.'

'Others? Police?'

'Police? Yeah, spose. Who else? Young blokes.'

'Not in uniform?'

Mrs Nugent looked at me with fowl eyes. 'Been in

uniform I wouldn't have to bloody spose, would I? Haven't gone that stupid.'

'No. Sorry. They take anything away?'

'Dunno.'

I got out my wallet. She held up a hand, palm outwards.

'Don't want no money. Just give the suitcase to the family. Tell em the neighbour says he was a nice young bloke. Had manners. Musta bin brought up right. Only saw him the coupla times in the beginnin, don't know he actually lived here.'

'I'll tell them,' I said. 'Thank you, Mrs Nugent.'

'And tell 'em I'm sorry.'

I was at the stairs, carrying the soft-sided black nylon suitcase, when the thought came to me. Mrs Nugent opened the door as if she'd been standing just inside it.

'Sorry,' I said. 'His car. Is it still in the garage?'

'Nah. Someone come and took it. Old Percy downstairs seen him.'

Percy wasn't at home. I drove the short distance from Abbotsford to my office in Carrigan's Lane. The greening brass plate said: *John Irish, Barrister & Solicitor*. As I put the suitcase on the old tailor's worktable that served as my desk, the feeling of guilt that had been with me for a while stabbed me. I should not have taken it from Mrs Nugent. I did not represent Robbie's family. I was just sniffing around for Cyril Wootton, and was being paid by someone who was probably not being entirely candid.

Take it back? And confess what? No. As for the client, who was I to worry? I was no stranger to economy in truth, economy and selectivity.

I opened the suitcase.

Robbie Colburne travelled light: leather toilet bag, two

pairs of black trousers, a pair of chinos, three black tee-shirts, three white shirts, a black jacket, a tweed jacket, a black leather jacket, a nylon windbreaker, an expensive-feeling woollen jumper, a pair of shiny black shoes, a pair of runners, old running shorts, a washed-out grey tee-shirt, black socks, underpants. And, on a wooden coathanger, a dinner suit, dress shirt, and black bow tie.

Nothing in the suitcase pockets. I looked at the shirts. Nice, superfine cotton by the feel, no labels. I picked up the black jacket, stroked it. It was light and soft—wool and cashmere, perhaps, no label. The tweed jacket was newish, beautifully cut. No label.

I opened the single-breasted dinner jacket. A product of Canali of Italy. A small label on the inside pocket said Charles Stuart. I knew Charles Stuart, they were men's outfitters in William Street in the city, men's outfitters to the big end of town. If you didn't fit that demographic, crossing the threshold of Charles Stuart's was a post-death experience: a buffed-up person wearing three grand's worth of the shop's stock examined you from top to toe, weighed up your clothing and footwear history, registered all your sartorial sins, made a judgment, came closer and said, lips like a cash-machine slot, 'May I help you, sir?'

I examined the shoes: Italian. I unzipped the toilet bag. It held a silver razor in a slim stainless-steel case, a bottle of Neale's Yard shaving oil, French deodorant, a toothbrush, French toothpaste, nail clippers, a Bakelite comb. I opened the shaving oil and sniffed. An expensive smell, clean. I inspected the toothpaste, squeezed some onto a fingertip, held it to my nose. Lavender.

Robbie Colburne might have been living in a one-bedroom flat in a low-rent block and working as a casual barman but his effects all shouted money and style.

That observation didn't advance things much. I repacked the suitcase, feeling the outside of pockets as I went. The dinner suit was last. I ran my hand over the jacket's outside pockets, felt something at the left hip. I lifted the flap, tried to insert cautious fingers, couldn't. It was a dummy pocket. Of course. What tailor would allow the line of a dinner jacket to be spoiled by something stuffed into a hip pocket?

Through the cloth, I felt the object again. Something the length of a pen cap, flat, no thicker than a stick of chewing gum. I opened the jacket and found the small inside pocket, a sturdy pocket designed to hold a single key, extracted the object. It was a plastic stick, dark-blue, a recessed button on one side. a hole in the front. I pressed the button. A red light glowed in the hole for a second or two. I did it again. The light went off even when the button remained depressed.

Today's mystery object. Nothing to identify it, say what it was for.

I put the device in my wallet, zipped the suitcase, put it in the small back room, sat at my table and eyed the unopened mail. Once letters held promise. Now I couldn't think of anyone who'd write an undemanding letter to me, pen your actual personal letter, fingers holding a writing instrument, hand touching paper. I thought about letters I'd read by fast-dying light, sniffed, imagined I'd caught a scent, held up, looked for a touch of sweat or the smear of a tear. Even, hoping against hope, the ghostly imprint of a kiss, just a touch of lips, leaving a mark.

Just a touch of lips. Lips left their mark, they all did, like branding irons, you felt them forever.

There was nothing left that I had to do or wanted to do. Midday Saturday. Once it had been the peak of the week.

I went to the window and looked at the street. Rain on the tarmac, oilslick-shiny pools in the bluestone gutters. Across the way, outside the clothing factory, a man in a four-wheel-drive had tried to shoot me one night.

The phone rang.

'Jack Irish.'

A sigh. 'Tried the boot factory, the furniture place, the mobile. Then I found this other number with Jack written next to it.'

Lyall. The dry, precise voice made the room seem brighter; no, the clouds must have thinned.

'I don't think we've ever conversed at my professional premises,' I said. 'Do you wish to consult me professionally?'

'I'm in Santa Barbara,' she said.

'Santa Barbara. What kind of trouble have they got there?'

'Understanding a sentence that doesn't mention Steven Spielberg or money. The ones I've met, anyway. I'm staying with Bradley.'

Staying with Bradley was fine from my point of view. Bradley was a former housemate of Lyall's, a film director. That wasn't what made him fine from my point of view. What made him fine was that he was gay.

'Extend my regards.'

'Brad's come out of the closet,' she said, voice low, serious.

'How many times can you do that?'

'It turns out,' she said, 'he's not gay.'

'They've done tests?'

She laughed. I'd been taken with her laugh from the outset, but it wasn't that laugh now. It was her laugh with something subtracted.

'He says he's never been gay, he's not even bi. He's been

58

celibate for twelve years. I just assumed that because he didn't want to screw me or any other woman he was gay.'

'Not an unreasonable assumption,' I said. I still remembered her exact words on that wintry night when we were still near-strangers.

I was in love with him for years. Never mentioned it. No point. He's gay. Huge loss to womankind.

I felt the weight of realisation, of knowing, on my shoulders, a dead weight, a bag of lead sinkers. A silence ensued.

'Jack.'

'Yes.' I could hear the soundless sound of her gathering courage.

'I'm attached, no, I'm in love with both of you. It's very difficult.'

'Torn between two lovers, acting like a fool,' I said. 'The old song. Or is it feeling like a fool? I've got something on the stove.' There are times when you will say anything.

'Jack.'

'Yes.'

'Don't dump me so quickly. This isn't easy. I've agonised over this.'

I said, without thought, 'Lyall, you're in Santa Barbie Doll or wherever and you're fucking Bradley, he's first-up from a spell, and you'd like to tell me about that and how difficult it is for you. Consider me told.'

Silence. Not even a hum from the copper wire that lay down there in the deep Pacific blackness consorting with the bottom-crawling sea life.

'Told,' she said. Click.

I sat there for a while, thinking that I needed a drink, needing a drink. Then I talked to myself for a while, recited the mantra about the black tunnel, and went home. There were things to do. It was time to clear the decks, to confront places long avoided. I cleaned the apartment from beginning to end, a ferocious attack on dirt in which I dusted pelmets and picture rails and skirting boards, washed floors, vacuumed carpets, defrosted the freezer, scrubbed the refrigerator, the stovetop, the oven. Then I turned on my grocery cupboard, threw out ancient spices, old flour, rusted cans of food I couldn't remember buying. Next, I laid into my clothes. Frayed shirts, unloved shirts, shapeless underwear, two old sweaters, lonely socks, a dark suit turning green, a jacket I'd never liked—they all went into a garbage bag and thence to the boot of the Stud. The Salvos could turn them into usable fibres. Then I stuffed two laundry bags with soiled clothes and sheets and table napkins and towels and delivered them into the cleansing hands of the Brunswick Street laundry. Next stop, King & Godfree in Lygon Street, where I bought exotic food and drink without regard for my penury.

At home, at the top of the stairs, a bag in each hand, the manic energy suddenly left me. I steeled myself for one final effort: pour cider over pork sausages in pot, put in oven. Halve tomatoes, quarter potatoes, put on tray, pour on olive oil, put in oven under sausages. Set oven on low. Open bottle of Carlsberg, lie on sofa, read the *Age*. Later on, I ate, drank a bottle of Cotes du Rhone grenache, watched the Saints get thrashed by West Coast, didn't care, a lot, wanted the phone to ring so much that it felt like a bodily ache.

In bed, I resisted the urge to burrow beneath the pillows and breathe carbon dioxide. I read my book. There should be a set number of endings in each life. No-one should have more. Experts could decide how many and enshrine that in the Charter of Human Rights.

But it would be too late for me.

I woke up thinking about Lyall and determinedly switched thoughts to my daughter, Claire. She was pregnant to Eric, her Scandinavian fishing boat skipper. Before my recent visit, I hadn't seen her for more than two years and, in full adult, barefoot, tropical bloom, she was shockingly different. She'd looked like my mother. My mother young and happy. I could not remember seeing my mother either young or happy, but I knew from the photographs that this was how she had looked. Claire was now very beautiful and my first sight of her had left me wrong-footed, unabled.

I had no guilt to carry in regard to Claire. Well, less guilt perhaps. It is all a matter of degree.

Her mother, my first wife, Frances, had left Claire's place in Queensland only hours before I'd arrived. She was still married to the man she'd left me for long ago, a surgeon, thin and pinstriped Richard, and Claire had two half-siblings, boys I'd encountered three or four times a year while Claire was growing up. Richard was your normal medical specialist: straight As for maths and science, no personality that would show up on any test. Nevertheless, he'd clearly touched something in Frances when he'd operated to fix an old tennis injury. Soon after, she departed without warning from the conjugal dwelling, taking with her one-year-old Claire. The next day, Richard arrived at my old law office in Carlton.

'Mr Wiggins to see you, Mr Irish,' said the secretary.

He was as pink and clean as a newly bathed baby and

wearing a suit worth more than I was making in a fortnight, gross. Primed to the eyebrows, hardly inside the door, he said, spitting it out, 'I'm here to tell you I'm in love with Frances and plan to marry her when she's free.'

I was late for court, looking for things. 'Steady on,' I said. 'Now what Frances is that?'

He coughed. 'Your, ah, wife. Frances.'

I said, 'Right, that Frances. You plan to do what with her?'

'Jack,' he said, 'I know this is a painful…'

'Wiggins,' I said. 'Aren't you her surgeon?'

Richard touched his razor-abrased chin. 'I did first meet Frances as a patient, yes, but…'

'Professional misconduct,' I said. 'I think your future lies in medical missionary work. Leper colonies, that kind of thing.'

His lips twitched. 'Jack, I assure you that I have not in any way contravened—'

'What's your first name?' I interrupted.

'Richard.' He saw hope, shot a cuff, put out a slim white-marble hand.

I ignored it. 'Save the assurances for the disciplinary hearing, sunshine. Now, I'm busy, so see yourself out will you?'

He gathered his dignity, head to one side. 'Unless the patient is the complainant, Jack, there really isn't…'

I was putting papers into my briefcase. 'Wiggy,' I said, 'you cut the flesh, I'll do the legal argument. In case she turns out not worth sacrificing a career for, try the sister. Some of the blokes prefer her.'

Cruel. Cruel and unnecessary, but the wounded animal is without compunction.

On this chilly Melbourne morning, many years later, time

having healed some wounds, put fragile scabs over others, inflicted new ones, I drove down Carrigan's Lane, its sole streetlight making gleams on the bluestone gutter. It was still dark as I unlocked the side door to Taub's Cabinetmaking, clicked on the lights, noted the bulbs gone: three. Charlie wouldn't have fluorescent lighting and no day passed there without me risking my life up a ladder replacing incandescent bulbs.

The workshop was as Charlie had left it on the day he flew to Perth to attend the marriage of his youngest grand-daughter to someone in the quarry business. His idea had been to be back inside 24 hours but he had been prevailed upon to spend ten days with another grandchild and his family.

Before he left, Charlie said to the workshop, not to me, 'For what do I need a holiday?'

I was under a three-metre-long table, made of red cedar cut in northern New South Wales before World War One. Charlie bought the timber in 1962, wrote the date on it in pencil. I was examining the perfect fit of the wooden buttons that fixed the tabletop to the frame and would allow the timber to move seasonally for a few centuries until it stabilised.

'You'll probably never want to come back,' I said. 'It's still warm. Hot. More than hot.'

He banged a huge fist on the tabletop directly above my head, causing me to feel that I was fainting.

'Hot? You tell me what's hot good for. One thing, you tell me.'

I crawled out, tympana still vibrating, got to my feet, braced myself against the table. 'People go outside and do things, go to the beach, swim.'

Charlie made his pitying noise, a sort of snort enhanced with nasal sounds. 'Exactly,' he said. 'They waste time. You think Mozart went to the beach? You hear that Liszt was a lot of the time swimming? What use is swimming, anyway?'

'It keeps you from drowning,' I said. 'In deep water.'

He rolled his cheroot between thumb and two fingers, puffed at it, shook his head in a worried way. 'Jack, Jack,' he said, 'don't go in the deep water, how can you drown? What use is swimming then?'

'I need some time on that,' I said. 'What do I do while you're away?'

He turned away, walked off towards his machines to touch them goodbye, said over his shoulder, 'Pack up and deliver the library, the lady's waiting.'

I followed him. 'Me? Are you mad? Mrs Purbrick's paying a fortune for Charlie Taub.'

'I told you already, Charlie Taub the woman got. You put a couple screws in the wall, that's it. When I come back, I check.'

'Charlie, that's not a good idea. I could ruin your reputation.'

He wound the blade of a table saw up, wound it down, an action serving no purpose. 'So ruin,' he said, subject closed. He turned his head in my direction. A new subject. 'The one with the horsetail, you know?'

I knew. The property developer who'd turned the old chutney factory in Carrigan's Lane into four desirable inner-city New York-style loft apartments, lifestyle choice plus once-in-a-lifetime blue-chip investment opportunity not to miss.

'I know,' I said, with an icepick in my heart.

'Six hundred thousand dollars.' Charlie pointed around the space.

'An offer?'

'From the agent. Clive, Clive somebody.'

'Clive Miller,' I said. The repulsive Clive, gone on from accepting fellatio in lieu of rent and from dudding poor tenants out of their rental bonds to sitting on boards and living in the best part of Kew. Clive Miller embodied the recent history of Fitzroy.

'That one. Nine hundred pounds I paid. One hundred and fifty cash down, five quid a week.'

'So?' I said.

Charlie straightened, ran a hand the size of an oven glove over the burnished surface of the cabinet, tested the stability of the fence.

'So?' I repeated, wanting to know, at that moment.

'So?' Charlie said. 'So?'

'Are you selling?'

'Selling?' The large head turned around, eyes under thatch bundles regarded me. 'My workshop? So I can go to Perth and learn to swim? So I don't drown?'

'Just asking,' I said, trying as nonchalantly as possible to get oxygen to my gasping little lung sacs.

Now I walked around the workshop, touched a few machines, just to comfort them, spent five minutes studying Mrs Purbrick's library. It was pure Charlie Taub: classical elements—pilasters, mouldings, cornices—but pared of all showiness. The eye was drawn first to the beauty of the wood, then to the perfect balance of the design, its understatement and severity, and then, perhaps, to the craft of the joiner.

The ensemble, missing only its top and bottom

trimmings, stood assembled in a corner of the workshop. It had been sanded, grain-sealed, shellacked and polished by Charlie's finishing man, the voluble Arthur McKinley, retired coffin-maker. That work had taken six weeks. To reach the stage where the finishing could begin had taken a mere eight months because Charlie had set aside three days a week for the library. Progress might have been even faster had he had someone other than me to assist him. But speed had never been a concern for Charlie. He didn't hear clients' questions about how long a job would take.

Once, in the early days, entrusted with a small table, anxious about my progress, I asked, 'When does this have to be finished?'

Charlie had been rough-planing an 18-inch walnut board with a block plane, working at an angle to the grain to avoid tear-out. The thick plane steel, sixty years old at least, honed and strapped, could clean shave a Gulf Country feral pig. With each stroke, long translucent shavings whispered through the plane's throat, bending back with the grace of a ballerina's arm.

'When it's finished,' he said, 'that's when.'

I went to the storeroom at the back and got out the packing blankets, World War Two army blankets Charlie had bought in the 1950s. Then I disassembled the library. There was not a screw in it; secret wooden locking wedges held it together. By 8.30 a.m., I'd finished wrapping and taping the pieces. I was waiting for the water to boil and thinking about my anchovy-paste sandwich when I heard the vehicle outside.

Cam was in his stockbroker gear—chalk-striped charcoal suit, blue shirt, silk jacquard tie—and carrying a dark-blue cardboard box. He put it on the steel trolley Charlie used as a table.

'Breakfast,' he said and opened the box. 'Scrambled eggs and barbecued pork New Orleans-style on Greek bread. Coffee. Blue Mountain.'

Fusion cooking was completely out of control. What chance did an anchovy-paste sandwich and a cup of tea stand? We got going, sitting on the chairs Charlie had rescued from a skip. The pork melted in the mouth, the scrambled eggs had a faint mustard and cream taste.

'Southern barbecued pork? Greek bread?'

'Good?'

'That's not strong enough. Who's the cook?'

'Greek bloke in Brunswick, used to live in New Orleans. He's got a brick oven out the back, looks like a rocket ship. Fat rocket ship. Little pig's in about eight at night, comes from his brother in the bush, the neighbour comes off shift at 4 a.m., checks it. Bit of bastin. Ready at seven.'

'Write down the address.'

He nodded, looked at me reflectively, tongue running over his upper teeth. 'Talked to Cyn again. She's gettin better, not so vague now.

'That's good.'

We chewed in silence.

'The one, he's got a tatt down the middle finger. Right hand.'

'What kind?'

'The Saint.'

'No, don't say that.' The stick figure with the halo was St Kilda's emblem.

'She says she was at the stove, it came to her. The head and the halo. Halo bigger than the head.'

I took the cap off the coffee cup.

'Can't drink it without sugar. Needs sugar,' said Cam.

'No.' I sipped. This was coffee, Harry Palmer coffee, sugar ruined it. 'That's it?'

'No. Ring each side she thinks, gold.'

'She should go back to the jacks.'

Cam opened his coffee, added sugar from two little paper bags, stirred with the plastic implement, tasted. 'She's not happy to do that.'

Our eyes conversed. I said, 'Yes. Leave it with me. It's an exceedingly long shot and I've exhausted my welcome. But.'

He nodded, not looking at me, eyes on his coffee. 'Can't find any other way.'

'The vehicle,' I said. 'I've been thinking about the vehicle.'

'The vehicle?'

'From a carpark.'

'A carpark.' Cam looked up, into the distance, turned the eyes on me, yellow eyes, the sinews bracketing his mouth showing. Nothing more to be said.

'Do the tatt,' he said, 'then we'll do the carpark.'

'This breakfast, I owe you.'

'Dinner. Owe me dinner.'

When he'd gone I made a call about the tattoo. The man at the other end groaned.

'Jesus, fuck,' he said. 'Use the phone book.'

'Robbery with violence, maybe serious assault. Not inside on February 20.'

'Use half the phone book. Tomorrow it'll have to be. Six-thirty.'

'Not fucking bad,' said the driver.

It was 10.40 a.m. and we were in the furniture van outside the wrought-iron double gates of Mrs Purbrick's neo-Georgian mansion in Kooyong. The greasy rain on Punt Road had turned to a soft, clean mist here, further testimony to the preferential treatment handed out to the extremely rich.

The driver's name was Boz and she was a film grip, an occupation whose essence, as I understood it, was the moving of things. When not gripping films, she used this skill to cart stuff around in her vintage van. I'd met her through Kelvin McCoy, a conman artist and former client of mine who leased the building across the street from my office. Boz transported McCoy's appalling creations to his gallery in the city. He had not been receptive to my suggestion that, on these missions, the Boz vehicle should display a Hazardous Waste sign.

'There's a side door,' I said. 'Just beyond, it's probably best.' I'd hired her for the day; one person couldn't move the library bits around.

I got out and pressed the button in the wall, could have smoked a full cigarette before David, Mrs Purbrick's personal assistant, came down the gravelled driveway. His hair was wet and he bore the telltale signs of someone not long vertical.

'My dear Jack,' he said. 'Apologies in full. I was on the phone, dealing with this most dreadful rug trader. Can you believe the man's tried the old switcheroo on us?'

'The switcheroo? That's impertinent,' I said.

'My word.' He held up a key. 'I have to unlock these now. It turns out all the high-tech electronic rubbish can't keep out a 12-year-old armed with an old remote control. So much for maximum security.'

The gates swung open on silent hinges. Boz drove in and lined up the truck with the side steps to within a centimetre.

She got out, broken-nosed, six foot two, near-shaven-headed, a woman in khaki bib-and-braces overalls and a white sleeveless tee-shirt.

I introduced her to David.

'I can see you work out,' he said admiringly.

'Work out?' said Boz. 'Work out shit, I'm a manual labourer.'

David was suitably taken aback. 'Well,' he said. 'Well, I'll leave you to it.'

It took us half an hour to move the pieces of the library into its home, an empty room with deep windows looking onto the side garden.

Then the real work began.

We started with the plinths, six of them. Their fit was snug but allowed for wood movement. More important were the levels. I worked my way around the room with a long spirit level and a box of maple shims. Fortunately, the floor was true; only three thin shims needed.

Next came the base cupboards, fixed to the plinths with Charlie's hidden locking wedges. Then we put the shelf cabinets on the bases, again fixing them with secret wedges. As instructed, I screwed each cabinet to the wall with two screws that went through prepared slots. Then I slid into place the decorative cover strips that hid the expansion gaps. Finally, I attached the cornices and the skirtings.

The room was transformed. Boz and I stood looking at it. We'd worked well together, said little as we turned a bare room into a library: woodwork softly glowing, bevelled glass catching the light. With books, a library table, a few chairs, the room would be complete.

'You blokes know what you're doing,' said Boz. 'It's beautiful. Best thing I ever carted.'

'Did your bit,' I said.

I walked around, tested a few locks, opened and closed a few doors and drawers, admired the fit, even admired my hand-cut dovetail joints and raised panels. This piece of furniture would be giving pleasure long after everyone alive on this day was gone, I thought. It was not a bad thing to have helped create.

A voice said, 'Oh my God, I'm dreaming. Heaven, this room is absolute heaven.'

Mrs Purbrick, owner of the house, danced into the room, head thrown back, came around me, pirouetted with arms above her head, finished leaning back against me. It would have been girlish had not Mrs Purbrick's girlhood been somewhere in the early 1960s. She was a short blonde with a formidable bosom, all of her lifted, tucked, sucked, puffed, abraded, peeled, implanted, stripped and buffed, and, today, packaged in a short-skirted dark-grey business suit.

'Mr Taub will check the installation when he gets back,' I said. 'This is Boz Bylsma, who did the hard work today.'

Mrs Purbrick was walking around the room touching the woodwork. Her eyes flicked to Boz, summed her up, nodded. She stopped, put her head back and shouted, 'D*aaviï*d.'

David appeared. He had clearly been waiting in the passage. He looked around the room. 'Marvellous,' he said.

'Quite marvellous. In exquisite taste.' He tugged at an earlobe. 'An island of good taste.'

Mrs Purbrick fixed him with her gaze. 'I want the books in by the end of tomorrow,' she said. 'Is that clear, darling?'

'Clear? What could be clearer? Any preferences? Leatherbound Mills & Boon? Collected works of Danielle Steel? I believe there's a special on Jeffrey Archer.'

'Use your *exquisite* taste,' Mrs Purbrick said. With difficulty, she raised her eyebrows and showed her top teeth. The teeth were perfect. Some cosmetic dentist probably lay warm and slack beside a pool in Tuscany on the proceeds of that achievement.

'How I wish that that were a standing instruction,' said David, not quite tossing his head.

Mrs Purbrick tried to narrow her eyes at him. 'On your way, you dear little man.'

'Well, that's it from us,' I said. 'On behalf of Mr Taub, I wish you well to use this library.'

Mrs Purbrick came over to me, came close, the torpedoes prodding my bottom ribs, put a short-fingered hand on my cheek. 'You are so old-fashioned and courteous, I can't believe men like you still exist.'

I caught the eyes of Boz, we were even-height, eyes level, some distance above Mrs Purbrick. She was expressionless, then she blinked, just a blink.

'Frozen in time,' I said.

Mrs Purbrick moved her hand down to my chest, traced a circle with a stubby finger. 'I'm going to have to have people for drinks to show off the library, make them envious. You'll be getting an invitation, you and Mr Taub. Nothing fancy, just drinkies after five. Mike and Ros Cundall will be coming. I'm sure you know them.'

'Not in the flesh, no.'

'Lovely people. And I'm sure they need a library. God knows, they've got everything else. I was at Sam's birthday party a few weeks ago, that's the son and heir, charming young man. In the recreation wing. Wing, mark you, it's like a resort, two bars, the pool, billiard tables, gymnasium, sauna. And then there's this games room—electronic shooting things, old pinball machines, you name it, my dear.'

'A library would certainly complete the facilities,' I said. 'I look forward to receiving your invitation.'

Mrs Purbrick saw us to the side door. On the way, she ran a hand over my buttocks, no more than an appraisal, the touch a trainer might give a horse's rump at the sales. It had been a while since anyone had done that to me.

'You will come for drinks, won't you, Jack?'

'It'll require legislation to keep me away.'

'And make sure the darling Mr Taub comes.'

Going back across the river, the empty van bouncing and squeaking, I studied Boz's forearms. Long, sinews showing, just a sheen of pale hair.

'So,' she said. 'Hangin out with the rich and famous. I was on a film set where Sam Cundall was big-notin himself.'

'In films too, is he?'

'Had money in it. Just for tax. And the possibility of sex. Dud film.'

'I haven't been to drinks for years,' I said. 'I'll have to go if the invite comes through. Charlie could use another library job.'

Boz gave me an unbelieving look. 'What about this Cannon Ridge business?' she said. 'Reckon it's bent?'

We talked about the politics of the state. She had no respect for anyone. Outside Charlie's, she said, not looking at me, 'That was quick. Short-time. What d'ya reckon?'

'The deal's the deal.'

She looked at me, left hand went over her stubble. 'No. Make me a lesser offer.'

I thought about it. 'You pay for a late lunch.'

Dodging drug dealers and their customers, we walked to a Lebanese place in Smith Street where they knew me.

Seated in the window, I said, 'How's the film business?'

Boz shook her head. 'Shithouse. I'm thinkin of givin it away. There's a bloke called Sewell moves a lot of art and antiques, wants to pack it in, sell the business. Problem is I can't work out what I'd be buyin.'

'How's that?'

'It's about 90 per cent goodwill, no contracts or anythin, just customers he's had for 20 years. They could take one look at me and say so long Maryanne.'

'You know that number? Tell him you want to go through the books. Work out the percentage of turnover from each of the regular customers. Then go and see them and ask if they'll carry on hiring the firm if you buy it.'

She looked at me, fork poised. 'I could do that?'

'If he says no, walk away. How old's this bloke?'

Through the window, a few metres away, I could see a boy of about 13, a thin boy, face sharpened by the street, peachfuzz on his chin. He was someone's child, lost into the world like a puppy into an open drain, now waiting for something, someone, agitated, scratching, licking his lips, rubbing his small nose. The person came, older, bigger, stood close to him, obscured him.

'Fifty maybe, around there,' said Boz.

The boy was gone. Two girls, older, late teens, dirty hair, faces pierced in three places, were on the spot, heads moving, looking in different directions. One clutched a plastic bag.

'You'll need a restraint of trade in the contract,' I said.

'Pardon?'

'How old are you?'

'Am I asking a stupid question?'

'No. I'm just losing touch with ages. I need a baseline.'

'Thirty-six. A week ago.'

'Happy birthday.'

'Thank you.'

Her eyes were the colour of wet slate.

'Restraint of trade. It stops him selling you the business and then starting a new one in opposition to you. He's young enough to try that.'

'Jesus,' she said, 'I know fuck-all about business.'

'Do the looking at the books bit,' I said, 'then come and see me about the contract. I'm cheap.'

'McCoy says living opposite your office is a risk.'

She'd been told the story.

'McCoy likes to generalise. He's had one unfortunate experience in the street. No-one forced him to throw his chainsaw into a passing vehicle.'

She paid and we walked back to Charlie's in half-hearted rain. I went around to the driver's side of the van with her. Her hair held drops of water. She brushed a hand over her scalp, dispelled the moisture. 'Got any other libraries to put in, I'm your person,' she said, getting into the cab. 'I like your libraries.'

'The person of choice. You will be that person.'

She looked down at me. 'Jack,' she said, 'not to fuck about, I suppose you're taken.'

So plain a question.

'At this moment in time,' I said, 'no.'

'I'm the same. Well, give me a ring. Business or social.'
She started the engine. 'Here's looking down at you, kid.'

I watched her take the top-heavy old van around the tight corner, stood for a while, thinking. Boz.

No. The world was already too much with me.

At the office, the answering machine was signalling me.

Jack, it's Morris. Listen, I want a letter to Krysis. The neighbour says the bastard's storing stuff in the garage again. Tell him he's trespassing and we'll kick his arse. Today, Jack, do it today. Cheers.

Morris, father of Stan the publican.

Jack, Morris again. I forgot to say the prick's pushed the offer up another thirty grand. I told him not interested. He says he wants to talk to you. Tell him your instructions are he should piss off and stop wasting my time. Okay? Cheers.

Ditto. Someone wanted to buy his two adjoining properties in Brunswick, a more than generous offer as I understood it, but Morris couldn't contemplate life without them.

Don't let them tell you Robbie Colburne was just a casual barman.

A woman. Them? Who would they be? Xavier Doyle and company?

Jack, the Brunswick Street one, that lease finishes next month. Bastard rang the other day, wants to talk. Don't want to know him, he's out.

Morris, again. His Brunswick Street tenant was indeed deserving of the slipper, an habitual non-payer.

I sat down and gave Robbie Colburne some thought. Queensland. He'd told The Green Hill he'd worked in Queensland. I rang a man in Sydney called D.J. Olivier. He said he'd ring me back. As far as my assets went, my credibility with D.J. ranked just behind my half of the boot factory. Then I opened my mail, threw most of the contents into the bin, took that into the back room and emptied it into a green garbage bag. After that, I made a cup of tea and sat at my table to read the latest issue of the *Law Institute Journal*. There were many things of interest in it, even some I understood, including recent findings of the legal profession tribunal regarding professional misconduct. Accounts of the venality of some of my colleagues left me greatly distressed. Distressed but not surprised.

I went to my window. Heavier rain now, steady plinks on the pools in the gutter. The lights were on in McCoy's abode across the street, presumably to assist him in committing some disgusting act on canvas. Or elsewhere.

The phone rang.

'Here's a number,' said D.J. Olivier. 'It's good for an hour or so.'

I drove around to the Prince, parked in the loading zone around the corner. Inside, I found no youthful pioneers of the cyberfrontier energising themselves with the fermented juice of radiated Russian potatoes. The nicotine-dark chamber held only a mildly alcoholic accountant called George Mersh, who played seven games for Fitzroy, and Wilbur Ong and Norm O'Neill, both strangers to the cyber and approaching a frontier from which no-one returned.

They saw me, mouths opened like demanding chicks spotting the parent bird.

I heard the words unspoken, raised a hand. The mouths closed.

'Not today,' I said. 'I don't want to hear about it today.'

We would speak of the Saints' inglorious performance but not while the memory was so fresh. Raw. I rapped on the counter and opened the flap.

Stan appeared.

'The phone,' I said.

'Your professional uses his mobile,' he said, and smirked.

'It's the new asbestos. Don't you read the papers, Stan? Worse than stuffing bits of asbestos into your ear.'

His eyed opened wide, then a knowing look came over his face. 'What do you take me for?'

'An enigma wrapped in a mystery. Three beers. And have something yourself. Have, what is it, a Wally?'

He shook his head. 'Jesus, Jack. Stolly. Really.'

I went into the pub's office/archive. The telephone was under one of Stan's jumpers, which I moved with a rolled-up newspaper. Cautiously. Then I cleaned the handset with a paper napkin I found marking a place in a paperback called *Get a New e-Life: Cybertactics for Small Business*, and dialled.

'Done the immediate stuff,' said D.J. Olivier. 'Queensland, driver's licence, issued 1992, renewed January 1996, and most recently six weeks ago. Otherwise, he's not on the books.'

Robert Gregory Colburne had no tax file number and was not registered with Medicare.

'MasterCard, six weeks old, limit ten grand, it's 600-odd in credit.'

'Address?'

'Brissie. Red Hill. 'Also for electoral roll. No phone in the name now or ever. There's just one possible lippy smudge on this collar.'

'Yes?

'The name got a passport in 1996. Departed Sydney, April '96, but there's no mention of a return arrival.'

'How can that be?'

'Well, sometimes they come back in a sailing boat, tramp steamer, fucking hang-glider, land in Broome, Top End,

Tassie somewhere, there's not always a record gets on file. Till they try to leave through Customs again, nothing shows.'

'Anything else?'

'No traces at the moment between April '96 and the licence renewal and credit card issue six weeks ago. Oh and he enrolled at Sydney Uni in '91. Seems to have dropped out in the first year. He's not there in '92.'

'What school?'

'Walkley. Up there somewhere to buggery over the mountains. You go through Bathurst. I think.'

I thanked D.J. and joined Wilbur and Norm. The subject of St Kilda could not be postponed. We had a fact-free exchange of views. The new development today was that both students of the game found some positive things to say about the Saints' appalling performance. Most of them would have escaped less scholarly eyes. It had been that way with Fitzroy through the many dark seasons, the times without comfort or hope, all our enemies grown taller and swifter, their hands bigger and stickier, their boots crafted to kick impossible bananas and their foul blows, trips and gouges apparently invisible to umpires.

Cheered, I left before the IT crowd arrived. If they were ever coming back. As I turned the corner, the rain paused. The air was cold, deceptively clean-smelling. I could hear water running in the gutters, a flow of toxic liquid heading for the river and the bay.

On the way home, Linda Hillier was on the radio, where I'd left her, on 3KB.

Congratulations. You're listening to Melbourne's smartest station, and that says something about you.

Tonight we're talking about drugs. Heroin users complained on radio this morning that they were treated like second-class citizens. Well, the

man I'm about to talk to, the Reverend Allen O'Halloran, says that's
what they are. What's your view? The number to call is, and bookmark
it in what passes for your phone's mind...

One day, I would phone in. One day when I had the
words to speak to Linda.

At home. A fire. No, too much effort. I put on the
heating, went to the kitchen, began the defrosting of
Sunday's stew and opened a bottle of the exemplary Mill
Hill chardonnay. Then I slumped in the armchair, switched
on the television for the news.

Innocents dying, the guilty walking free, nature mocking
the frailty of human habitations, a hijacking, a royal birth, a
supermodel on drug charges, a politician caught out in a lie,
a cat's incredible sewer journey, the death of a revered
pornographer and the legal battle over his archive of people
doing things. Sport. And weather, a map, a man who knew
about weather: cold, rain, the possibility of periods without
the latter.

Watching this necklace of images strung in some
electronic bunker, a part of my mind that bicycled along dull
streets and sat on benches overlooking nothing was thinking
about Robbie Colburne.

What to make of Robbie? Gets into university. Drops out.
Runs up debts. Departs for foreign shores in 1996. Not
recorded as coming back. Four years later, back nevertheless,
renews his driver's licence and, notwithstanding his credit
history, gets a credit card with a $10,000 limit. Appears in
Melbourne with a small but expensive wardrobe, gets a
casual job as a barman, dies of a drug overdose.

A short but puzzling life.

Someone had to know more about Robbie. Someone had
to be able to put some coherence into this narrative. It was

just a question of who. The woman who left the message on the answering machine knew something. But I didn't know who she was.

I rang Cyril Wootton on his latest mobile number. The numbers changed all the time.

'You wish to make contact with me?' he said. 'How unusual. That's twice in a few days. The hole in the ozone layer, El Pino, to what do I owe this?'

'Niño. El Niño. Pina Colada. Expensive, this thing.'

'How much?'

'Yes or no. I'm happier with no.' I didn't want to go travelling.

'Yes, if properly accounted for.'

'Was it not ever thus?'

'Ever thus my arse,' said Wootton.

'Really, Cyril,' I said, 'at times your vocabulary is at odds with your appearance. Your carefully cultivated appearance.'

The town of Walkley was a long and narrow blanket thrown over the spine of a ridge running out the back of the Great Dividing Range. To get there, you drove out of Sydney and on through hard country, high, gaunt, dry. Everywhere black rock broke the thin skin of soil, erosion gullies furrowed the slopes. The light was white and offended my city eyes.

I drove around until I found the school, it wasn't difficult, parked the hired Corolla outside the only brick building. The wind was a shock, buffeting, frozen hands pressing against my face.

A sign took me past murmuring classrooms to the principal's office. In the anteroom, a stone-faced woman, big, sat on a stool behind a counter. She looked at me and asked, 'You're not Telstra, are you?'

'No.'

'Bastards. Kin I do for you?'

'Carly?'

'Yes.'

'I spoke to you yesterday. Jack Irish. The lawyer from Melbourne.'

'Oh.' She looked less stony. 'Well. Melbourne. My little sister lives in Doncaster.'

'I'm told it's a great place to live. Does she like it?'

Wince, shrug of big shoulders.

'He's a paramedic. She met him in Bali. This bloke with them, he was dancing, fell over. Heart. Young, too. Everyone panicked. Denzil just went over, pushed everyone away, sat on the bloke, got the ticker going.'

'Saved his life.'

'No. Well, for a bit. Anyway, Carol's down there with him. In Doncaster. Supposed to get married but it's bin six years.'

'It's a big step. Giving it a lot of thought.'

'Yeah.' She passed a hand over her right temple. 'That or he's got somethin else goin.'

Time to move on from Doncaster. 'The principal's in?'

Carly rose with difficulty and went to the door at the back of the room, knocked, waited, opened it and put her head in.

'The man from Melbourne's here,' she said. 'Mr Irish. He rang yesterday.'

She waved me in.

The principal was behind a bare desk in a big, light room with school photographs on one wall and a large whiteboard covered with diagrams and lists on another. He stood up and put out a hand.

'David Pengelly.'

'Jack Irish.'

We shook hands and sat down. He had wispy hair combed across his scalp and a thin, worried face, the face of a farmer forever anxious about weather and weeds and the bank.

'Long way to come.'

'Excuse for a drive. I had business in Sydney.'

'Carly says you're asking about a student.'

'He would have finished about ten years ago. Robert Gregory Colburne.'

'What's it in connection with?'

'He died suddenly. No-one knows anything about his

family, next of kin. I was asked to look into it.' All true.

Pengelly scratched his scalp with one finger, taking care not to disturb hair. 'Ten years,' he said. 'That's a problem.'

I waited.

'The records used to be in a demountable out the back,' he said, pointing. 'Burnt down in '94, my first year here. Couldn't save anything. Kids. Year 12s, just after the exams.'

'Anyone still on the staff from 1990?'

He pulled a face. 'Ann Pescott. That'd be about it. Been packing it in, all the senior ones.'

'Could I talk to her? It would only take a minute.'

Silence while he studied me. Then he got up and went to the door. 'Carly, ask Ann Pescott to step in for a minute, will you?'

He came back. 'Died suddenly?'

'Drugs,' I said. 'Accidental.'

'Not much accidental about drugs. I used to teach in Sydney, in the west. Kids shooting up in the toilet block. Got away first chance I could.' He looked out of the window at a sad stand of eucalypts moving in the wind. 'Can't get away from it though. Can't get away from anything, can you?'

'No, I suppose not.'

'No.' He was studying me again. 'I wanted to be a lawyer. Had the marks. My parents didn't have the money.'

I didn't have anything to say to that. There was a knock at the door and a woman in her forties came in, not confidently. I stood up.

'Ann, this is Mr Irish, a lawyer,' said Pengelly. 'It's about a kid from years ago. What was the name?'

I shook hands with Ann Pescott. She had an intelligent face, lines of disappointment, nervousness in her eyes: cared too much, waited too long.

'Robert Gregory Colburne. He started at Sydney University in 1991, so 1990 would probably…'

Her face was blank. 'No,' she said. 'Colburne, I don't remember a Colburne. But I didn't have the seniors then.' Her eyes apologised for failing me. 'Sorry.'

'He'd have been a bright student.'

'No. He didn't come through me.' She swallowed. 'Must have arrived in eleven or twelve. There were a few new kids around from Forestry around then.'

'Forestry?'

'Conservation and Forestry, whatever it was called then, changes its name every year. They sent a whole lot of people up here from Sydney. Regionalisation I think it was called. Total disaster, city people, they all hated it and then the government changed and they all went back.'

'So people around here would remember them?'

She shrugged. 'Well, yes. Some. I suppose.'

'Where should I start?'

A siren sounded, a harsh noise.

Ann Pescott's eyes went to Mr Pengelly.

'They'll probably find their own way out,' he said. 'Animals generally do when the door's open.'

'Terry Baine at the newsagents,' she said. 'He would have been around in 1990. And they know everything, the Baines.'

I thanked Mr Pengelly and Ann Pescott for their time, together and separately. He seemed sad to see me go. I understood. On my way out, I thanked Carly.

'Got a card?' she said. 'You never know. My sister might need a lawyer in Melbourne.'

'You never know.' Relationships made in Bali are not known for their durability. Six years was probably some sort of record.

I parked outside the newsagent in the main street. There wasn't a great deal going on in Walkley. A bullbarred ute rumbled by. Two men were talking outside the bank, faces and hats shaped by hands and wind and rain and gravity. A shop door opened and a child in a stroller came out, followed by a woman inside many handknitted garments. I could see only the tip of the child's nose, a tiny pink nipple.

Two customers were in the shop, browsing the rack of magazines. The man behind the counter, fat advancing, hair receding, was staring at a computer monitor, frowning, rapping keys. He saw me in his peripheral vision, didn't look around.

'Sometimes I think it's a blessing the old bloke's gone,' he said. 'Christ knows what he'da made of this crap.'

'Terry Blaine?'

He turned his head. 'Help you?'

I introduced myself.

'Melbourne.' He beamed at me. 'There the other day. For the Grand Prix. Stayed at the Regency, me and me brother, nothin but the best. Casino, you name it. Treat for the wives.'

'They like motor racing?'

'Nah. They went shoppin. Had to take the credit cards off em after the first day, mind. Outta control. So what's yer business up here?'

'I'm trying to find the family of someone who died in Melbourne recently. He finished school here.'

'Yeah? Who's that?'

'Robert Colburne.'

Jesus,' he said. 'Robbo.'

'Remember him?'

'Oh yeah. What happened?'

'Drugs. Accidental overdose.'

Terry whistled, shook his head. 'Robbo. Mad, bad and dangerous to know.'

'Knew him well?'

'Yeah. A bit. Came in Year Eleven. Clever bloke, very smart. Went to uni after. Him and Janice Eller were the only ones.'

'Know his family?'

'Only Mrs Reilly.'

'A relation?'

'His auntie. She went back to England, oh, six, seven years ago. Robbo said his mum and dad split up when he was a kid, left him with someone. Then his dad got some tropical wog, PNG, I can't remember, he died. His mum didn't want to know him, she was in England, I think.'

He paused, sniffed. 'Mind you, Robbo was a bit of a bullshitter. Bit of the poof in him, too. Arty-farty.'

'So Robbie wasn't part of the Forestry move up here?'

'Nah. Just came the same year.'

A projectile-nosed woman with a scarf tied over her narrow head came to the counter, copy of *New Knitting* in hand.

'Sellin things today?' she said. 'Or just natterin?'

Terry didn't look at her, took the magazine and passed a barcode reader over it. It appeared not to work. He sighed, jabbed at the till keyboard.

'Voted for this government, mate,' he said. 'Make no secret of it, never have. I can tell you, never again. This GST…no, don't get me goin on the subject.'

'Shockin, the price of this,' the woman said. 'You put it up every second month.'

'Don't blame me,' said Terry. 'That's the pound done that, pound and the GST. Beats me how the pound can be worth more than the dollar. I need that explained to me. That's four twenty-five change. Thank you, Mrs Lucas.'

'Profiteerin goin on, no doubt in my mind.'

He watched her go, slit-eyed. 'Old bitch,' he said. 'Shit I have to put up with.'

'So there's no family around that you know of?'

'Nah.'

'He didn't come back here?'

'Nah. I heard he dropped out of uni, Janice Eller's mum told me that.'

I said, 'I might talk to Janice Eller. How would I do that?'

He blinked, ran a knuckle over his pink lower lip. 'Dead, mate,' he said. 'Thredbo.'

Thredbo was a one-word Australian story, a tragedy on the snowfields, a large piece of hillside coming unstuck, people dying under collapsed buildings.

'What about her family?'

'Only had a mum. She died.'

Not your most profitable expedition, this trip to Walkley. Nothing gained and nothing in prospect but an indigestible meal and a night in some sagging motel bed.

'Anyone around here who'd know anything about Robbie?'

He shook his head. 'Nah, don't think so. This girl came up here from Sydney with the Forestry, hung around Robbo. What was her name? My mate Sim had a thing for her...Sandra someone.'

'Your mate around?'

'Gone barra fishin, way up there in the Territory, lucky bugger. Should be back soon.'

I got out a card. 'I'd appreciate it if you could ask him to give me a ring.'

I got as far as Lithgow. I'd got as far as Lithgow once before, in the largely blank period after my second wife, Isabel, was murdered by a client of mine. At least I think it was Lithgow. I wasn't paying much attention in those days, only sober for as long as it took me to drive from one town to another, any town with a pub to any other town with a pub. If it was Lithgow I remembered, some kind of miners' strike was going on and, in the pub, a drunk miner accused me of being a journalist from Sydney. I didn't deny it, didn't care to, just had a fight with him.

No pub fights on this visit. I drove into the cold valley town, breathed the coal smoke from the fires, bought two stubbies of Boag and a bottle of mineral water from a drive-in bottle shop, found a place that made hamburgers and got one with the lot, except the egg. In a room at an unlovely brick-veneer motel, I drank the beer and ate my supper in front of a television set that changed channels on its own. Then, tired in many ways, I went to bed with my book, *Dying High: Lies About a Climber's Life*, bought on impulse months before, grabbed on my way out to get a taxi to the airport. There is something about the stupidity of climbing mountains that appeals. Perhaps it's the clinging by the fingertips to inhospitable surfaces. I could claim some experience in this area.

In the night, I was woken by the sounds of quick sex close by, intimately close, centimetres away, just beyond the plasterboard wall. Startled, for a moment unsure of where

I was, saddened when I remembered, I wrapped the sour foam pillow around my head, lay thinking about Robbie Colburne. Then I moved on to Cynthia and her attacker with the Saint tattoo, drifted off, listening to the trucks hissing, groaning, whining on the highway, thinking about my life, why equilibrium escaped me, why I couldn't find a steady state, chose to ask questions of strangers, lie down in beds too short, turn and turn again between cold, slithery, electric nylon sheets.

I rose just after dawn, creaks in my knees, happy to be going. I'd only had brief times in my life when I wasn't happy to be going. Sneakily, shamefully happy. Cleansed in a cramped, stained fibreglass chamber, I went outside. In the coal valley, the air was freezing. White breath hung on the face of a man walking two small dogs, clung to a few pale shiftworkers coughing on the first of the day. They were all I saw on my way to the steep, winding road out of the valley. There was a moment on the heights when I could look back: nothing to see, the place gone, buried in sallow, yellow dawn-mist.

On the plane home, I sat next to a middle-aged dentist from Collaroy. Shortly after take-off, and without the slightest encouragement, he told me that he was leaving his wife and two children, aged eleven and thirteen, to be with a Melbourne person he had met at a cosmetic dentistry conference in Hawaii.

'These things happen,' I said. Another man grateful to be going.

'I wasn't looking for it to happen. It just happened. Like a…like a bolt of lightning. Can you understand that?'

'Without any difficulty.' I got out my book, found my place.

'Well, you don't do something like this lightly, do you?'

'No. You wouldn't.'

The dentist leaned over, looked at me from close range. I suppose they get used to doing that, a life of looking into people's mouths. After a while, you lose the feeling of intruding.

'I feel like I'm on a personal journey,' he said. 'The road less travelled.'

I looked at him briefly, a mistake.

'Know what I mean?' he said, licked his lips.

'Yes.'

Complicit, I didn't say that it was not so much a personal journey on a road less travelled as a trip in a crammed bus on a six-lane freeway. All I wanted to do was read. This would stop me thinking about the distinctly unhealthy coughing note I'd detected in the port engine.

My companion went on exploring metaphors for his condition all the way to Melbourne. From time to time, I fed him a new one to keep him from asking me questions.

Home. The comforting feel of one's own tarmac.

On the way from the airport, I got off the suicidal freeway before the tollway began, perversely took to choked Bell Street, and at length found my way to St Georges Road and Brunswick Street. It was early afternoon, overcast. I lucked on a parking spot near Meaker's, went in and ordered a toasted chicken sandwich from Carmel, the worldly child.

'Tell him it's for Jack,' I said. 'That sometimes stops him leaving the bones in.'

'I'll write it down,' she said. 'I'm too scared to speak to him.'

Enzio the cook was subject to mood swings. From bad to much, much worse, and back. I'd almost finished reading the form for Mornington when his squat figure emerged from the kitchen, scowled at the room, came over and put a plate down in front of me: big sourdough slices containing Enzio's secret filling of chicken, red capsicum, ricotta and other unidentifiable stuff, the whole flattened under a hot weight. I felt saliva start.

Enzio sat down, looked around, pointed his blunt and unshaven chin at me. 'Listen,' he said. 'Hair transplants. What you think?'

'Can we talk about this later? Hair and food don't mix.'

He ignored my plea. 'This woman,' he said, 'she likes hair.'

'A new woman?'

'At the market. Her husband died. She talks about his hair all the time, lovely hair, strong hair.' He ran his hand over the surviving strands on his scalp. Unlovely, unstrong.

I looked at my sandwich. The point about a toasted sandwich is that it is eaten warm.

'Talks where? Where are you when she talks about hair?'

He jerked his head. 'Where you think? Where you talk this kind of talk?'

I gave him the lawyerly eye. 'Enzio, if this woman wanted hair, she wouldn't be talking to you in bed about hair. She's feeling guilty because she's having such a good time. Her hairy husband, all he had was hair. That's all she can find to say about him. You, on the other hand, you've got something else.'

I paused, bent my head closer. 'It's not hair she wants, Enzio. Get me?'

The ends of Enzio's mouth bent down, slowly, a sinister, knowing look.

'Fuck hair,' he said. He made a gesture with his right forearm that brooked no misinterpretation.

'Exactly. Now get back to work.'

He left. In the doorway to the kitchen, he turned. Our eyes met. He gave me a confident nod. Several nods.

Next patient, Dr Irish. Would that all problems admitted of such effortless solutions. In particular, my problems. The sandwich was still warm. Halfway, I signalled for the coffee, the short signal, thumb and index fingers a centimetre apart.

Carmel brought the potent eggcup of coffee and a yellow A4 envelope. 'Enzio says this came yesterday.' She touched the tip of her tongue to her upper lip, a kissable upper lip. 'He's whistling,' she said. 'Is there a secret?'

'Make them come to you,' I said. 'Never use force.'

She nodded, no expression. 'Thank you. I believe some call you the cookmaster.'

'The knowing do,' I said.

Carmel was clearing the table next to the door as I left. 'Your work here will never be done,' she said.

The office was cold and I noticed dust. How could anyone trust a solicitor whose office was dusty? I put on the blow heater and the smell of hot dust filled the room. How had this dust problem crept up on me?

Cyril Wootton on the answering machine, twice, a Wootton urgent but not irascible, which was unusual. My sister, Rosa, mildly exasperated, which was not. Drew Greer, saying unkind, mocking things about St Kilda's performance against West Coast. Sad but to be expected from someone rendered agnostic by the death of Fitzroy. And Mrs Purbrick.

Jack, darling, such short notice but you must come for drinks tomorrow, six-ish, no excuses accepted.

It's business, I thought. And my chance to meet the Cundalls. Everyone else had.

I rang Cyril.

'As always, Mr Wootton will be delighted to have made contact with you,' said Mrs Davenport. Every day, she sounded more like Her Royal Highness Queen Elizabeth II.

'But do we ever really make contact, Mrs Davenport? We talk, we may even touch, but do we make contact? I mean, in the sense of...'

'Putting you through,' she said.

'Jesus, Jack,' said Wootton, 'mobile that's not switched on, what the fuck is the purpose...'

'Silence is the purpose, Cyril. The silence in which to do one's work.'

He gave me a silence. Then he made a noise, not so much animal as vegetable, the noise a sad carrot or potato might make, the noise of something deeply, hopelessly embedded in mud.

'The client would like a progress report,' he said.

Spoilt rotten, judges. Associates and clerks and tipstaffs and witnesses and defendants and jurors and learned counsel in silly wigs, all hanging on their every word, many of them hanging and fawning.

'Tell the client I'll report when there's something worth reporting.'

Wootton whistled, put the phone down. He'd be one of the fawners. I'd have to ask Cyril how it was that Mr Justice Colin Loder brought the problem of Robbie Colburne to him.

I sat down and thought about my progress. Nil, really. Robbie left the country and didn't appear to have come back. That was about it. It was strange but there were possible explanations.

Time to go home. Dawn in cold Lithgow seemed days away.

Halfway to my car, I heard a car slowing behind me, looked around, flight-or-fight coming into play: a red Alfa, new, two men in it. At an unthreatening crawl, it drew level, and the passenger window slid down.

'Jack Irish?'

The man was young, sleek dark hair, a mole beside his mouth. He was wearing a grey polo-neck and a soft-looking black leather jacket without a collar:

I nodded, kept walking.

'For you,' he said, holding out a brown paper bag. 'From a friend.'

Without thinking, I took it. The car pulled away, braked before it took the sharp corner, a double pulse of red light in the gloomy day.

The bag held a video cassette, new, unlabelled. Courtesy, presumably, of Detective Sergeant Warren Bowman.

At home, I half-filled the bath, drowsed in it for a long time with a glass of single malt, the end of a bottle given to me by Lyall, bought duty-free in some airport servicing a trouble spot. Or Santa bloody Barbara. It was peaceful in the big room, a bedroom when I bought the building. Once upon a time, a fire had sometimes been lit in the brick hearth on a cold Sunday afternoon, one person had read in the bath, the other had sat in the armchair.

I thought more about Robert Colburne. The judge was paying to find out what had really happened to him if he hadn't accidentally overdosed. He said he was acting on behalf of someone who knew Robbie, lost touch with him for a long time, then made contact again in Melbourne.

I didn't like the feel of that story, the distance it placed between Mr Justice Loder and Robbie.

Musing in the claw-footed bath, a bath big enough for two, if they arranged themselves.

I dismissed that memory, rose and donned unironed but clean garments and began the preparation of a modest meal.

I drank some red wine, moved roughly-chopped onion around for a while, kept away from the hot spot that the famous and expensive French frying pan wasn't supposed to have. The French are the finest conpeople in the world. I added garlic and mushrooms, a tin of tomatoes.

The video. Delivered by hand by men in an expensive car. Undercover cops? I switched off the gas, took my glass to the sitting room and plugged in the cassette, went to the couch and used the remote. The video flickered briefly, began.

A young man got out of a cab. This would be Robbie Colburne. He was tall and slim and, from on high and zooming in and out on him, the camera caught a certain athletic insouciance: chin up, arms moving freely, first two fingers extended pistol-like. It was night but made day by spotlights recessed into the building on his left. Light gleamed on his cheekbones, on his straight black hair combed back. He was handsome, all in black, a jacket worn over a tee-shirt.

The camera followed him to where he disappeared beneath a cantilevered porch bearing the name of the building, incised in polished concrete: CATHEXIS.

Daylight this time, someone sitting at a table on the pavement from across a busy street, traffic blocking vision for seconds at a time. Then a new camera angle, nothing obscuring the man now but the camera unsteady. He had a small glass on a saucer, the shortest of short blacks, drank a teaspoonful, looked around, newspaper in his hand, a half-amused look. He was dark, balding, a fleshy intimidating face.

Early evening, the young man again, Robbie, seen in profile, side on, waiting to cross a busy street, finding a break in the traffic, walking diagonally, the confident walk.

Night again. A long shot in bad conditions, rain, a car window coming down, the camera zooming in, the young man behind the wheel, in a dinner suit now, white shirt, black bow tie, saying a few words to someone outside the vehicle.

End of moving pictures.

I'd asked Warren Bowman for a photograph of Robbie.

I'd expected a still, a mortuary picture. Instead, he sent me a collection of surveillance video clips showing Robbie under expensive observation, moving, in the street. Good of him but why? I could ask Detective Sergeant Bowman. But he would probably say that he was just being helpful.

And why did a casual barman like Robbie deserve this kind of photographic attention? Was it because he wasn't just a barman, as my anonymous caller had suggested?

Warren Bowman said senior drug squad officers were on the scene quickly after the uniformed cops reported finding Robbie's body.

Expensive surveillance, two cameras on one occasion. That only happened to persons of great interest. Unless Robbie was an accidental, someone filmed in the surveillance of someone else. But, in that case, he would be someone close to the target; there was no other way he would be caught on camera so many times.

Robbie caught up in the surveillance of someone else. Was that it? The fleshy man?

Back to cooking. Time to add the tuna, get the rice going.

I was eating in front of the television when the phone rang. Cam.

'Little trip in the morning,' he said. 'Won't take long.'

'I got talkin to the bloke at the hotel next door,' Cam said. He wound down his window, flicked his cigarette end out, raised the window. We were in the V-8, passing the Fawkner Crematorium on the Hume, a sunny morning, petrol tanker ahead, Kenworth behind, stream of heavy metal coming the other way.

'What's the connection?'

'Hotel's part-owner of the carpark. Guest parkin. Carpark employs three blokes on eight-hour shifts, hotel provides security. In theory. This fella, he worked there eighteen months.'

'The name again?'

'Rick Chaffee. Two complaints about extra K's appearin on the clock while he was there. One bloke from Adelaide had a logbook, he reckoned someone took his Discovery for a 200K spin.'

Cam edged out for a look, came back in. He was wearing Western District casual attire today, navy-blue brushed-cotton shirt, heavy moleskin trousers, short riding boots. 'On the day, this Chaffee, his story is he was on the phone, he thought he recognised the driver of the Land Cruiser, let him out without checkin ID. Honest mistake.'

'They buy that?'

Cam shrugged. 'What can you prove? Sacked him. Cops run the tape over him, the hotel bloke says. No form to speak of, some kid stuff in WA, he's a WA boy, Mangoup, Banjoup, one of those up towns, they got hundreds. Plus he's got an assault when he was a bouncer in King Street.'

He was steering with his fingertips, head back, index fingers tapping to the music, soft Harry Connick. 'Worth a yarn, I reckon.'

'If the bloke's in this,' I said, 'it'll take more than a yarn.'

Cam's dark eyes lay on me for a moment.

I went back to reading the *Age*. The story at the bottom of page one was headlined: *Call for Cannon Ridge tender probe.*

It opened: *The State Government was last night urged to hold an inquiry into the tendering process that awarded a 100-year lease on the Cannon Ridge snowfield and a mini-casino licence to a company associated with Melbourne's millionaire Cundall family.*

The company, Anaxan Holdings, has a glittering list of shareholders, including some of Australia's Top 100 richest. A spokesman for shortlisted rival bidder WRG Resorts told a press conference yesterday that WRG has evidence that Anaxan knew details of all tenders before the vital second round of bidding.

The Minister for Development, Tony DiAmato, said WRG Resorts had not approached him. 'I have no idea what they're talking about. The previous government awarded this tender. We fought the whole idea of a private snowfield and another casino, everyone knows that. But it's done, it's history.'

Cam said, 'I read that stuff you sent me. The Saint's big with your crim tatt artist.'

I folded the paper. 'That's what my bloke said. Use half the phone book.'

I'd sent him the yellow A4 envelope left for me at Meaker's, sent it by express courier, fat and silent Mr Cripps behind the wheel of his burnished 1976 Holden.

'It's down here,' said Cam.

We turned right off the Hume, drove through a light industrial area, bricks, concrete products, pipes, turned left and went a long way, to the end of an unpaved road. Ahead, a sign on a wavy corrugated-iron fence was falling over. It said, no punctuation, Denver Garden & Building Supplies Plants Sand Soil Gravel Pavers Sleepers. The gate was half-open, drawn back until its sagging tip dug into the ground.

Cam nosed around it, parked in front of a long cement-sheet building, flat-roofed, meagre shelter over the door, one small window. Beside the door, three bags of cement had solidified, fused. We got out.

To the left of the gate was what remained of the Plants division of the business: a copse of birch trees in black plastic root bags, leaning inward, touching, dead; a conifer fallen over but indomitable, roots broken through the seams of the plastic bag and penetrating the packed soil; a row of concrete pots growing couch grass in abundance; some sad roses clinging to life, sparse leaves spotted with yellow.

The sound of a machine came from beyond the building. We walked around, passed an old pale-blue Valiant, buffed up, saw an expanse of dark, wet, rutted ground, big concrete pens holding gravel and sand, mulch, compost, other dark substances, everything untidy, spilling out of the enclosures, crushed into the ground.

The machine was a mid-sized lifter and it was moving rocks from one part of the yard to another, television-sized rocks for adding character to small, flat blocks in the outer suburbs.

We walked towards it and the driver saw us coming, the light glinted on his dark glasses as he looked our way, kept on going to his new pile, dumped the load with a crash, reversed the machine, gunned it back to the mother lode, took the bucket down, stuck it in with a ghastly screech, lifted, rocks falling out, swung around, went back, lifted the bucket to dump.

We were close, in the noise. The man turned his head towards us. Cam raised a hand, palm outward.

Bucket poised, the man cut the motor. He was big, no neck or chin to speak of, peaked cap too small for his long hair, tiny nose, arms like sewer pipes, belly hanging over a wide leather belt.

'Yah?'

'Rick Chaffee,' said Cam. It wasn't a question.

'Want somethin?' The man's voice was reedy, not congruous with the body.

'Few words about the parking garage.'

'What?'

'Curtin parking garage. You worked there.'

'Jacks?'

'No.'

'I'm workin here,' the man said. 'Busy.'

'Be a good idea to talk to us,' Cam said.

'Yah. Why's that?'

'You could be in trouble.'

Chaffee shook his head. 'Not cops?'

'No.'

He swivelled in his seat, stood up on the platform of the machine, towered over us, our heads at his knee-level. 'What's your name?' he said to Cam.

'Bruce,' said Cam.

Chaffee drew on his sinuses, not an engaging sound, and spat to Cam's right.

'Bruce's not a coon name,' Chaffee said. 'You look like you got a bit of coon in you.'

Cam turned his head to me, eyes full of resignation.

'Far as I'm concerned,' he said quietly, 'you stayed in the car.'

'We should leave,' I said, more than uneasy, much, much more. 'There are other ways.'

'Won't take long,' Cam said. 'Since we're here.'

He turned back to Chaffee. 'All I want to do is ask you about the Curtin carpark.' Pause. 'Mr Chaffee.'

Chaffee put a hand into an armpit, scratched. 'Busy, boong, fuck off.'

Cam looked down, shook his head, coiled, sprang, hooked his right arm around Chaffee's knees, pulled the big man out of the machine with one twisting movement, brought him over his head and dumped him.

Chaffee made a sound like a kicked dog as he hit the wet ground. He rolled over, balled himself, he was no stranger to being kicked, would try to grab the foot, the leg.

Cam stood back. 'Get up, Ricko,' he said, ordinary tone. 'I'm in a good mood.'

Chaffee got up, wary of a surprise, but when he was on his feet, I could see he liked this turn of events. 'Hey,' he said, taking off the dark glasses, throwing them to one side, his eyes flicking to me. 'Hey, no reason to fucken do that, really fucken stupid. Fucken boong stupid.'

Cam took a step closer, inside the range of the big arms, his hands at shoulder height, loose fists. He was as tall as Chaffee but 20 kilograms lighter. Chaffee put his head to one side.

'Cocky fucken boong,' he said, then grabbed at Cam's shirtfront, lunging, forehead dropped for the butt.

Cam went forward, into the lunge, his right hand travelled upward no more than 10 centimetres, a corkscrewing fist that made contact with Chaffee's nose, brought the man's head up, opened his eyes wide with pain, his arms falling to his sides, cap falling off.

Cam took another pace, in close, hit him again, the same short, twisting punch, this time high in Chaffee's chest, in the left collarbone. I thought I heard it break.

Chaffee went down, on one knee, both hands at his nose, blood running through his fingers. Cam put his hand in the man's hair, pulled him forward, dragged him across the muddy, rutted ground, Chaffee moaning, not resisting.

'Open the car door, Jack,' said Cam, nothing different about his voice. 'Wind the window down. Take the keys out.'

I opened the driver's door of the Valiant, did as I was told. Cam pulled Chaffee up to the open door, dropped his head on the seat, got behind him, kicked him in the backside with his right boot.

'Get in, Mr Chaffee,' he said.

Chaffee crawled in, using the steering wheel to drag himself. Cam helped, gripped the man's wide leather belt in both hands, pushed him in, slammed the door, a solid thunk.

Feeling his knuckles, flexing his fingers like a surgeon about to operate, Cam went over to the lifter, swung himself up, started the motor, gunned it, reversed, swung the machine savagely, came up to the Valiant.

'Ricko,' he shouted.

Chaffee was holding his chest now, his mouth open, blood in it, running over his lower lip. He looked at Cam, fear, wonder, in his eyes.

'Who'd you lend the Cruiser to that day, the one they sacked you for?'

'Dunno what you…' Chaffee coughed blood.

'You know, bubba,' Cam said. 'Ran your own car-hire business at the Curtin. Tell me now. Quick.'

'Know fuck-all about—'

'Your mates nearly killed a woman that day, know that, Ricardo?'

'Nah, don't—'

Cam raised the hopper.

I stood back.

He dumped the full load of stones, big landscaping stones, on the Valiant.

Stones bounced on the roof, one went through the windscreen, stones fell off the sides, rolled onto the bonnet, the boot.

The roof collapsed, the right-hand door pillar buckled, the back doors popped open.

Cam reversed the machine, swinging around, screamed across to a pit of yellow paving sand, dropped the hopper, drove it into the sand, filled it, sand spilling, raised the hopper, reversed and swung, came back.

A last grey volcanic rock toppled off the Valiant roof, rolled down the crazed, opaque, holed windscreen, over the stoved-in bonnet, fell into a puddle.

In the car, Chaffee was making sobbing, wheezing noises, noises of terror. The roof was pressing on his head and he was trying to open his door, jammed by the impact.

'Jesus, Ricky,' said Cam. 'You come through that alive. You're tough, you WA boys.'

He pulled the lever, dropped most of a cubic metre of sand on the Valiant. The springs sagged, sand poured into the car through the hole in the windscreen, filled the depressions, slithered to the ground.

The Valiant was disappearing under rocks and sand.

Chaffee screamed.

'There's more comin, Ricko,' said Cam. 'Then I'm givin you the gravel shower.' He waited. 'The Cruiser. Who'd you lend it to? Last time I'm askin you, fat boy.'

'Artie, Artie, I only know Artie.' Chaffee's voice was weak, he could barely speak.

Cam revved the engine, calmed it.

'More, bubba,' he said, 'more.'

'God'smyfuckenwitness, Artie's all...I'm dyin...'

'Damn straight,' said Cam. He emptied the rest of the sand onto the car, switched off, climbed down, dusted his moleskins, hands brushing. He went over to the wrecked Valiant, tested the door handle, gripped the door pillar in his right hand, and jerked.

The door came open. Cam reached in with both hands and pulled Chaffee out, jerked him out, let him fall into the mud. Paving sand was stuck to the man's blood, blood and sand all over his big chest, it was in his long hair, and he had a mask of yellow sand on his face, new black blood from his nose eroding it, creating thin furrows of blood.

'Dyin,' said Chaffee. 'Help me.'

'You'll be fine,' said Cam. 'WA boy like you, Buggerup, the old home town, take more than a few roccks, bit of sand. What's that word you called me? I forget. Want to say that again? That word?'

Chaffee put his head back, rolled his face away, into the mud, the white of an eye showing. 'Mate,' he said. 'Sorry, mate.'

'Well, that's okay than,' said Cam. 'Sorry is such a good word. Pity more people don't use it. Tell me some more about Artie.'

Chaffee groaned.

On the Hume, cruising, listening to Harry Connick again, I said, 'A really good trip. A short bloke called Artie. Chaffee's probably going to die back there and all we got was a short bloke called Artie.'

Cam was tapping his fingertips. 'Only hit him twice, can't die of that. Short Artie's good too.'

'How's that?'

'How many short Arties can there be? Short Arties with a Saint.'

The answering machine was speaking to a caller as I opened the door of my office. I took the two steps and picked up the phone.

'Ignore those words. Jack Irish.'

'Jack, Gus.'

Augustine, Charlie Taub's granddaughter. Alarm, a stab.

'Charlie?'

'What?'

'He's alright?'

She read my anxiety, laughed her sexy laugh. My shoulders and my chest untightened.

'Never better. He said to tell you he's staying another week. He's playing bowls every day, he's playing in a tournament next week. He said, and I quote, "Tell Jack, hot's good for one thing."'

I sighed.

'Means something, does it, the message?'

'Yes. Exactly as I feared. Will you marry me? Take me to Canberra with you?'

Charlie's granddaughter was a fighter for the oppressed workers and, said the gossip, being courted for a safe federal Labor seat. That or in due course Australia's highest union office.

'I'm not going to Canberra,' she said. 'You've been reading that idiot in the *Age*. Anyway, I don't think harem life would suit you.'

'The zenana. We'd sit around, the boys, playing cards,

crocheting, waiting for you to come home and pick one of us.'

'I may need to give this Canberra business more thought,' she said. 'Stay close to the phone.'

It was just after noon. Much of the day ahead, much already accomplished: a trip down the bright golden Hume, the witnessing of a man having his nose broken, his collar-bone fractured, tonnes of rock dropped on his prized car, followed by a coating of paving sand, enough sand to provide the base for a nice barbecue area.

Moving on. I settled down at my aged Mac and attended to the affairs of my bustling legal practice, to wit, a letter to Stan's father's tenant, Andreas Krysis, asking him to desist from storing things in Morris's garage, which was not part of his lease.

Hunger struck. I went around the corner and bought a salad pita, came back and ate while reading the sports section of the *Age*. The daily bulletin on all football clubs said that, notwithstanding the team's atrocious performance against West Coast, the St Kilda club president was standing firm behind the coach. 'He has our full confidence. We have always said that we are with him for the long haul.'

In football-speak, these sentiments translated as: *Full confidence*—most committee members want to sack the bastard. *The long haul*—until the next game. Saturday at Docklands Stadium was Waterloo for the coach.

I rang Drew. He was in court. I rang my sister.

'So,' Rosa said, 'to what?'

'To what what?'

'Do I owe this honour?'

'I've been away a bit. I went to see Claire.'

'I know that. I talk to her every second day. You may recall that I'm her aunt.'

It was hard for me to grasp that people saw themselves as aunts or uncles. I had neither, had never felt a vacuum in my life.

'Anyway,' she said, 'you've been back for over a week.'

An edge to her voice, not anger, not the usual exasperation. Worse. Knowingness.

'Lunch,' I said. 'It's been a while. Your choice of venue after the cruel things you said about mine last time.'

'Lunch.' She managed to roll the word around in her mouth, endow it with sinister meaning.

'What about The Green Hill?' I said. 'Very fashionable, I'm told. They know me there at the highest levels, the boss shouted me a tankard of Leprechaun ale the other day, Leprechaun, some name like that, very ethnic.'

Silence.

'Andrew Greer stood me up,' she said finally.

The masticating on *lunch* now meant something.

A moment of calculation.

'Drew? What, a legal matter?'

'No. A *lunch*.'

'I didn't know you knew Drew. In a lunching sense.'

Sparring. A spar.

'I don't. I thought I was going to have the opportunity.'

'To do what?'

'Get to know-him in a lunching sense.'

'Well, he's a busy man, things come up, that's the law.'

'Lawyers don't work on Saturdays.'

'The lawyers you know. Lawyers in name only. Accountants in drag. Tax avoidance, mergers and acquisitions. Drew is a criminal lawyer. They never stop, never sleep. Never eat, some of them.'

She knew. She could not know, but she knew. Some

psychic vibration had reached her, bounced off a star, found her.

'I don't know what this is about,' I said. 'What time are we on? What time is it on your side of the river?'

Silence.

'Well, I rang you, so whose prerogative is it to end the conversation? Tricky point of etiquette, not so?'

'Sometimes I hate you,' she said and put the phone down.

On the other hand, she could know if Drew had told her.

I sat back in my captain's chair and my shoulders sagged. Why had I been so stupid as to speak my mind to Drew? What did it matter if he became entangled with Rosa? What was one more clear-felled forest, one more toxic waste dump, one more nuclear test site in my immediate vicinity?

I sat in this mood of despond for a while and then, for want of something to do, I dialled Telstra inquiries. Since the privatised utility wanted to encourage people to use this free service, it took six minutes to get the number of Baine's Newsagency in Walkley.

'Baine's,' said Terry Baine.

'Terry, Jack Irish, I talked to you—'

'Mate, telepathy, mate, on the verge of ringin ya,' he said. 'Got the name of that girl, Sim come in this mornin.'

'How'd the barra go?'

'Yeah, well, big as great whites ya believe the bastard. Sandra Tollman, that's the name.' He spelled it. 'Sim says she married a Forestry bloke. Says he heard that. Christ knows where he'd hear that.'

I said my thanks.

'Got your number, mate. You're on the record. Comin down for the vroom-vroom next year, look you up.'

Adult life was all desire and expectation. Until it was too late. I went home to change for Mrs Purbrick's library-warming.

David, Mrs Purbrick's personal assistant, opened the huge black front door. His smile seemed genuine.

'Jack,' he said, extending his beringed right hand, the hand with the green stones, 'we're delighted you could come.' He dropped his voice. 'I must say I found the muscle you brought with you last time rather intimidating.'

'Just her manner of speech,' I said. 'She works with film people most of the time. I gather they only respond to a rough touch.'

He nodded, serious. 'I've heard that too. They like the firm smack of something or other.'

'The smack and the other, probably.'

David laughed. 'This way. Everyone's in the library telling madame how clever she is.'

We went through the gallery-like hall, through the open double doors into the wide passage, eight-paned skylights high above, parquetry and Persian rugs beneath our feet.

Music was coming from somewhere. Gershwin. We were close to the library door before the voices within became audible.

'Please,' said David, waving me in.

There were at least two dozen people in the room, more women than men, standing close together, laughter and teeth flashing. For a moment, I looked, wished Charlie were there to see his elegant bookcases filled with books, glowing in the lamplight, the people in the room made handsomer, better somehow, by being in the presence of his craftsmanship.

'Jack, Jack. Darling, so distinguished.'

Mrs Purbrick, on heels so high her toes had to bend at near-right angles to touch the ground, in business gear again, a dark suit, jacket worn over an open-necked white shirt unbuttoned for a considerable distance, great mounds beneath, ceremonial mounds. And, in keeping with the after-work nature of the occasion, severe horn-rimmed glasses. She took me by the lapels and brushed me on both cheeks with her inflated lips, the kiss of balloons, turned to face the room.

'Everyone, everyone, meet Jack Irish, who helped Mr Taub build this magnificent library.'

I cringed. There was a polite round of applause. Then I was taken around the room and introduced to people, youngish people, summer-in-Portsea, winter-in-Noosa, week-in-Aspen people. Over someone's shoulder, I recognised the face of Xavier Doyle, the boyish charmer from The Green Hill. He smiled, threaded his way over, patted me on both arms, a form of embrace.

'And here you've bin tellin me you're a legal fella, Jack,' he said. 'Why didn't ya just come right out and say you're an honest workin man?'

'Shyness,' I said.

'You know each other,' said Mrs Purbrick, touching Doyle's cheek. 'How lovely. Two of my favourite men.'

Doyle shook his head at her. 'Now, I won't share you with him, Carla,' he said. 'That's a warnin.'

To me, he said, 'This lovely lady is one of my investors, my angels, a person of faith in The Green Hill and its future.'

'A commodity required in abundant measure.' A tall man in his early sixties, solid, with a full head of wavy grey hair,

115

was at Doyle's side, a head taller. He put out a hand to me. 'Mike Cundall. Congratulations, beautiful piece of work.'

'Thank you, on behalf of Charlie Taub,' I said. 'I'm the helper. Just here as the front man. Charlie's in WA. Also he hasn't worn a suit since his wedding.'

Cundall nodded. He had grey eyes, clever eyes, appraising, in a lined, stoic face. He'd been drinking for a while. 'Carla tells me you're also a lawyer,' he said.

'In a small way.'

'My father was a lawyer who liked woodwork. He made garden things. Benches that fell over. He'd come home from Collins Street, out of his suit and into overalls, straight to the workshop and stay there until dinner.' He looked around, moistened his lips. 'Which he'd devote to shitting on me.'

A bow-tied waiter with a tray of champagne flutes appeared. We armed ourselves.

'Well,' said Cundall, 'this is probably a good moment.' He coughed and raised his glass above his head. People stopped talking.

'Carla's invited us around,' he said, 'to admire her new library. I must say I'm quite stunned by its elegance, stunned and jealous. And we have with us one of the builders of this thing of beauty, Jack Irish. I'd like to propose a toast: to Carla and her library, may it give her much pleasure.'

He raised his glass and everyone followed. A happy murmur.

'Thank you, Mike darling, thank you,' said Mrs Purbrick, waving her glass at the room, 'and thank you all for coming, you busy people, my dear friends.'

Xavier Doyle moved off, winding his way towards two blonde women, tanned, golf and tennis tans. They broke off their conversation, turned to him, faces opening.

'A mind like Paul Getty behind all that Irish boyo crap,' said Mike Cundall. There was no admiration in his tone.

'Nice place, The Green Hill,' I said. 'On the basis of one visit.'

Cundall was lighting a cigarette with a throwaway lighter. 'Do you smoke?' he asked. 'Forget your manners, nobody smokes any more.'

I shook my head.

'Yes. The Green Hill.' He blew smoke out of his nostrils. 'Money shredder, the Amazon dot com of pubs. Thousands of customers, own vineyard, Christ knows what else, sinks ever deeper into the red.'

'You're an investor?'

'Don't insult my intelligence. My wife's thrown money at The Green Hill. Her own money too. Was her money, I should say. It belongs to the ages now.'

The waiter was back. He had a crystal ashtray on his salver.

'I'll put this here, sir,' he said, drawing a thin-legged table closer to us and placing the ashtray. Then he offered more champagne.

'Nice drop,' I said.

'Roederer, sir. The Kristal.'

We lightened his tray. Another bow-tied man arrived with a silver tray of hamburgers, on sticks, exquisite miniatures, each the size of a small stack of twenty-cent coins, to be eaten at a bite.

Cundall twisted his cigarette in the ashtray. 'Smoked salmon's not good enough any more,' he said, 'too common.' He put one hamburger in his mouth, took a second. When he'd finished both, his mouth turned down. 'Instant indigestion these days.'

117

'How's Cannon Ridge going?' I said.

'That's my son,' said Cundall. 'My son and assorted rich boys. Sydney rich boys. The fucking dot com brigade. New economy.' He put down most of the champagne in a swig, held up his glass like an Olympic torch. 'Still, Cannon Ridge's old economy. Real asset, real business, combines leisure and gambling. Boys got a fantastic bargain.'

The waiter arrived. Cundall finished his glass, took another. 'Get me a whisky, will you?' he said to the youth. 'Something drinkable. With Evian. Just a bit.' He looked at me. 'Whisky, Jack?'

'That would be nice.'

'Decent shots,' said Cundall, blinking.

'Sir.'

'Good lad.'

'I see there's some unhappiness about the handling of the tenders,' I said.

'Politics of business,' said Cundall, slurring slightly. 'WRG wants to build a whole fucking town on the Gippsland Lakes. Get the new government in some shit over Cannon, good chance they won't get knocked back on that.'

He eyed me. 'Good practice, anyhow,' he said. 'Always takes a while to sort out a new lot, find out who to pay, who to play.'

'Jack, darling, you haven't met Ros Cundall.' Mrs Purbrick was holding the arm of a tall, dark-haired woman, once beautiful now merely good-looking.

We shook hands.

'I'm very taken with this room,' said Ros Cundall. 'I've always wanted a library. Do you think your Mr Taub would build one for me?'

'At least you can be sure it'll hold its value,' said Mike Cundall. 'Unlike that cocaine palace.'

Ros Cundall didn't look at her husband, made a wry face. 'Mike built a Las Vegas wing onto our house,' she said. 'All it lacks is the bedrooms for the harlots.'

'I thought you could go on using the house for that,' said Mike Cundall.

Mrs Purbrick laughed, an unconvincing trill. 'Oh, you two,' she said, 'so wicked.' She was watching David talking to one of the waiters.

Our whiskies arrived. We made small talk. Then, all at once, everyone was leaving, much brushing of lips on cheeks. Ros Cundall asked me for a card. So did two other people. Charlie might be building libraries full-time in future.

Near the front door, Xavier Doyle came up behind me.

'Jack,' he said. 'Mind I see you down the pub now.'

'Count on it.'

'That Robbie, you find out anythin more about the lad?'

'No,' I said. 'He's a mystery.'

Sandra Tollman had become Sandra Edmonds but was now Sandra Tollman again. She looked up from a tray of seedlings as I came down the greenhouse aisle. I'd found her easily, through her father, who still worked for the forestry department in New South Wales.

'Sandra?'

'Yes.' She was tall, with dark, curly hair cut short, wearing green work clothes.

'I'm Jack Irish.'

She took off a rubber glove and we shook hands. A long, slim hand, strong. I'd spoken to her on the phone at home the night before. She lived outside Colac and worked for a commercial tree nursery.

'I'll take my break,' she said. 'We can talk in the kitchen. The bosses are in town.'

I followed her out of the greenhouse and down a gravel path to a weatherboard building. We went in the back door, into a kitchen with a wooden table.

'Sit down. Tea or coffee?'

'Tea, please.' I sat where I could look out of the window, at a green hill with mist hanging on it.

She switched on the kettle, put teabags in mugs, got a carton of milk out of the fridge, stood waiting for the kettle to boil.

'Nice place to work,' I said.

'It is. I'm lucky. Nice bosses too, easygoing, no problems about starting times, that sort of thing. My little girl spends the afternoons here with me.'

'Rare thing, a nice boss.'

She nodded. 'I've had a few shits.'

The kettle boiled. She poured water into the mugs and sat at the end of the table.

'Robbie hasn't crossed my mind for years,' she said. 'What's this about?'

I hadn't told her on the phone. 'I'm afraid he's dead,' I said. 'Died of a drug overdose.'

She put a hand to her mouth, eyes wide. 'Jesus.'

'I'm trying to piece together his history,' I said. 'No-one seems to know much about him.'

'Well.' She scratched her head, bemused look. 'Well, I haven't seen him since, it must have been 1994. I had a terrific crush on him at school, I thought he was just the most divine thing, it ruined my school work...anyway, yes, 1994.'

'Where was that?'

Two birds were on the windowsill, looking around calmly, lorikeets, their colours startling in the grey day.

'In Sydney, in Paddington, bumped into him. He was with a woman at least ten years older, more maybe, you can't tell with some women.'

'A friend?'

She had dark eyes, clean whites, no guile in her eyes. 'I was walking behind them and the woman put her hand in the back pocket of Robbie's jeans.'

'Not looking for something, you'd say?'

'No.'

'And then you talked?'

'Just for a minute. In the street. The woman walked away, looked in windows.'

'What did Robbie say?'

'Small talk. Said he'd dropped out of uni. But I knew that, someone else told me, a girl in our class.'

I put a teaspoonful of sugar in my tea, stirred. 'Janice Eller.'

Surprise. 'How do you know that?'

'Terry Baine told me about her.'

'Terry Baine. The fat shit.'

'Sim's still carrying a torch for you,' I said.

She smiled, dropped her head, covered her eyes with a hand. 'God, you know everything,' she said. 'I cringe at the memory. Me walking around behind Robbie like a puppy, Sim sending his mates to give me messages. Really dumb messages.'

'I'm sure it was an extremely serious matter at the time,' I said. 'No other contact with Robbie?'

'No.'

I took out the still photograph I'd had printed from the video, the best shot of Robbie Colburne, almost full face, held it between thumb and forefinger. 'This is the person we're talking about?'

Sandra Tollman looked at the picture, looked at me, shocked.

I'd known. In the unfathomable way of knowing, I'd known since I watched the video clips, since D.J. Olivier told me that there was no record of Robbie returning to Australia.

'No,' she said. 'This is Marco.'

'Marco?'

'Robbie's friend.'

'Marco who?'

'Marco Lucia. Does this mean Robbie isn't dead?'

'You're sure this is Marco?'

She took the photograph. 'It's Marco. He doesn't even look much older. When was this taken?'

'Recently.'

'Why did you think it was Robbie?'

'He was calling himself Robert Colburne. He had a driver's licence in the name.'

'So Marco's dead and Robbie's not?'

'Marco's dead. I don't know about Robbie. Possibly alive.'

I didn't think that. 'Tell me about Marco.'

'I loved the name. Marco Lucia. He came up from Sydney in the holidays after year eleven to stay with Robbie, second most divine boy I'd ever met. Everyone in Walkley was just so Anglo-Irish. Blaines and Smailes and O'Reillys and McGregors. Marco could've been Robbie's brother, both pale, this black, black hair. Janice thought it was the second coming.'

We looked at each other for a while. She was back there, in Walkley, age seventeen.

'And after the holidays, did you see Marco again?'

'No. It was just those weeks, two weeks, I was in love, teenage love. Janice and I were the class smarties, readers, suddenly Robbie arrives, then his friend, this half-Italian boy, so exotic, they were both so clever and you could talk to them about books and poetry. Very un-Aussie, two boys who weren't petrolheads.'

'Half-Italian?'

'He said his mother wasn't Italian.' She looked out of the window. 'I think his mother left his father, went off to be a hippy, in Nimbin, somewhere like that. His father brought him up. That's all I know about him.'

'Did you know where he came from in Sydney?'

'No. Janice would have known. You know about Janice?'

'Yes. You heard nothing more about Marco?'

'No. I ended up at ag college in Orange. Pressure from my father. Not much talk about books and poetry there, I can tell you.'

'Robbie went overseas in 1996. Did you know that?'

She shook her head. 'That day in the street, that was it.'

I finished my tea. 'Thanks,' I said. 'You've been a great help, saved me from wasting more time.'

She walked to the Studebaker with me. 'This is weird, isn't it?' she said.

'Yes.'

'Was Marco an addict? she asked.

'The dead man had needle marks.'

'I'd like to know how it turns out,' she said.

'Me too. I'll let you know.'

'This come out of the blue,' said Harry Strang. 'People I done some transactin with, '87, '88, thereabouts. She's got the full licence, smart lady. He's a bit of a dill. Often that way, mind. Anyway, we had a bit of luck. Here's the turn now, memory serves.'

We were in open country, sere, rocky outcrops, going down a deeply rutted track.

Cam was driving the big BMW. 'Nice around here,' he said. 'No sheep.'

He'd rung me on the mobile on my way back from Colac. I found the pair waiting for me outside the boot factory. I hadn't asked any questions, just fallen asleep before we reached the tollway.

'When did this happen?' I said.

'Awake are you, Jack?' said Harry. 'Admire a man can kip anywhere. Sign of a clear conscience.'

'Sign of someone who wants to escape life,' I said. 'When?'

'After the night racin at the Valley last week,' said Harry. 'Jean's very upset. Said we'd come out and have a word.'

He was silent for a moment. 'Got through to me, possibly not a personal problem we're havin. Get my meanin?'

'This it?' said Cam.

A sign on the fence said: Kingara. David & Jean Hale. We crossed a cattle grid and drove down a lane of young poplars. There were horses in the paddocks on either side. Straight ahead was a bluestone-faced house, long and low with a slate-tiled roof, behind a struggling privet hedge. We parked next to a Holden ute with a history.

'Stretch the legs,' said Harry. 'Meet the lady. Can't hurt you blokes to meet normal people.'

'I dunno,' Cam said. 'Might find you like normal, ruin your whole life.'

As we sat there, a tall woman, slim, thirties, early forties, strong features, long blonde hair pulled back, ears showing, came around the corner of the hedge. She was wearing horse gear: checked shirt, Drizabone vest, jeans, gumboots. At the same moment, a wheaten labrador with the faintly puzzled but amiable look of its kind came through a hole in the hedge, tail wagging.

'Normal,' Cam said. 'I suppose I could like it, somebody shows me how.'

We got out, cold after the car.

'Come with a crowd,' Harry said to the woman. He went over. They shook hands. She put her left hand on his shoulder, leaned forward and kissed him on the cheek.

'Thanks for comin,' she said, voice a little blurred. 'After ten years, you still took the trouble…'

Harry put up a hand. 'No trouble.'

He introduced us. We shook hands and I resented the fact that her hand seemed to linger in Cam's longer than it did in mine. She had light-blue eyes, a little puffy: she'd been crying. I'd seen my own eyes like that in many a mirror, some of them spattered with substances whose composition or origin one did not wish to guess at.

'I've got scones in the oven,' she said. 'Haven't made scones for yonks. You used to like scones, Harry. Still?'

Harry dry-washed his hands. 'Still,' he said. 'Always. Good memory. Lead the way.'

On the verandah, Jean paused to take off her gumboots, quick, supple movements, rubber boots off, feet into worn, receptive shoes. We went through a sitting room with a stone fireplace into a big kitchen, smell of baking, cast-iron stove, sash windows in the north wall, painted cabinets and a big pine table, eight chairs. The view was of an old orchard, much older than the house, in need of heavy pruning.

'Live in here,' said Jean. 'Warm. You don't mind the kitchen?'

'That's where you eat scones, kitchen,' said Harry.

The scones were steaming, pale yellow inside. Butter lay on the rough surface for a second, liquefied, sank. Quince jelly, lemon marmalade and Vegemite. I started with the Vegemite, two scones, moved on to the quince jelly, two scones, pretended I'd had enough, consented to eat one with marmalade. Two, three.

Harry and Jean talked horses. Winter sun slanted in from the north-west. We drank tea out of white mugs, tea made in a pot. 'Sorry, no coffee,' Jean said. 'Can't afford proper coffee these days, can't drink the instant stuff.' She looked at Harry. 'Thought we'd be able to afford a new ute after last week, never mind coffee.'

Harry didn't say anything, ate his sixth scone, all with quince jelly. Cam was on his fourth. Jean offered him another one.

'No,' he said. 'Don't stop now, spoiled for life. Come out here and pitch a tent.'

'So,' Harry said, last morsel swallowed with tea. 'What happened?'

She pushed hair off her forehead. Her nails were cut short. 'We lucked onto this horse, Lucan's Thunder. Owners wanted a new trainer. Complete amateurs, the owners. I thought, same old story, it's always the trainer's fault. But it was. Dave knows him a bit, says he's an arsehole. Piss artist. Dougal Mackenzie? He's had one or two in town?'

'The name rings,' said Harry.

'Christ knows what Mackenzie'd been doing with this horse. I'd say very little and then badly. I put in a bit of time with him, got the diet right, you could see early on he was a rung up from the usual.'

'New South form, that right?' Harry retained form the way teachers used to remember pupils.

Jean nodded. 'Griffith, around there. Won two from seven, picnics really, then these owners bought him and gave him to Mackenzie and he was a dud from then on. Six starts, six–zero.' She paused. 'Anyway, when we started gettin some really good times from him, we thought we had a chance for a bit of a collect.'

'Owners inside?' said Harry.

'Yes. We said we'd talk to you, they didn't want to know, didn't want to share it around. Got a bit greedy, I spose.' She looked down, put a hand to her forehead. 'Wouldn't have happened if we'd gone to you.'

We looked at each other. Harry nodded to Cam.

'Doesn't follow, that,' said Cam. 'We got turned over a while back.'

'You?' She looked at Harry.

He nodded.

'Hurt the commissioner bad,' said Cam. 'How'd they do you?'

'Dave's mate put this bunch together. Sandy Corning, he's a local, a really nice bloke, straight as they come. Got these blokes he knows. Did okay to start but then the owners buggered it, the mates, the aunts, nannas, the lot, all shoving

128

money at the books. So in the end, the collect was only about sixty grand after commission.'

'Where?' said Harry.

Jean drank tea. 'Near the course. The Strand, near Mount Alexander, know that part?'

We all nodded.

'Dave didn't want Sandy to carry the money home, they were going to meet on The Strand. Dave was there first. He talked to Sandy on the mobile, Sandy was in the carpark, collectin…'

'Not clever,' said Cam.

'No, well, the whole thing's not clever. This car blocks Sandy near The Strand, the other one's behind him, his door's locked, the animal smashes the window with a sledge-hammer, one of those little ones, y'know?'

We waited.

'Sandy's got the money in this bag, it's a kid's schoolbag. He just offers it to the bloke. No, they pull him out…'

She sniffed, found a tissue, wiped her nose. 'Anyway, the bastards bashed him.'

'How bad?' said Harry.

Jean looked at the table. 'This woman from across the road hadn't come out, she's a nurse, he'd a died there. Rib punctured his lung, jaw broken, nose broken.'

She looked at us. 'He was offerin them the bag.'

We sat in silence.

'Cops say what?' Harry asked.

Jean looked at the table again, shrugged. 'Nothin. Lookin for them.'

More silence.

'You can say anythin,' Harry said.

She sighed. 'Dave's on the piss before lunch, smokin

129

again. Eight years off em, back to sixty a day. Doesn't sleep. I'm scared. We've had it now, goin down the tubes here for three, four years. More. Bloody owners. First they love the trainer, then the trainer's ratshit, horse's better than the trainer…'

'What about the horse?' said Cam.

'Took him off us. The next day. The one bastard rings up, says they've decided they want him with a more experienced trainer. Jesus, I could've…'

She caught herself, put a hand on top of Harry's, rubbed it. 'Last luck we had was with you. Thought that was the start of big things.'

Harry put a hand on hers, briefly, a hand sandwich.

Jean got up, galvanised, brisk. 'Shit, you don't want to hear this. More tea? I can make fresh.'

We shook our heads.

She made the gesture of helplessness. 'Well, that's all.'

Silence. The labrador came into view in the orchard, stately walk, tree to tree, the honorary colonel inspecting the regiment. One tree offended him and he peed on it.

Harry looked at his Piaget, a slim instrument that cost as much as a good used car, put his palms together. 'Bit of urgency creepin in,' he said, getting up.

We all stood up.

I said, 'See you outside in a minute.'

They left and I turned to Jean.

'The blokes Sandy recruited. Locals?'

'From the pub in town. The Railway.'

'Jean,' I said, 'I need the names and addresses of everyone—owners, owners' relatives, Sandy's blokes, everyone this thing touched, don't leave anyone out. Have you got a fax?'

She nodded. I gave her my card.

'Tomorrow?'

'Today,' she said. 'Tonight.'

We went outside. Jean hugged Harry, kissed him on the cheek, shook hands with us, some moisture in her eyes.

On the way back to the city, on the tollway, after the brief rolling bumps of the cattle grid, the trip up the hard, lined track, on the made road, the freeway, Harry said, head back on the leather rest, 'This would not be a personal problem, am I right?'

'Could be personal,' Cam said. 'Could be local, could be global.'

'Put on Willy,' said Harry. 'Haven't had any Willy for a while.'

'This Sandy,' I said. 'He put the team together. In a pub.'

'Oh, sweet Jesus,' said Cam.

Long before they dropped me it was night, Friday night, dripping.

I drove the youth club to the Prince after the game, very little said on the way. Very little needed to be said. A supporter near us had screamed most of it at the coach at three-quarter time, two sentences:

Lookitthescoreboardyafuckenmongrel. Seewhatyafuckendonetous.

Us. Done to *us*. The coach wasn't one of *us*. Coaches were transients and carpetbaggers. And only a few players in any era in any club ever became one of *us*. The supporters were *us*. They were the investors. Gave the club their hearts, dreams, they expected a return. Every game was an annual general meeting.

'That Docklands stadium,' said Eric Tanner. 'That's not a proper footy ground.'

'Like playin in a circus tent,' said Wilbur. 'It's not right.'

I prepared to reverse park. It was going to be tight.

'Loadin zone,' said Wilbur Ong. 'No can do.'

'No can do?' said Eric Tanner. 'No can do? It's bloody Satdee, no bloody loadin goin on.'

'Not the point,' said Wilbur, calmly. 'Loadin zone.'

I went in, put a back wheel on the pavement. I didn't care. 'Well,' said Wilbur. 'A lawyer, Jack, expect to find a bit of respect for the law in a lawyer.'

'Last place you'd find it,' I said. 'Look elsewhere. It's a loading zone. Am I unloading you lot on the Prince or not?'

Wilbur sniffed, faith in the law's majesty undiminished. We departed the vehicle, burst into the Prince in a low-key way.

It was a low-technology evening. In residence, six silent people and a dog. The cybermeisters were hanging out elsewhere this evening, perhaps at The Green Hill in South Melbourne, sipping a Green Hill pinot noir, flipping through The Green Hill cookbook.

Stan came over, very much the happy hangman today. 'My,' he said, 'you boys really know how to pick a team. Yes, I take my hat off to you. These Sainters, they could be the Roys come back in another jumper…'

'This place still serve beer?' said Eric Tanner. 'Mind you, there's some says you haven't bin able to get a beer here since Morrie retired. Not what you'd normally call a beer.'

'Touchy today. Beer comin up.'

When we had our beers in front of us, had a sip, wiped off our moustaches, Norm O'Neill, next to me, said quietly, not a register I knew he commanded, 'Well, made up me mind, Jack.' He looked to his left, at the others. 'Speakin for me, that's all.'

I didn't say anything. There wasn't any defence to mount for the Saints. This was execution day.

'Yes,' said Norm. 'Reckon I'm stickin with the team. Can't give up on a side that's so bad. Be inhuman, like leavin a hurt dog in the street.'

Wilbur nodded. 'The boys'll come good,' he said. 'Sack the coach, that'll be a start.'

'Things wouldn't a bin so bad today,' said Eric, 'if that bloody ump hadn't found a free for the bastards every time they get a hard look.'

I looked into my beer. It had happened. The graft had taken. The donor hearts hadn't rejected the recipient.

'Hero, that Harvey,' I said.

'And Burkie,' said Norm.

'What about that Thompson boy?' said Eric. 'Kid's all heart.'

And so it went. The years fell away: we might have been talking about Fitzroy. I signalled for another round. Stan took his time. When he arrived with the first two, he said, 'Gets worse from here too, don't it. Next week, your girls play the mighty Roys.'

Norm put a hand under his cardigan and produced a fixture card, studied it through his thick, smudged lenses. 'Says here,' he said, 'next week St Kilda plays Brisbane.'

'After Brisbane, there's another word,' said Stan. 'Lions. L-I-O-N-S. Brisbane Lions.'

Norm folded the card and put it away. 'Don't say that on my card. And it never bloody will. Only Lions left are right here.' He waved around the room at the photographs. 'And you, Stanley, you're a disgrace to the memory of these great men.'

He looked at me, looked at Eric and Wilbur. 'Am I right? Am I right?'

'You're right,' said Wilbur.

'Damn right,' said Eric.

'Beyond right,' I said.

A chastened Stan brought the other beers and slunk off. We resumed our discussion of the virtues of individual Saints. Then I drove home and set about making Saturday night bearable. Ten minutes into this, the phone rang. Wootton.

'Just checking the out-stations,' he said, full of gin, jovial Saturday-evening Wootton, back from his golf club, stuffed with nuts and little sandwiches and bonhomie. 'Anything to report, old sausage?'

'The out-stations? I think you've got a wrong number. Wrong century too.'

'If you have,' he said, 'the client will be at the same spot on the dial tomorrow morning, 9.30 a.m. Precisely.'

The judge was in a zippered white cotton garment that slotted in somewhere between a NASA spacesuit and Colonel Gaddafi's overalls. He ordered orange juice and a toasted wholewheat muffin with honey.

'Breakfast,' he said. 'I'm on my way to tennis. You don't want to eat too much before tennis.'

'Fatal,' I said.

We were back at the window table at Zanouff's in Kensington, the less-hungover weekend breakfast crowd beginning to straggle in.

The juice arrived. Colin Loder drank half the glass at a swig.

'The dead man's name is Marco Lucia,' I said.

'I beg your pardon?'

It was too early for this kind of rubbish, even from a judge. I said, 'You didn't hear me?'

He gave me a surprised look, weighed up the matter. 'I don't know the name, Jack. An expression of surprise.'

I'd rung D.J. Olivier after Wootton's call the night before. D.J. was part of the seven-day-week world, Saturday night was just another night. A woman rang back at 10.30 p.m., found me deep in melancholy and self-loathing.

'The subject,' she said in a private-school voice, 'has no criminal record. Passport issued March 1996, left the country in April that year, returned January 1998. Name mentioned in reports of a criminal case in July 1999. An article in the Brisbane *Courier Mail* in September '99 refers to someone who may be the subject.'

'What's the criminal case?' I said.

'Assault, unlawful detention. Subject was the complainant.'

'And the article?'

'Organised crime in Brisbane and the Gold Coast. Someone interviewed refers to someone of this name as, I quote, Milan's fucking star, unquote.'

Milan's fucking star.

I liked the way she said that. 'Thanks.'

'Our pleasure. Let us know if you need a broader inquiry.'

Mr Justice Loder's muffin arrived, golden honey in a bowl. When the waiter had left, I got out the photograph of 'Robbie' and put it next to his plate. He looked around, unzipped a pocket and took out a spectacles case, put on a handsome gold-rimmed pair, looked at the picture without picking it up.

'Well,' he said, put a finger to his lips. 'As I said, this inquiry is on behalf…'

My hands were palm-down on the table. I kept my eyes on the judge and raised the fingers of the right one. 'I'm working for you,' I said. 'You get the bill.'

He breathed deeply, looked out of the window, closed his eyes for a second. He had long eyelashes. 'You'll understand this isn't easy,' he said.

'I understand.'

He held my eyes for a few seconds. 'I met him in Italy several years ago. In Umbria. I was staying at a friend's house. The friend was away, and this young man arrived on the doorstep with a letter of introduction to my friend from someone in London.'

He had the diction of a schooled witness. 'Calling himself?'

'Robbie Colburne. He said his mother was Italian, from the Veneto, and his father was Australian. He spoke good Italian.'

'Eat your muffin,' I said, 'it's getting cold.'

He looked at the plate, broke off a piece of muffin, held it like a dead spider, put it down. 'I think I'll skip the muffin.'

I said, 'I only need the pertinent bits.'

'A relationship developed. I had a week left of my holiday. He said he was planning to spend a few years in Europe. I didn't see him or hear from him again until a month ago. He rang me one night. My wife was away. She's often away.'

Without looking at it again, Loder slid the photograph over to me. 'He was an attractive person. Intelligent, full of life. And a lot of sadness in him.'

'Most people have to settle for one of those things,' I said. 'Generally, the last one.'

Loder smiled, cheered up a little. 'That's what's pertinent,' he said. 'I suppose.'

Zanouff's was filling up, people wearing dark glasses, two couples with trophy children, dressed to be cute, caps worn backwards, expensive running shoes. One of the fathers had a tic in his right eye, a stress tic. He kept touching it but it wouldn't stop.

'You resumed the relationship?'

'Yes.'

'I won't put icing on this,' I said. 'Are you scared of something?'

The judge smiled, made a gesture of openness with his arms, spread his fingers. The smile didn't have any staying power. Nor did the gesture. He gave up, closed his arms, put one hand over the other.

'Something's missing,' he said.

'Robbie?'

'Yes.'

'Of what value?'

A sad smile. 'How do you value a career?'

'Not talking about the degree certificates?'

'No.'

A train was leaving Kensington station, an empty rattle of train, windows flashing sky.

'Anything happened since you noticed the loss?'

He closed his eyes again. 'Nothing. I'm petrified. My dad's still alive.'

'And then there's the dignity of the law,' I said, cruelly.

He revived, face turning stern. 'I suspect that the dignity of the law transcends and outlasts that of its humble servants, Mr Irish.'

A dignified response from the Bench.

'Silly remark, allow me to withdraw it,' I said. 'Let me tell you what I know about Marco Lucia.'

When I'd finished, Loder said, 'Can you be sure it's the same person?'

'Pretty much. Only one person matches.'

We watched another train, saw the faintest tremor in the plate-glass cafe window.

'Your advice,' said the judge.

'Option one is that you save yourself a lot of money by popping around to your local jacks and telling them what you're missing.'

'And read the first rumour in the paper tomorrow? Option two, please.'

'I can keep looking. There's always the possibility of turning up something.'

'Keep looking,' he said.

'The missing item?'

'Photograph album. Red leather.' He gave me his sad smile again. 'You're asking yourself how I could be so stupid.'

'No,' I said. 'I've stopped asking that question. I know the answer.'

He got up. 'Thanks, Jack.' A pause. 'It's silly but I find the fact that you're a colleague strangely comforting.'

A judge calling me a colleague. As he went out, it occurred to me that this was probably the high-water mark of my legal career.

I caught the 6.05 a.m. flight to Brisbane, two hours in the air, hired a car and drove for 90 minutes, never once lost, to reach the imposing gateway to Haven Waters. It was half-way across a 500-metre land bridge just wide enough for two lanes.

A man in a police-style uniform, light blue and dark blue, armed, left the gatehouse, came out into the white-porcelain light.

'G'day,' he said. 'Have to ask for your name, address and purpose of visit, sir.' He was a wiry man, ginger and freck-led, big freckles. Cold and grey climes would have suited him better.

I gave my particulars. He wrote them down on a clipboard. Then he asked for two means of identification. Fighting my instincts, I handed over my driver's licence and my Law Institute card. Forever on another record. One day D.J. Olivier might find me there and a young woman with a private-school voice would tell someone.

'Only take a minute, sir,' he said and went back. I saw him pick up a phone, talk, nod, put it down. There was someone else in the gatehouse, a movement. Expensive, a two-person guard, six shifts, that would cost management two hundred grand a year, plus benefits. Just to check tickets. Perhaps the second person also did patrols, that would ease the strain.

Gates opened. The man was waiting for me inside, gave me a map printed on card, laminated.

'Down this road, sir. At the T-junction, turn left. Then first right, go past the golf clubhouse and the village.'

He was English, I caught that now.

'First residence after the village. The entrance is on your right, first gate. Adriatica, that's the name. It's marked on the map. And the name's on the gate.'

He pressed a small plastic disc, the size of a fat ten-cent coin, onto the windscreen above the registration sticker. 'So that we can find you if you get lost, sir,' he said. 'We'll take it off when you leave. Enjoy your visit, sir.'

Bugged, I drove across the bridge, down a curving road, through a landscape sculpted by bulldozers, blanketed with imported soil, planted with thousands of mature sub-tropical trees, grassed, lavishly watered. Water was always visible, on both sides deep inlets. I saw two fat joggers, a thin runner, half a dozen walkers, a woman in jodhpurs on a high-spirited chestnut horse. Then the golf course was on my left, greens like great dollops of pureed spinach, people on motorised buggies. I watched a man duff a tee shot.

The golf clubhouse was low, sinuous, heavy with flowering creepers, and then the village appeared on my right, a semicircle of whitewashed buildings of different heights, different roof shapes and pitches, a clock tower in the middle, someone's idealised Mediterranean village, water glimpsed beyond the buildings, flashes at the end of narrow lanes. Two small parking areas were as snobbish as stockbroker bikies, European metal only, nothing Japanese here.

This was where big money came to die, water without, guards within.

I found Adriatica behind a white creepered wall broken by bays housing big shrubs, leaves large and polished. Its gate was black wrought iron, ornate metal stems and leaves. It was a gate for cars. No-one arrived on foot in this place; there was nowhere to walk, nowhere to park, no pavement, no kerb, no gutter.

I parked in front of the gates, got out. It was warm. I took off my jacket and approached the gates.

'Take off the coat,' said a voice.

'I'm not wearing a coat. I'm carrying my coat.'

He came into view from the left, a thin man, not young, slicked-back hair, one eyebrow like a furry caterpillar stuck to his forehead. The weapon held at his side, pointing at the ground, was extravagant, a long-barrelled .38.

I said, 'Put that fucking thing away. I've got an appointment to see Mr Filipovic.'

He shrugged, opened the gate.

I walked up a paved driveway to where a path through tropical jungle branched off to the house. The air was dense with exotic scents.

At the front door, a huge studded Moorish creation, another man, young, tee-shirt and jeans, was waiting, holding a device like a cordless telephone. 'Gotta check you over,' he said, then ran the metal detector over me.

'Give him your coat,' he said.

The man with the revolver had come up behind me. I complied.

'Arms up,' said the detector of metal.

I raised them. 'Looking for a wire?' I said. 'Go very carefully.'

He smiled at me, excellent teeth. 'I'm very careful. Loosen your tie, unbutton your shirt, cuffs too.'

You sensed a lack of trust in him.

When he was finished, he said, 'Come in.'

We went through a hallway decorated with oversize

Grecian-style urns, down a passage and into a sitting room the size of a four-car garage. It was full of white leather chairs and sofas and glass-topped tables holding heavy bowls of tortured coloured glass. On the wall above a fireplace hung a huge picture of a red rose lying on stone steps. The blowsy petals held perfectly rendered drops of dew the size of oranges.

Through the open French doors, you looked over a broad deck to where a boat was tied up, at least ten metres of gleaming white craft with a flying bridge. A man was working at the stern, kneeling on the deck, straightening up every few minutes to relieve his back.

'Welcome to my house.'

The man had come into the room from a door to the right of the French doors. He was in his fifties, heavily built, oiled silver hair combed back, wearing only striped shorts and boat shoes. His skin was the colour of fudge and his chest was grey-furred, like the belly of an old dog.

I put out a hand. 'Jack Irish.'

'Milan Filipovic.' He applied a challenging grip and I gave it back.

'Strong hand,' he said. 'Don't work behind a desk all the time, hey?'

'Thanks for seeing me,' I said.

'Not a problem, mate.'

Another man had come into the room, a younger man, strong looking, a bodybuilder, with dark hair cut short. He was in shorts, a golf shirt and boat shoes.

'Steve,' said Milan. 'He works for me.'

Steve didn't offer to shake hands, just smiled, another mouth of first-rate teeth. Something in the local water, perhaps, or a good cosmetic dentist.

'Hey,' said Milan, 'we're jus goin out on the boat, test the engines. Steve, ask that cunt if he's finished?'

Steve went out.

'This place, what you think? Nice, hey?'

'Very nice. Must be good to live on the water.'

'The best. Cost a fucken bomb. What you reckon they want for management, upkeep, security, all that shit?'

'Quite a bit.'

'Forty grand a year. How's that?'

'That's a lot, that's steep.'

He scratched his chest pelt. 'I told em, I don't need your fucken security, look after myself. Little cunt says it's not an option.'

I watched Steve come back. His legs were too short for his torso.

'Ready,' he said.

'Pineapple juice,' said Milan, 'get a coupla litres.'

He led the way to the boat. We passed the man who'd been working on it. 'She's ace, Mr Fil,' he said. 'Runnin smooth.'

'Good boy,' said Milan, patting him on the chest. 'Tell Denny I said cash.'

We were at the centre of a bay, a big expanse of water. The village's long curving boardwalk was on the right, two-storey boathouse-like buildings lining it, people sitting under market umbrellas. Perhaps forty other waterfront houses were in sight, most of them with boats tied up at their landings, big white muscle boats, here and there a yacht supplying some class.

'Like it?' said Milan.

'Top spot,' I said.

'You gotta earn it.' He was first onto the boat.

Steve and the young man who'd searched me arrived, Steve carrying a big pitcher of yellow juice. The young man cast off, went up to the flying bridge, Steve went below.

'Take a seat,' said Milan, waving at the banquettes. They were gently scalloped into individual seats.

I sat down. He sat opposite me, his pectorals sagging, dark nipples peeping out of the dense hair like the noses of inquisitive forest creatures.

The engines fired, a satisfying sound, a growl that made the deck beneath my out-of-place leather soles vibrate. My searcher took the boat away from the landing, howling off at forty-five degrees from the land. In a few minutes, we were passing through a broad opening to the sea, a dead calm sea, blue-black.

Milan got up, climbed the steps to the bridge, muscles showing in the big calves, said something to the helmsman, who throttled back the engines, settled on a modest cruising speed.

Back in his seat, Milan looked at me, opened his arms, palms upward, smiled. 'Fucken paradise, hey? Whatya think?'

I looked around. There wasn't much to see. An endless flat paddock of ocean, a boat here and there. 'Very close to it,' I said. 'You're a lucky man.'

He laughed, ran a hand over the oiled hair. 'Lucky? Jack, listen, mate, I come to this country with fuck-all, I work like a dog, anythin, mate, anythin, cleanin gully traps, that's what I did. Cleaned a gully trap?'

I shook my head. I had, actually, but this wasn't the moment to compare experiences.

'Yeah, well, don't talk lucky to me, mate. Qualified fitter and turner, you think I get a job? No way, they don't want a fucken wog can't speak two words of English.'

Steve emerged with the pitcher of yellow juice and two heavy-bottomed tumblers. 'Yellow peril ready to go,' he said.

'Just a small one. I'm driving,' I said. It sounded lame.

Milan laughed as if I'd said something very entertaining. Steve poured two full glasses, handed me one.

'Pineapple and vodka,' said Milan. 'Good for you, builds up acid, cleans the bowel.'

He put back half his glass. 'No, mate, I'm just a fucken Serb. Nobody likes Serbs, right? Be fine if I was a Kosovar. Right? Remember that lot?'

I nodded.

'Everybody bleeding about fucken Kosovars. Mate, they not even Christians. Christian country this, right? Those people are fucken Arabs. Not from Europe. You see the women? Hide their fucken faces. Got no pity, either. Kill children. Right, mate?'

I didn't say anything. What was there to say to six hundred years of breeding?

'So what's this Marco shit?' he said. 'You NCA, Feds, what?'

I shook my head. 'I saw you mentioned in the newspaper. I've got a client who needs some information. That's it.'

Now he had a good laugh. I was becoming funnier every minute.

'Listen, you not from the Feds, okay, you give the Feds a message from me. Okay? Okay?'

'If they ask me, okay.'

'You tell those bastards, Jack, I tol em, they don't listen. They never gonna make this drugs stuff stick on me. I don't deal drugs, I never deal drugs, never will. Not interested. People come to me with offers all the time. I say no. That's right, Steve?'

'Right,' said Steve.

'Right. I'm not sayin I don't know some stupid people, they get involved in this shit. Not sayin that. Everybody knows stupid people. You can have a stupid brother, how's that your blame, hey? But I tell them, keep away from me, keep that shit away from me.' He leaned over, belly creases deepening. 'Jack, you think I'm such a dumb cunt I'm dealin while I've got the fucken Feds on my fucken hammer?'

'It wouldn't be smart, no,' I said.

'Tell em that, Jack, tell em. Tell em to get off my fucken back. Adult entertainment, that's my business. That's fucken all. And property, I got a bit of property. Plus a couple investments. All in the open.' He looked at Steve.

I said, 'Can I ask you about Marco Lucia?'

'You ready?' Milan said to Steve.

'Ready.' Steve went below and came back with a flat case. He opened it and took out a small machine-pistol and two long magazines. A magazine made a snick as it went into the butt.

Milan took the pistol, showed it to me. 'Nice, hey? Ingram. Better than a Glock. Don't trust fucken Austrians.'

Steve shouted something from the bow of the boat. We slowed to walking speed. A blow-up pool toy drifted by: a swan.

Milan stood up, went to the side and fired a short burst at it. The swan collapsed without a sound.

'And another thing, Jack.' Milan turned to me, took on a sad look, a man injured to his core. 'I'm hurt there's no gratitude.'

'Gratitude?'

'Gratitude. What these pricks in Sydney do when their fat boy gets in the shit with whores? They come to Milan, that's what. I squeeze that cunt Papagos for them like a grape, end of problem. So where's the gratitude?'

'You deserve more,' I said.

'Fucken right. You tell them, Jack.'

'Any time I get the chance. About Marco Lucia?'

A blow-up crocodile came by, followed by several big balls, two ducks and Mickey Mouse. Milan went into a firing frenzy, changing magazines in mid-carnage. The objects deflated, slumped on the water.

'Marco,' I said.

Steve appeared. 'Hey, shootin,' he said.

'Pretty boy cunt,' said Milan. 'People say I topped Marco. Bullshit. Wouldn't fucken waste my time. Cut his cock off, that's somethin else. Find him, I sew it up in his mouth.'

'Have to stick half down his fucken throat,' said Steve. He laughed, showing his teeth.

'Gimme another drink. Jack, have another one.'

'No thanks. Why do they say you topped him?'

'He just fucked off, noone seen him, so they say he's dead, they point at me.'

'Why at you?'

Milan eyed me over the top of his glass, lowered it. 'Warm as piss,' he said. 'More ice, Steve. Why?'

'Why do people point at you over Marco?'

'He did some work for me.'

'What kind of work was that?'

Steve was putting ice into Milan's glass with tongs.

'Just work,' said Milan. 'Things I give him to do.'

'Marco's dead,' I said.

Milan looked at Steve, eyes eloquent, looked at me. 'Says who?' he said.

'Drug overdose in Melbourne.'

149

Milan drank some pineapple juice. 'Melbourne,' he said, as if hearing the name of some remote cattle station. 'What's he doin in Melbourne?'

'Working as a part-time barman.'

I could see a huge powerboat coming our way at speed, foaming bow waves. It slowed, veered away to increase the distance between us when we passed. Perhaps the idea was to lessen the risk of spilling Milan's drink.

The three men and a woman on board all waved. Milan moved a hand at them. 'Everybody knows Milan,' he said.

'Marco was calling himself Robbie Colburne,' I said.

Another exchange of looks.

'Robbie what?' said Milan.

'Colburne.'

'You sure the dead one's Marco?' said Milan.

'I've got a picture. It's in my jacket. Inside pocket.'

Milan looked at Steve. Steve felt around in my jacket, found the photograph, showed it to Milan without looking at it.

'Hey,' said Milan, a broad smile, real pleasure. 'The pole. Marco Polo.'

Now Steve looked. 'Good fucken riddance,' he said. He was smiling too.

'Overdose?' said Milan. 'What?'

'Smack.'

Another boat came from nowhere, rocked us with its wake. 'Arsehole.' Milan shook his head. 'So a needle?'

'Yes.'

Milan puffed out his cheeks. 'Needle's a big fucken surprise to me,' he said. 'What's the Feds' interest?'

This was not progressing. 'What kind of work did Marco do?'

Milan smiled at Steve. Steve smiled back. 'What you reckon, Steve? What kinda work Marco do?'

'I dunno, Milan.'

'Marco's all cock,' said Milan. 'Work it out.'

'If someone wanted to kill him, why would that be?'

Much laughter. Milan held his empty glass out to Steve. 'More,' he said. 'Whattabout you, Jack?'

I shook my head. 'I'm not getting anything here,' I said. 'You want me to pass on messages, you won't answer a simple question.'

Milan considered this, working his tongue over his teeth. Then he leant over. 'Listen, Jack, the cunt's just a big prick and a thief. Maybe he stole somethin, made people angry. He's no fucken loss.'

He straightened up. 'But don't lookit me. You know how I'd a killed Marco? You know?'

I shook my head.

'I bring him out here, I open him up a little, just for blood, tie him to a 200 kilo line. Then I throw him over and I tow the cunt around lookin for sharks. Tow him till all I got on the line is a bit of bone.'

Steve's mobile shrilled. He said a few words, handed it to Milan.

Milan listened. 'Tell him to fucken wait,' he said. 'I'm comin.'

He gave the phone back to Steve. 'Home,' he said.

The first you saw of Haven Waters was the clock tower. What need did these people have of the time?

Tired, the feeling of the whole body being tired, not the earned tiredness of exercise, of physical work, just tired in the bone marrow. I went down the dark passage to the kitchen without bothering to switch on a light. The clock on the microwave said 9.14. I'd been up for seventeen hours, four hours in aircraft seats, three hours driving.

And bubbles of sour pineapple juice kept rising. Milan was right. It built up acid, it would probably clean the bowel. Scouring, they called it in horses.

Milk. I needed milk, drank two glasses, not terribly old. Then I opened a bottle of red and sat on the couch in the sitting room waiting for the place to warm up. Food I had no need of – I never wanted to eat again.

The buzzing of the tired brain.

Marco Lucia. Milan had not spoken well of him. But what had the judge said?

…an attractive person. Intelligent, full of life. And a lot of sadness in him.

There would certainly have been a lot of sadness in Marco if Milan had had his way and towed him around the Queensland coastline as live shark bait. Bleeding bait.

Listen, Jack, this cunt's just a big prick and a thief. Maybe he stole somethin, made people angry. He's no fucken loss.

A big prick and a thief. Would the judge agree with this description? Yes, if I understood the term relationship properly.

Marco Lucia on the run from something in Queensland.

He comes to Melbourne. Many people think Melbourne is a long way from Brisbane.

Marco takes on the identity of his school friend, Robbie Colburne.

How was it possible to do that?

Groaning, I got up and found my notes.

Robbie Colburne and Marco Lucia both left the country in April 1996.

School friends. They'd gone to Europe together. But only Marco came back. Was it the case that Robbie didn't need his identity any longer? Because he was dead?

Marco could've been Robbie's brother, Sandra Tollman had said. Both pale, with black, black hair.

I poured some more wine, put the video in the slot, sank into the couch with the remote in hand.

Marco going into the Cathexis building. The new Melbourne landmark. Hideous but the very edge of architecture.

The unknown man at a pavement table, dark, balding, a fleshy face seen from across a busy street, then a new camera angle, a second camera, unsteady. The man drinking the shortest of short blacks, newspaper in his hand, looking around, half-amused.

Worth trying to identify the man? No, too hard.

Early evening, Marco in right profile, side on, several parked cars between him and the camera. He is waiting to cross a street, a narrow street, vehicles flashing by. He takes a break in the traffic, walking diagonally, the confident walk.

Nothing there.

Marco in his dinner jacket in a car.

I sat in the half-dark thinking about the origin of the

clips. State cops? Feds? I thought about Marco waiting to cross the street, wound back.

Marco waits to cross, waits, a gap, he walks, he's in the middle of the street. Freeze the frame.

To Marco's right, on the other side of the street, is a parked car. There is someone in the driver's seat.

Was Marco walking towards the car?

I looked at the clip in slow motion. Definitely someone in the car, that was all. And the number plate was visible but unreadable.

Too tired to think any more. I needed Milo and my new book, bought at the airport and only just violated. It was called *Love and Football*. The warm, innocent liquid and a brief read of my book, that would be my reward for a long day in the field.

Tomorrow, I'd take the video in to get some enhancements.

In the cracking dawn, I shambled around Edinburgh Gardens and along the pavements of North Fitzroy, nothing on my mind but the signals coming from all regions of my body—distress calls, warnings, entreaties.

Home, I raided my shrinking store of new shirts, stock-piled in more prosperous times, and showered long and hard and hot, adjectives that could be applied to Marco Lucia if I'd got the drift of the exchange between Milan Filipovic and his white-fanged and complaisant colleague.

After a cup of tea and, at the kitchen table, a few more pages of my new book, a moving tale of innocent passions corrupted by corporatism, I departed for Meaker's. There I breakfasted on fat-trimmed bacon and mushrooms on toast, lavish quantities supplied by an Enzio who appeared to have been irradiated. Twice he winked at me from the kitchen door, both times running a hand over his scalp. The message seemed to be that my reading of the widow had been correct: hair she had not been pining for.

At 9 a.m., I was at Vizionbanc in South Melbourne, just around the block from The Green Hill, showing the manager the images I required.

'Eleven,' she said. 'We're a bit slow today. A morning sickness problem.'

The problem of morning sickness I understood perfectly.

I used her phone to ring Mr Cripps, the postman who wouldn't retire, and arranged for him to pick up the prints. This was done through Mrs Cripps, who could relay messages to the puttering Holden without using a mobile phone, a device her rotund husband once told me he abhorred. That was, in fact, the only thing he had ever told me. Telepathy was not ruled out.

On the way back, I passed the casino, even at this early hour vacuuming in hapless poker machine addicts. It was one thing to put your faith in your scientifically arrived at choice of beautiful creature, to be urged to realise its full potential by a small and muscular person. Hoping a flashing and programmed electronic device would give you money was another matter. Entirely.

At my professional chambers, I found that the fax machine had extruded paper: Jean Hale's list of everyone associated with the Lucan's Thunder plunge. Guilt assailed me: I had given the matter no thought.

And, on the answering machine, Mrs Purbrick.

Jack, I'm experimenting with a new caterer and I need a man of taste. Give me a ring soon, darling.

Pause.

I'm in my beautiful library constantly. Devouring books. And Ros Cundall is green with envy.

Would it hurt to be Anne Purbrick's taster? What could she tell me about Xavier Doyle, Robbie's employer?

Drew was next.

Woodmeister, you're listening to a man who's had a mystical experience. I think I'm in love. In lust and in love. Ring and I'll share this with you.

Not Rosa. Please, God, not Rosa.

I read Jean Hale's list. Plumbers and electricians and painters and redundant teachers. It was even worse than I'd expected.

I rang her. The ring went on for a long time. A man answered, gruff. I asked for her. She was outside with horses.

'What's your name?' he said.

'I'm associated with Mr Strang.'

'Right. Sorry, I'll get her.'

Jean Hale came on.

'Jean, Jack Irish. How's Sandy Corning?'

'Better. He's going to be okay. We're going to see him today.'

'Good. Can you ask him to rule out people on the list? People he has complete confidence in?'

'Yes. Sure.'

'And fax it to me again?'

A hoot outside. Mr Cripps. I said goodbye, found a $20 note, went out and exchanged it for a stout envelope.

'Exemplary service, as always,' I said. He nodded, expressionless as a whale. The yellow Holden puttered away, its waxed surface dotted with fat beads of rain. Beading. You'd done the wax job properly when the result was beading.

Thinking about how little beading had occurred in my life, I returned to my chair and opened the envelope. The cassette and four prints, two enlargements of Robbie crossing the street, two of the man at the pavement table.

The registration number on the car Robbie was walking towards was now readable. And the person in the car was a woman, half her face visible, looking in Robbie's direction over the top of dark glasses.

I studied the fleshy man in the other pictures. There was a reflection in glass behind him, that would be the cafe window, a reflection of writing on something, not a flat surface, the word *asset*.

Asset?

It didn't matter. I strolled around to the Lebanese and rang Eric the Geek, Wootton's attenuated computer ace, prince of hackers. There were redialling sounds and science-fiction lost-in-space noises before he answered.

'Yeah.' Not an interrogative inflection. This was about as expressive as Eric got but the single grunt conjured up his gloomy, damp-jumpered, patchily-shaven presence.

'It's Jack. I need a name.'

I read out the registration number.

'Minute. Number?'

I gave him the number. While waiting, I studied the notices on the board near the phone. House-minding, dog-walking, appliances for sale, a new homemade wanted poster with a photograph of a thin, dark-haired young man described as a heroin addict, missing dogs, cats, a budgie, probably now inside one of the missing cats. The phone rang.

'Jack.'

Return of the cyber-Visigoth.

'Exactly,' I said.

He sniffed, coughed, a cough that needed attention. 'Hang on,' he said.

Keys tapping, silence, more taps, silence. A tap.

'Company car. Syncred Nominees.' He spelled it out. 'Address 27/6 Kelling Street, Crows Nest, Sydney.'

I wrote it down, said thank you, and rang Simone Bendsten, an expert fisher of companies and the people in and around them.

'How's business?'

'Good. Looking up. I owe you. Max's given me a lot of due-diligence research and he's passed me on to another firm.'

Max was a corporate lawyer I'd recommended her to. I told her what I needed.

'Work of minutes, hold on, I'm at the machine.'

More listening to tapping. Outside, a police car pulled up and a cop got out and went out of view. He came back holding a scruffy, emaciated teenager by the arm, shoved him in the back seat. Was I witnessing your actual drug bust? A Mr Big removed from circulation?

'Jack. Two directors. James Martin Toxteth, Colin Leigh Blackiston.'

'Mean anything to you?'

'No. I'll look around. Ring you?'

I gave her the mobile number.

At the office, in the captain's chair, in a patch of sunlight, I looked at the pictures again. Drowsy. Up too early. Too much exercise. The doomed dog had not fronted today. Scared? Somehow cognisant of my murderous instincts? Aware of my total lack of ruth?

People filming Marco or filming the fleshy man or filming the woman in the car?

They were filming Marco. He wasn't the bit player, he was the star.

A fuck star.

Milan and Steve both showed real pleasure at the news of Marco's death. Death of a fuck star.

A star.

An evil star.

And grapples with his evil star.

The sight of my grandfather, my mother's father, came to me, the lean figure sitting in his buttoned chair, quoting Tennyson, every word a universe of meaning.

The old man was referring to my father's evil star. In my childhood, no week went by when the old man did not find an opportunity to speak ill of the dead man. He made it clear that there was something in me of my father that he had a duty to exorcise. I was well into my teens before it dawned on me that the sum total of my father's evils appeared to be beer, the odd punch-up, and fully paid-up membership of the working class and the Communist Party. The last two vices my grandfather found particularly heinous.

I'd had the old man in mind on my first visit to the Prince of Prussia, empty that autumn afternoon, light from the western windows lying on the scuffed floor, on the dented and cigarette-burnt bar, dust motes and my cigarette smoke hanging in the weak sunlight.

Morris had put down my beer that day, eyes fixed on me. 'In mind of Bill Irish when I look at you,' he said. 'Funny.'

'My father,' I said.

Morris studied me for at least 30 seconds, then he said, head on one side, indignant, 'Where the hell've you bin?'

The mobile jerked me out of my reverie. Simone Bendsten. 'Jack. Those directors. James Martin Toxteth is a former merchant banker. Colin Leigh Blackiston was an investment fund manager. They're in business together in a Sydney venture-capital company called Toxteth Blackiston Private Equity. That's about it.'

No illumination there.

'Thanks,' I said. 'Send me the bill.'

'You're in credit here. Buy me a glass of wine one day.'

'That'll be for pleasure. This is work, someone's paying. I'll use my credit another time.'

Back to drowsing. Should I be brave, ring Drew, find out the identity of the love object? It couldn't be Rosa. He'd stood her up. But nobody stood Rosa up. She'd simply have driven around to his office, fronted up to him. Rich, spoilt people were like that. The phone.

'Jack, the other day, you wanted a snap.'

Detective Sergeant Warren Bowman, he of the telegraphic eyebrows.

'I'm grateful,' I said.

'Sorry I've been so long, mate. No luck, can't be done. Cheers.' Click.

After a while, I put the phone back in the cradle.

The two men in the new red Alfa. The one who gave me the video cassette was young, a mole beside his mouth, wearing a collarless black leather jacket.

Not the messengers of Warren Bowman.

I rested my forehead on the tailor's table.

The rest of the day I spent on the half dozen files I had open: a few letters of demand, a complaint about harassment by a landlord, a protest against an unjust parking fine. Then I did my hours and expenses for Cyril Wootton and faxed them to him.

Driving home in the early dusk, I put on the radio, caught the wheedling tones of a drive-time host called Barry Moran, a seminary flop who had joined the legion of other faith-challenged but inordinately sensitive people on radio. Barry was sensitive to the concerns of the young, the old, ordinary people, extraordinary people, the poor, the rich, the short, the tall, the middling, all religious beliefs, and the legitimate concerns of both sides in every dispute. He strove to be fair to everyone but had a tendency to be snappish with people who disagreed with his reasonable views. Unless they were powerful people, in which case his views quickly came to encompass theirs. He was saying:

...The Development Minister Tony DiAmato joins me now. Thanks for coming on the program, Minister. Last week you washed your hands of the Cannon Ridge controversy because the previous government awarded the tender. It's done, it's history, you said. Now this is a tricky one, I know, Minister, but if the tender process was corrupted, don't you have a duty to declare the tender void and hold an inquiry?

I thought about the library-warming, my attempts to make conversation with Mike Cundall. 'Politics of business,' he'd said. 'WRG wants to build a whole fucking town on the Gippsland Lakes. Get the new government in some shit over

Cannon, good chance they won't get knocked back on that.'

Now the Minister cleared his throat.

Barry, we're talking about allegations here. We've had a pretty good look at the documents and we can't find any evidence of corruption.

Barry, ever the unctuous ex-seminarian, said: *That's a reasonable approach. Now Minister, I'd like to put a tricky one to you. WRG Resorts says a member of the tender evaluation panel was quote placed under duress unquote. Now I wouldn't dream of saying the name but every media person in town has heard it. Do you know who the alleged person is?*

The Minister sighed, tired at the end of the day.

No, I don't. And Barry, I'm surprised at a person like you not recognising that WRG's on a fishing expedition. They say they've got evidence. Where is it? They've yet to approach me with it.

Barry, nimble as ever: *Of course, it might well be a fishing expedition, Minister, as you point out. We might take a call. Its Steven from Doncaster.*

A confident voice said: *Hi Barry, love your show. About this Cannon Ridge business, everybody knows that in opposition this government put up a pissweak resistance to the sale of Cannon Ridge. Pissweak. They let the previous government sell off part of our heritage. Why'd you reckon? Because they're in the Cundalls' pockets like everyone else in this town.*

Barry: *Minister?*

DiAmato, weary: *Well, for a start, Anaxan has five major shareholders…*

Caller: *And one's a Cundall. One's all it takes. You know that…*

It went on this way. I parked beneath the trees outside the boot factory, listened for a while, went upstairs and switched on the radio in the kitchen, tuned to Linda's station.

…breaking up is hard to do. That's what the old song says. But do men take it harder than women? Yes, says writer Phil Kashow in her

new book, published today. It's called Healing Your Broken Bits. *I want your views on the subject. The author's on the line from Sydney. Hello, Phil…*

I stood in the room listening to the exchange, Linda's mildly amused tone in dealing with the publicity-hungry woman. Then, without thought, I went into the sitting room and dialled the talkback number, pressed the redial button a dozen times until I got through to the producer.

'Hello, you are?'

'Jack from Fitzroy.'

'And you want to say?'

'I'm a psychotherapist and I'd like to shed a little…'

'Stay on the line please, Jack.'

A wait, listening to people emoting, then Linda's voice. 'Jack from Fitzroy's next. What's your view, Jack?'

'If breaking up is hard, how much harder is making up? That's the question I'd like to pose to Phil. And to you, Linda.'

'Excellent point, Jack,' said Phil. 'No simple answer. I deal with this in chapter sixteen of my book, called "Be proud and be lonely"…'

She talked rubbish for a good while, then Linda said, quickly, 'And insofar as that question included me, not hard at all, Jack from Fitzroy. Moving on, Phil, you say…'

I switched off, found a bottle of Cooper's Sparkling in the back of the fridge, stood around drinking it, thinking about Linda, what the remark meant, about who would want to give me the video of Marco and why. In the way of minds, I then veered off to Sandy the bashed plunge organiser, to my sister, to a despondent survey of the clutter of my life. A life that had no pivot, no fulcrum, no axis, no…

The phone.

'Jack Irish.'

'I'm in the ad break.'

Linda.

'Ad break. I'm in the life break.'

'Where?'

'Donelli's?'

'Shit,' Linda said. 'Doesn't anything change?'

'Not if I can help it.'

'Eight-thirty?'

For a Tuesday night, Donelli's in Smith Street was crowded. It had recently been redecorated, which included knocking a large hole in the wall between the dining room and kitchen. Now it was a theatre-restaurant: diners could watch the fat *faux* Italian patron and chef, Patrick Donelly, fussing around and abusing his staff.

I'd rung to book. The patron spotted me entering and came out to escort me to my table. 'You're a lucky man, Irish,' he said. 'Two servings left of the stuffed squid braised with white wine and tomatoes.'

'That'll be fine,' I said. 'Anything I don't have to watch you both stuff and cook.'

'The watchin's by popular demand,' he said. 'Punters can't get enough of the chef. Sex objects, that's what we are.'

I looked at the man, torso like a wrapped fridge. 'Speaking for myself,' I said, 'I'd rather have sex with the squid. Now, a decent bottle of white. Any of that little Tuscan number left?'

'Two bottles. I was savin them for the cognoscenti.'

I patted him on the white arm, as thick and round as a fire extinguisher. 'Well, they're not coming tonight, Patrick. I'll have theirs.'

'You'll be dinin on the bill, will ya?' he said.

'I think you can take that as read.'

Donelly owed me a large sum, payment for hundreds of hours of skilled labour over a messy legal matter finally resolved in his favour. Since getting actual money from the man was impossible, I'd been extracting my fee in food and drink.

Linda came in the door. Her hair was different, longer, parted in the middle. She was wearing a black raincoat and she took it off to reveal a black polo-neck and jeans. Lean and handsome, that was the same. She came over and kissed me, on the cheek, touch of silk, throat-catching hint of perfume.

'Now this closes the circle,' she said.

Our first social meeting had been at Donelli's, at this table.

We sat down.

'How can circles be circles before they're closed?' I said.

She smiled. 'When I think of the years I've wasted wrestling with that problem.'

My desire was to take her by the hand and go home, but nothing was that simple. Except in beginnings.

'I've ordered squid. Stuffed. Braised with tomatoes and white wine.'

'Sounds good, excellent.' She pushed her hair back. 'Somehow, I never saw you as a talkback caller.'

'I've always wanted to be. Full of potential. Just never heard a talkback host I wanted to talk to.'

We sat looking at each other, smiling, neither of us sure how to proceed.

'How've you been?' she said.

'I've known better. You're looking good.'

'For radio, I'll pass. You're thinner.'

'Worry.'

Silence again. The wine arrived. I waived the tasting ritual.

Linda sipped. 'Nice. I heard you'd taken up with a photographer.'

She'd never been one to step around subjects. I tried the wine. Much too good for the cognoscenti. 'Who told you that?'

'Gavin Legge. He rang me. Trying to get publicity for a book he claims to have written.'

Legge was a journalist, a client of mine in the old days when I was practising criminal law. I'd got him off a charge of assaulting a female restaurateur. He had also introduced me to Linda.

'The Legge is quicker than the eye,' I said. 'But he's out of date. I've moved on. Now I'm seeing a supermodel. She's eighteen. Stalked me, a thing for older men. What about you?'

She made a gesture of dismissal. 'Too much bother. And there's this internet service that home-delivers men— yourfuck dot com. It's all a working woman needs.'

I nodded. 'Do they take them away again?'

Linda frowned. 'They say they're working on that bit. Four in the garage the last time I looked.'

I laughed, she laughed, and the awkwardness was over, the long time apart contracted to nothing. I felt buoyed, light-headed. We talked about things that lay in our common ground, laughing a lot. She'd always been able to make me laugh and I'd had some success with her.

The squid was served by a small and intense young man. It was delicious. Donelly arrived, lifting Linda's hand and bowing his head to kiss it, reverent.

'Deeply honoured, my dear,' he said. 'I remember when ya first graced my establishment in the company of this ruffian. And now the whole kitchen loves ya. Station of choice while we're preparin the finest food in this city.'

'Thank you,' said Linda. 'I appreciate you saying that.'

I realised that people said things like this to her all the time. It was nothing new to her. She was a celebrity. I took the opportunity to order another bottle of the Tuscan.

'And in the circumstances, how could I say no?' said Donelly, shaking his head at my opportunism.

'Exactly.'

Donelly sighed. 'Consortin with this famous lady, Irish,' he said. 'How ya do it, legal extortionist that you are, defies the imagination.'

'She sees in me what is invisible to people like yourself, Patrick,' I said.

He went off, stopping here and there to bestow benedictions on tables of chef groupies, all eager to have sex with him.

'I've been consorting with other famous people,' I said. 'I met Mike Cundall last week. And the beautifully preserved Ros.'

I told her about Mrs Purbrick's library.

'The son and heir's in with a fast crowd,' said Linda. 'Comes from spending too much time in Sydney. Sam's been trying to get out from under Mike for years but everything he touches turns to dog shit. The nasty coke habit and the gambling don't help. Then along came Cannon Ridge.'

'What's the story there?' Linda knew Melbourne.

'The Sydney smarties put together this consortium to tender. It's full of funny money. They brought in Sam because they reckoned the Cundall name could swing the thing. Not an unreasonable assumption. I mean, Mike Cundall used to just front up to see the last Premier, no appointment, shown straight in. And people heard him shouting at the Premier. Now that kind of thing cuts ice in Sydney.'

And Linda knew what cut ice in Sydney. She'd left Melbourne, and me, to be a current affairs television star in Sydney. That was where it all went wrong between us.

'And he did swing it?' I asked.

She forked up the last of her squid and chewed thoughtfully. 'Let's say it was swung,' she said. 'No-one quite knows how. WRG, the other bunch, they thought they had it stitched up. Australian company, experienced resort operators worldwide, went through the probity stuff without a hitch, pitched the tender on the high side to be sure and threw in some sweeteners. Cometh the hour, they find Anaxan has got them covered on all counts. Into shock they went.'

'I heard Barry Moran saying everyone in the media knew the name of a tender panel member who'd been put under duress.'

Linda looked around. 'Said to be a bloke called Rykel. A conservation bureaucrat on the panel. The whisper is that a large sum arrived in his wife's bank account just after the winner was announced. A transfer from a numbered account at the Bank of Funafuti or some such.'

The wine arrived. Then our plates were removed.

'According to Mike Cundall,' I said, 'and Mike tells me things all the time, this leak stuff is just WRG's way of screwing the government into letting it bulldoze a large section of Gippsland. Presumably the section that houses the last known breeding ground of an endangered creature.'

'With tiny pink nose. Yes, Anaxan's got the spin doctors putting out that story. Best in the business. Ponton's. Did you know Gavin Legge works for them now?'

'Openly? He's come out?'

'This mole has lost his value on the inside. Damaged goods is Gav.'

'What's his book called? *Living Off the Land: How to Take With One Hand While Also Taking With the Other?*'

'*Media Relationship Management in the Cyberage.* It's a slim volume.'

'I beg your pardon? Are we talking about the Gavin Legge who offered to get the name of the man who was tiling his shower into the paper? As a contra deal?'

'We are. Ponton's keep people chained up in New York to write a book for every new consultant. It's called WTB cred.'

'What? Wing Tailed Buzzards?'

'Wrote the Book. As in, the expert on the subject. Then they subsidise publication and bribe the reviewers in the business press to say things like succinct and definitive work, brilliant insights, etcetera. All easy, cheap. One decent contract, Pontons are in profit.'

'Shocked, that's all I can say,' I said.

She gave me the Linda eye and half-smile. 'Yes, well, you would be, pottering around as you do exclusively in Christian outreach circles.'

'Have a heart,' I said. 'Not just Christian. I don't discriminate on grounds of faith.'

She raised her glass, serious, put out her left hand and touched my face for an instant. 'To old friends new again.'

We touched glasses. I also thought I felt a leg touch mine and an erotic charge went through me, through the core. I often thought about her athlete's legs. 'That's a good toast,' I said. 'Welcome home.'

'I may never leave Melbourne. Well, maybe not never.'

'No. They say never is now down to six months.'

Donelly appeared, beaming smoked-salmon face moist above his surgical garb. 'You'll be wantin somethin to close with.'

I shook my head. Something about this personal attention was nagging at me. Celebrity-sucking, yes, but there was something else.

'I want the memory of your stuffed squid to stand alone,' said Linda. 'So a short black would be lovely.'

Donelly smiled at Linda, smiled at me, bowed and departed.

I poured the last of the wine, having had the sense to come by cab. 'You're not driving?'

'The station pays for after-work limousines,' said Linda. 'It's in my contract.'

'Good.' We looked at each other, smiles beginning.

'As someone steeped in the lore of Sydney,' I said, 'do the names James Toxteth and Colin Blackiston mean anything to you? They're venture capitalists, but that's all I know.'

'Jamie Toxteth, yes. Are you planning an IT start-up? Involving horses?'

'I'm trying to find out about someone who ran away with someone else's album of naughty snaps, died of smack, turned out not to be who he said he was.'

'This doesn't sound like Jamie Toxteth country to me,' said Linda. 'Jamie plays polo. The Toxteths are landed gentry. They own Mount Toxteth station. It's huge, like a small country. A country of sheep. Prince Charles spent weekends there.'

'He'd like a country of sheep. They have no problem with following the most stupid. What would a woman in Melbourne be doing driving a car owned by a two-dollar company Jamie owns?'

She raised her cup. 'This place is closing. For all I know, women all over Australia drive cars owned by Jamie. I may be the only one left out. This was a lovely evening.'

Linda found her mobile and rang for a cab.

We rose. Linda went to get her coat. I appreciated the way she looked from behind as I strolled towards the waiting Donelly.

'Show me where to sign,' I said. 'And may I say that if I were a squid, you would be my preferred stuffer.'

He ran fingers over his brow, disturbing the long strands of hair that originated well to the west.

'That'll be $38.50,' he said, a light in his eyes, a glow, an unearthly glow. He'd been waiting for this moment for three years. 'Your outrageous bill paid in full plus $38.50. And we'd prefer cash. If it's a cheque, you'll have to leave your watch.'

An era ended, closed. A watershed, a turning point. Dining out would never be the same.

I gave him a $50 note, said, 'I presume there's a discount for cash.'

'Certainly.' Donelly went away, he was gone for a few seconds, and when he returned, he counted out $11.50 in change. Then he said, 'And here's your discount.'

He put half an unshelled peanut in my palm.

'You're being petty, Donelly,' I said. 'Give me the other half.'

Outside, rain and cold had driven everyone except a few drug desperates into shelter. We stood against Donelli's window. 'I'm back at the boot factory,' I said. 'What about you?'

'I bought a place in Carlton. On Drummond Street, near your old office. It's nice, an old building, used to house nuns.'

'I can understand you feeling at home.'

She put a fist under my chin. Her cab arrived. 'I'll drop you,' she said.

Seize the moment? No. Patience. I shook my head. 'Wrong direction. We'll do this again, I hope.'

She opened her hand, touched my lips with three fingers. 'Call me.'

I was at home on my way to bed, in a better mood than I'd known for some time, when the phone rang.

Cam said, 'Somethin we should do tomorrow morning. You okay?'

'Any luck on short Artie with a Saint tatt?' I said.

Cam shook his head. 'That Braybrook address, he was there for three months in '98 after he came out. Three years for serious assault.'

Artie's name was Arthur Gary McGowan, he had form going back sixteen years, and he lived outside the world of telephone books, credit cards, Medicare, voters' rolls, and phone, power, gas and rates bills. He was out there in the cash economy and all we had was an old driver's licence address.

Today, we were in a non-threatening vehicle, a new Subaru Forester, dark green, parked outside the Royal Melbourne Institute of Technology on Swanston Street, just up from the ugliest new facade in the city. The architects had played an end-of-century joke on the university. Needless to say, the university hadn't caught it yet. Universities never do catch the joke until it's too late. Many a French fraud had died laughing while earnest Australian academics were still doing PhDs on his theoretical jokes.

'She finishes at twelve today,' said Cam, eyes on the passersby. 'Fashion, that's what she does. Whatever that is.'

He was talking about Marie, the 18-year-old daughter of Cynthia the commission agent.

I watched the throng of students, many of them the sons and daughters of the old colonial world, the Asian part. We'd closed our factories so that we could exploit the cheap labour their parents provided. Then we had a second cunning and rapacious thought: we could convince them that our universities were intellectual powerhouses and charge huge fees for admitting their children.

It worked.

'What'd Cynthia say?' I said.

'The boy told her Marie's got a habit. Coupla days ago. She says she went wild, grabbed Marie when she came in the house. Marie says it's over, she's clean, clean since Cyn got bashed.'

'That's all?'

He nodded.

'This Cynthia's idea?'

'No. She doesn't make any connection. I never said anythin. There she goes. You start.'

Cam was out of the car, walking round the front, long strides in his moleskins. He caught up with a slim young woman in black jeans and a purple top, said something. She turned her head, smiled, stopped, obviously knew him. He gestured at the car. She nodded, came back with him.

Cam opened the back door for her.

'Hi,' she said.

I turned and said hello. Her spiky hair was the same colour as her top, her lipstick was green, and she had ear and nose rings. The overall effect was innocent, something a five-year-old let loose on her mother's things might achieve.

Cam got in. 'Marie, Jack Irish. Your mum knows him. He's a lawyer.'

'Hi,' she said again. 'I've only got a minute. What's it about?' Her speech was rushed, nervous.

Cam took out his Gitanes, offered her one. She took it, leaned across for a light, had a coughing fit.

'Jeez,' she said, 'what is it?'

'There's somethin milder here somewhere,' said Cam.

'No, it's cool.' She coughed again. 'Just a shock.'

Not turning, I said, 'Marie, we're trying to find out who bashed your mother.'

I could hear her exhale smoke. 'Yeah,' she said. 'Yeah, that's good. It's like a nightmare. Weird.'

I waited a few seconds. 'How long have you had a habit?'

Silence. 'Christ, what's this shit? I'm out of…'

Cam leaned over the seat, draped his arm. 'Marie, listen, it's not about you and drugs, right? It's about who nearly killed your mum. You love your mum, don't you?'

More quiet. Marie began to cry, a sniffle, throat noises.

'Don't you? Love your mum?'

Then she was making crying noises, not loud, and saying, 'Oh, Jesus, oh Jesus…'

We waited.

After a while, I said, 'Tell us about it, Marie.'

She did a lot more sniffing, then she said, 'Mum sent you?'

'No,' said Cam. 'Your mum told me you'd had a problem, but that now you're clean. She's proud of you, your mum.'

The sniffing resumed. Then she said, courage plucked, 'There's nothing to tell, like. What's this—'

I said, 'Last chance, Marie. You could go to jail for this. Conspiracy.'

This time it was a cry from deep down, a wail, then more sobbing. I looked at Cam. He was looking at Marie, flicked his chestnut-brown eyes at me. I thought I detected a hint of compassion. Probably just the light.

We waited.

'I just told this bloke my mum did big-money bets,' she said, sad voice. 'Don't even know how it works—'

'Which bloke?'

A long silence.

'Can't go back now, Marie,' said Cam, gently. 'Which bloke?'

'Around the bike shop. He deals, everyone knows him, it's safe.'

'Why'd you tell him?' Cam said.

Sigh. 'I dunno, I just told him one day.' Sigh. 'Like I thought it was smart, like my mum didn't do ordinary kind of…Just stupid. Mum always said…Oh, shit.'

'You told him that and then what happened?' I asked.

She became matter-of-fact. 'He said, give us the word when you've got a horse. I didn't know anything about that, mum never said a word, all I knew is some days she's got something on at the races, she's phoning people, you can't understand what she's saying to them.'

'You told him you never heard the names of horses?' I said.

'Yeah. Then one day he says, tell me when your mum's going to the races and I'll give you a hit.'

Silence, waiting, Cam leaning over the seat, looking at Marie, tendons like cable in his neck.

'And?'

'That day, I was hanging out, didn't have a cent…'

'You told him,' said Cam.

'Yes.' Tiny voice. 'I'd've cut my wrists before I told him if I knew what…'

'Where's the bike shop?'

'Elizabeth Street.'

Cam started the vehicle and waited to pull out.

'My mum,' said Marie, 'you're going to tell mum?'

'No,' said Cam, getting into the traffic, 'you've got your punishment. This bloke always there?'

Marie sniffed. 'Most of the time. He sees you're chasin and he meets you at the Vic Market. Keeps the stash there.'

'We'll drive by. See if you can point him out.'

We went around the corner into LaTrobe Street, turned right into Elizabeth Street.

Marie saw him almost immediately.

'Next to that white car, the bloke on the bike.'

'Sit low,' said Cam.

He was across the street from the motorcycle dealers, sitting on a black BMW, helmet on his lap, talking to someone in the passenger seat of a car. We got a good look at him—tall, curly red-brown hair pulled back in a ponytail, short beard around his mouth.

We took Marie back to Swanston Street. As she was getting out, she said, 'Cam, I'm so scared my mum'll find—'

'Not from us,' said Cam. 'Stay clean or you'll break her heart.'

'I'm staying clean. That's over, over.'

We watched her go, long-legged walk, bag swinging.

'Get that number run?' said Cam.

'Five minutes. Find a public phone.' Cam took out a mobile. 'Safe phone,' he said.

I didn't ask what that meant. I took it and dialled Eric the Geek.

There was a fax from Jean Hale waiting at the office. Two names on the Lucan's Thunder betting team were circled. One was someone called Tim Broeksma. In the margin, Jean had written: *He's new. Sandy doesn't know much about him. A plumber.*

The other name was Lizard Ellyard. There were quotation marks around Lizard.

He's got a firewood business. Bit of a sad case, was in a bad accident, I think. Anyway, he didn't show up on the day so he really shouldn't be on the list.

I drowsed in the captain's chair, mind picking daisies. Cam and I had lunched well at a pub in Abbotsford. It was a place frozen in time like the Prince, except that this pub had been deliberately frozen, used as a television series location for years, and it was in excellent shape. Halfway through the sausages and mash, I felt a hand on my shoulder.

'Straying out of your territory, Mr Irish.'

Boz, in jeans and a jerkin. I introduced her to Cam. She sat down for a few minutes and I told her about Mrs Purbrick's party.

'You'll end up choosing her books, Jack,' said Boz. 'I saw the signs.'

She was getting up to rejoin a table of people, all talking, telling stories, film people if I read the signs, when Cam said, 'I do a fair bit of movin. Got a card?'

Boz shook her head. 'Got a pen?' She wrote her name and phone number on a drink coaster. He put it in an inside pocket.

I saw the signs.

Now, half-asleep in my office, I was thinking again about who had given me the Marco video. The people who'd taken it? I'd assumed it was a cop video—federal, local. That might still be true. But I had to assume that the cops hadn't given it to me.

Who then? And why me? Why would someone other than the cops give me a surveillance video? What could they want from me?

Who else knew that I was interested in Robbie/Marco? My anonymous caller knew. But there was no way to find out who she was. Had the judge told someone? Not likely. The people at The Green Hill knew. But why would they be interested in helping me find out more about a dead man they had employed under another name? And where would they get the video?

This line of thought wasn't going to produce anything. If I knew more about Robbie/Marco, the questions would probably answer themselves.

I got out the enhanced pictures and looked at them again. Trying to identify the woman in the car belonging to Jamie Toxteth and his partner hadn't met with any success. That left the fleshy man at the sidewalk table.

How to begin?

I was looking out of the window. I could see Kelvin McCoy's front door. A young woman came into view, dressed in what from this distance appeared to be a garment fashioned from colourful rags, offcuts from a tie factory perhaps, and carrying a big flat folio bag. At McCoy's portal, she paused, uncertain for a moment. Oh God, she had been invited to show the unwashed charlatan her drawings. I felt I should open my door and shout a warning. Too late, she knocked. A brief wait, the door opened, I glimpsed the brutal shaven head, she was drawn in. The beast would see a lot more than her drawings before the day was out.

Ah well. Life went on.

The fleshy man. In the glass behind him, the cafe window, a reflection of writing on an uneven surface, the word *asset*.

Written on what outside a cafe? What was uneven?

An apron, it was on an apron, a long black apron of the kind favoured by Melbourne cafes. A reflection of a name on a waiter's apron.

Asset?

My stupidity dawned on me.

I walked up to Brunswick Street and weaved and jinked my way along a pavement crowded with young artists, fashion students, actors, directors, scriptwriters, drug dealers, filmmakers, fashionistas, off-duty *baristas,* models, writers of forgotten grunge novels published by Penguin, *Age* lifestyle journalists, internet entrepreneurs, meme-carriers of every description. Many of them were on the phone to like-minded people. Why did people have so much more to communicate these days?

At my destination, a good bookshop next door to what had been a good gun shop with a bad clientele when I came to Fitzroy, I bought a copy of a guide to cheap Melbourne eating places. Cheaper.

Near the office, I heard the phone ringing, ran, wrestled with the lock, got in, panting.

'Jack,' said Wootton, 'the client wants to meet very, very urgently.'

I took the book with me. You never know how long you'll be kept waiting.

The door was huge and studded and the steps before it had hollows worn in them big enough for birds to bathe in. I pressed the button and waited no more than a minute or two.

A tall, thin man in a dark suit opened the door. 'Mr Irish?'

'Yes.'

'Please follow me.'

We went up a curving staircase to a lobby, then down a grand corridor, stopping at a door near the end. The man opened it with a key and ushered me into a panelled reception room with desks and computers, no-one at work. He knocked at a door to the left, listened, opened it, and said, 'Mr Irish, Your Honour.'

He stood back for me to enter and closed the door behind me. I stood in an impressive room: high ceiling, dark panelling, cedar bookcases tight with bound volumes, small oil paintings in gilt frames lit from above. It was exactly the chamber I'd expected a judge to inhabit. Only the computer station was out of place.

Mr Justice Colin Loder, no jacket, was coming around his leather-topped desk. 'Jack,' he said, 'thanks for coming.'

'Your Honour.' We shook hands.

'Colin. I should've said that before. You know too much for formality.'

'Something's happened.'

'Sit down.'

I sat on a chair with buttoned green leather upholstery.

The judge went back to his seat, sat upright, forearms on the desk. A long yellow envelope lay in front of him. He touched each of his cufflinks, modest silver ovals, checked them, pointed at the envelope with his eyes. 'The worst,' he said. 'Worse than I expected. Left downstairs an hour ago.'

I waited. He pushed the envelope over.

'Read it, please.'

It had been opened with a paper-knife. I removed one sheet of white paper, twice folded. A good computer printer had produced half a page of type:

Mr Justice Loder,

The accused in the so-called 'cocaine jackets' hearing before Your Honour are innocent victims of a Federal Police conspiracy. In its eagerness to make up for its incompetence, this agency has often resorted to illegality in the past and has done so again in this matter. As you will know only too well, an option is available to you when this matter resumes. Choosing it will be in keeping with your well-deserved reputation as a defender of the citizen against improper conduct by government agencies. Therefore I am sure Your Honour will see fit to use your discretion to exclude evidence relating to importation, from which it follows that the accused must be acquitted, since without this evidence the prosecution must fail.

In passing, may I say how sad it was to hear of Robbie's death. The album of photographs you lent him, so touching in their intimacy, will be returned to you at the appropriate time. You will not, of course, wish to recuse yourself or to find some other reason for not hearing this matter. Such actions will have the unfortunate consequence of your reputation being damaged beyond salvation.

Naturally there was no signature. I folded the page, put it on the desk, looked into the judge's brown eyes, eyes the colour of strong tea, the bag left too long in the mug.

'Appropriate is a bad word,' I said. 'What's the cocaine jackets?'

'Cocaine concealed in ski jackets. Two men charged. It's what's called a controlled importation. The Federal Police ran the thing using an undercover agent, an informer. I don't think it would be unjudicial of me to describe the operation as a massive cock-up.'

'The demand. Lawyers wouldn't be stupid enough?'

'No. Not even lawyers are that stupid. They wouldn't know about this. This is from people associated with the accused. Trying to make sure it goes their way.'

'What kinds of people are the accused?'

'They're not Mr Bigs, these two, they're mules, really. But they're all the Feds could lay their hands on. Desperation stuff after spending huge amounts of money.'

'Why wouldn't the people higher up simply let them go down?'

He turned his mouth down, raised his hands. 'Don't know. They may know something. And should they get long gaol terms they might agree to co-operate with the police. Could be other reasons. Family, who knows?'

'Distinct legal tone to the letter. Lawyer in there some-where. The finding it suggests, could you make it?'

'Are you familiar with *Ridgeway*?'

'Familiar's probably not the right word.' It was the landmark High Court decision on police entrapment.

'Well, that's what they'll be arguing. And yes, it's a poss-ible finding, depends on what happens when we resume.'

'When's that?'

'Next Thursday.' He sighed, made a resigned face. 'I suppose I should call the police in now, issue a statement to the media. This'll kill my father.'

185

'You could ignore the letter. See what happens. It may be bluff, they may just go away.'

The judge shook his head. He'd aged years in a few hours. 'No, Jack. Any finding I reach would be tainted by this. The well's poisoned.'

'Give me a few days.'

His chin sank a little. 'Any point?'

'We have to assume that Robbie took the album with this or something like this in mind. If I can find out what happened to him, it's possible I'll know who the blackmailer is.'

Another sigh.

'I won't keep you in suspense,' I said. 'If I'm not getting anywhere by Tuesday, I'll pack it in.'

Silence for a while. The sounds of the city didn't reach the room.

'I'll give you a mobile number,' he said. 'It's not in my name. I've borrowed it.' He took out a notebook, flipped through it, wrote down a number on a desk pad, tore off the page and gave it to me. 'I feel as if I've entered the under-world myself.'

I stood up. 'Can I get a transcript of the proceedings?'

The judge stood up too, went to a wooden filing cabinet and found a yellow folder, gave it to me. He walked me to the door. We shook hands.

'We could get lucky,' I said. 'Chin up.'

He smiled. 'Thanks, mate. Thanks for everything.'

'Don't say thanks till you've seen Wootton's bill.'

The thin man was waiting outside to escort me to the side entrance. On the way to Fitzroy, stuck in Little Lonsdale, I picked up the cheap eats guide, flicked through to the index.

There it was, on the first page I scanned.

La Contessa, assetnoC aL in reverse, was a narrow place in Bridge Road, Richmond, that looked as if it had been there longer than those on either side in what was now a smart strip.

Although it was cold and too early for the after-work crowd, the half-dozen tables outside were taken. Inside, there were only a few customers. I found a seat near the kitchen. The man operating the coffee machine was not of the new generation of cafe people; he had the pained expression of someone too long standing to perform a repetitive task: the assembly-line worker's look.

A young man, possibly the son, came out of the kitchen. He was wearing the apron in the picture, a long black apron with La Contessa printed on it. I asked for a short black. When it came, I had the picture out, facing him.

'That's probably you,' I said, tapping on the reflected apron.

He was intrigued, had a good look. 'Yeah,' he said.

'Who's that?' I said, my finger on the fleshy man.

'Alan Bergh,' he said, suspicion starting. 'What's this, what's this about?'

'I'm a lawyer.'

This statement often has the effect of briefly paralysing the brain of the hearer.

'Right.' Uncertain. 'What do you—'

'I'd like to get in touch with Alan.'

'Yeah, well, he's away.'

'Away from where?'

'Where? His office.'

'Where's that?'

He indicated with a thumb. 'Vietcong supermarket. Upstairs.'

He'd learned that from his father. The war in Indochina was not over. The battle for the hearts and minds of the invaders had still to be won.

I didn't pursue the matter. The waiter left, went outside.

The coffee was terrible, sour, third-rate beans, old, probably black market.

'Come again,' said the father, giving me my change.

'Can't wait to.'

I walked in the direction indicated by the son's thumb. Halfway down the block was a business that satisfied his description. Beyond it, a heavyweight door with a mail slot carried the names of two businesses on the first floor: VICACHIN BUSINESS AGENCY and CORESECURE.

The door was locked. I pressed the buzzer on the wall.

'Yes,' said a woman's voice, hissing through holes in a slim stainless-steel box beside the door.

'Client of Coresecure,' I said. 'Here to see Alan.'

'Mr Bergh not here,' said the voice, staccato.

'When's he coming back?'

'Don't know.'

I accepted that, wrote down Vicachin's phone number. Coresecure didn't have one on the door. Then I went home, a slow journey in failing light in the company of irritable people.

Coresecure wasn't in the White Pages. Nor was it in the Yellow Pages in any category I could think of. I packed up for the day, not a great deal to pack, and drove around to

Lester's Vietnamese takeaway in St Georges Road.

Lester was alone in the shop, in the kitchen. When the door made its noise, he looked up and saw me in his strategically placed mirror.

'Early, Jack,' he barked. 'How many?'

'I need a favour,' I said.

'Ask.'

I asked. He nodded, took the piece of paper and went back to the kitchen, held a long, rapid-fire conversation in Vietnamese on the phone.

He came back and returned my slip of paper. 'They talk to you,' he said. 'You can go there tomorrow.'

I drove home in drizzle, tail-lights turning the puddles to blood, listening to Linda on the radio taking calls on Victorians' gambling habits. The daylight was gone before I found my mooring beneath the trees.

Upstairs, I put on the kitchen radio to hear a man say:...*accept that the state's now on a gambling revenue drip and raise the tax till the bastards scream.*

Linda: *You're saying gambling's a fact of life, so get the most public benefit out of it?*

Caller: *Exactly. And this Cannon Ridge casino, the Cundall casino, slug it. Playground for the rich, double the bloody gambling tax.*

Linda: *Thank you, Nathan of Glen Iris. Now there's a challenging point of view, even if the logic may be slightly fuzzy. What's your view, Leanne of Frankston?*

Leanne: *Linda. I'm a compulsive gambler, I've had treatment…*

Enough. She would ring or she wouldn't. It was probably better if she didn't. We could meet from time to time as friends. Old friends. We'd made a good start at that.

Had she rubbed her left leg against my right? Not a rub, but a linger. A touch and then a linger.

How old did you have to be before this kind of rubbish stopped?

I got a fire going, bugger cleaning the grate. Everything was dirty in my life, why worry about a pile of soft, clean ashes?

Now, a drink. I looked in the cupboard. Campari and soda, Linda's end-of-day drink, the bottles not touched since

Linda. I poured a stiff one, settled on the couch to think. The phone rang.

'No doubt,' said Drew, 'I find you poring over your footy memorabilia, sniffing old Fitzroy socks, marvelling at the size of your antecedents' jockstraps, lovingly preserved.'

'Large in their day but dwarfed by those to come,' I said. 'I gather you've found a form of happiness with some unfortunate.'

Tell me that it is not Rosa, please.

He sighed. 'To find joy and to share it, that is life's purpose. You probably have no idea who said that.'

'No. Let me have a stab. You.'

'Spot on. Anyway, you can't dwarf a jockstrap.'

'The courts will decide what you can and cannot do with a jockstrap. Who?'

'A corporate lawyer. International experience. Top-tier firm, I might add. With a personal trainer.'

I gave silent thanks. 'Trains her to do what? Find 48 billable hours in the day? Render the simple incomprehensible? Conspire with the other side to shake their clients down?

I could imagine the pained Drew look.

'Slander your fellow servants of the law if you will,' he said. 'This delightful creature has been slumbering, awaiting the kiss of an awakener.'

'Slumbering? Form?'

'Unraced.'

'Age?'

'I'm not filling in an application here.'

'I'll put it to you again.'

'The thirties. Thirty-five, six. Thereabouts, I suppose.'

'That's quite a slumber. How did this happen?'

'Her secretary was in a bit of strife. Vanessa came

along to give the poor woman moral support. You'll have noticed the effect a commanding physical presence, razor-sharp intellect, and professional brilliance can have on women.'

'I have. How'd you get Vanessa to notice you?'

'I can feel waves of jealousy passing through this instrument.'

'I hope you're talking about the phone. You got the secretary off?'

Drew sighed. 'Actually, no. Could've been worse though.'

'Moving away from your erotic fantasies,' I said, 'as a man of affairs, does the name Alan Bergh mean anything?'

'It does.'

'Tell me.'

'An employers' secret agent, Mr Bergh. Years ago, when the unions could still get up a decent strike. Before a Labor government broke the Builders' Labourers.'

'Does everyone except me know that?'

'Unusually, no. Bergh planted thugs in marches, demos, the blokes at the back who lob the first unopened can of VB at the cops, that sort of thing.'

'How do you know?'

'Appeared for one of his thugs. You were on sabbatical then.'

He was saying that this was in the time, the long time, when I was drunk, half-drunk, getting drunk again, after my wife Isabel's murder.

'The client told you?'

'We were pleading guilty, mate, as befits people shown on television poking what looks like an electric cattle prod up a police horse's bum. A former racehorse. With not unpredictable consequences.'

'Took off at great speed?'

'No. Reared and endangered lives, jockey fell off.'

'Surprising. Given a touch of the jigger, your racehorse generally shows a bit of toe, leaves the field behind. That's the idea of jigging them. So the client told you about Bergh?'

'Not him. Another bloke came in. An extremely dubious character. I got the impression that he'd hired my client and was a bit worried about what I'd do in court. I didn't want to discuss the matter with him, so he said, listen, just don't do anything that'll piss off Alan Bergh.'

'And?'

'Over a cheering glass with the labour aristocracy down at the John Curtin, I asked about Bergh. The word was that he did jobs for employers. The nasty work. Not still in business, is he?'

'He's in some business. Haven't worked out what it is yet.'

I was still trying to work it out in the last moments before sleep. I tried to find a thread in everything I knew about Robbie/Marco. Hopeless. It wasn't a fabric, it was a heap. And now there was a sophisticated attempt to blackmail a judge of the Supreme Court sitting in a drug importation case.

Marco was murdered. He was being watched, and then he was murdered. The supplier of the surveillance clips knew that and wanted me to know that. Milan Filipovic hadn't thought it likely that Marco had stuck a too-potent needle in his arm.

'Needle's a big fucken surprise to me,' he'd said.

But Detective Sergeant Warren Bowman said the dead man had needle tracks.

Alan Bergh and the woman in the car belonging to a Sydney high-flier. How did they fit into Marco's life and death?

Sleep claimed me, troubled sleep, full of strange places, peopled with strangers.

Up early stumbling around the streets, back to Richmond in peak-hour morning traffic, thinking about Colin Loder and his dad. That was what worried him most: his dad finding out that he had it off with non-women.

Not his brilliant legal career crashing. Not his wife and children finding out. Just his expectation of his dad's horrified reaction. His dad probably had his suspicions anyway.

Mr Justice Loder should announce that he was being blackmailed because he was gay or bi, had been silly enough to appear on camera.

Was that all Colin was worried about? Consenting adults? Did his album hold photographs that told a different story?

In Bridge Road, I parked in a loading zone and rang the bell at Vicachin Business Agency.

'Yes,' the voice hissed again.

'Lester rang about me. Yesterday.'

The door bolt unlocked.

The stairway was dark. Upstairs, the offices of Coresecure and Vicachin faced each other across a dim corridor. Vicachin's door opened and a young woman, unsmiling, beckoned me into an office, walls decorated with travel posters. She opened an inner door and stood back.

A balding middle-aged man in a black suit and striped shirt was behind a desk. He stood up and put out a hand. 'Call me Tran,' he said, briskly.

'Jack Irish.'

'Sit, Jack.' He sat down and adjusted his glasses. 'Your

friend tells me you want to know about Alan Bergh. There's not much I can tell you.'

He had an American accent.

'He's gone somewhere?'

'Well, he hasn't been in for a couple of weeks.'

'Have you told anyone?'

'No.' He wasn't looking at me, looking down, fiddling with his glasses.

'Something may have happened to him.'

He shrugged. 'I don't like to interfere. Mind my own business.'

'Do you know much about Coresecure, Tran?'

Tran held up his hands. 'God knows. Something to do with company security. I think Alan was a soldier once. He speaks some Vietnamese.'

'Who's the landlord?'

'I collect the rent.'

An answer to a question I hadn't asked. 'That's up to date?'

'Oh yes. Three months in advance.'

'What did you find when you checked his office?'

'Nothing.'

As he said it, he knew he'd been taken, tugged at an ear lobe, perhaps thinking about the mind-my-own-business problem.

'You worry whether someone's collapsed, heart attack, you know,' he said.

'Of course. Would you mind if I had a look?'

Tran's eyes said nothing. 'I don't understand. Your friend says you're a lawyer. What is your interest in Alan?'

'It's complicated. I think it's important to find Alan. Very much in his interests. You can trust me not to involve you in any way.'

A long think.

'I can't let you into his office.'

'You don't have to.'

More thought. Then he opened a drawer at his right and took out two keys on a metal disk, put them on the desk. He stood up, turned his back on me, went to the window. I took the keys.

'Thank you for talking to me, Tran,' I said. 'I imagine a security consultant's office would be guarded by the latest alarm system.'

He turned. 'No. Nothing of value, I suppose. Sorry I couldn't be more help.'

We shook hands and I left. The outer office was empty. I crossed the corridor and unlocked the Coresecure office. Inside, it was dark and musty.

I felt like a burglar.

In many ways, I was a burglar, always intruding, taking things I had no right to.

There was little to take in the Coresecure office. It consisted of two rooms, the front one not used, the back one minimally furnished. There was a desk, nothing on it except a telephone and a box of tissues. The drawers contained printer paper, an ink cartridge and a box of ballpoints. A printer was on a stand next to a filing cabinet, empty. To the right of the desk, a bookshelf held capital city telephone books, copies of an American magazine called *CORPORATE SECURITY*, and a dozen or so books, company histories and books about business failures and corporate crime.

The wastepaper basket was empty.

I went behind the desk, picked up the telephone and pressed the redial button.

Nothing. Last call cleared.

Standing behind Alan Bergh's desk, in his boring office, his telephone in my hand, a feeling of disgust, of failure and futility, settled on me. This was not the way an adult should spend time.

I pulled a tissue out of the box, wiped the instrument, replaced it, realised how silly this was for a member of the legal profession, gave the phone an extra rub anyway and went around looking for other things I'd touched. Paranoia satisfied, I clicked off the light.

In the near-dark of the outer room, reaching for the doorknob, I saw the mail basket. The mail was collected downstairs and someone, Tran's assistant no doubt, posted it through Coresecure's slot. It fell into a basket attached to the door.

A burglar. A thief.

I did a quick sort of Coresecure's mail and left, posting the firm's keys through the mail slot after closing the street door.

Back to Fitzroy, to the office. I'd never spent so much time there. I didn't want to be there. I wanted to be at Taub's, making things. Any things.

At my table, I opened the purloined mail. I'd stolen two bank statements, a credit card statement, and a mobile-phone bill.

I read the bank statements. One was for a cash management account holding $66,354. No transactions in the statement period, an interest credit. A cheque account statement showed three deposits adding up to $28,730 and cash withdrawals, two a week, four or five hundred dollars each time. Six cheques had been drawn against the account, the biggest for $3024. The most recent transaction was a cash withdrawal of $500 two weeks earlier and the account was $12,340.80 in credit.

On to the credit card statement.

Alan Bergh spent money on restaurants, hotels, plane tickets and hire cars, bought clothes at expensive shops, and paid the account balance inside the interest-free period. Rich and prudent.

The last account was the mobile-phone bill: four pages detailing how Alan had incurred a debt of $2548.20. The man gave good phone. I got a pen and asterisked the frequently called numbers and the long calls. Then I rang for Mr Cripps. He was at the door inside fifteen minutes.

Coffee.

Urgent, compelling was the need. I walked swiftly, bought the *Age* on the way, found Meaker's near-empty. A new waiter, a thin young man, took my order.

Waiting for my long black, I postponed reading the paper, watched a man taking things out of the back of a van in the loading zone. A sign-writer: Beems Brothers, Sign-writers.

My coffee came. I sipped.

Foul taste of uncleaned machine, reused grind.

Poised to complain, I realised that I didn't recognise the large person lolling against the counter in front of the machine. Fat, in fact.

I raised a hand. There was anxiety in me.

The new waiter came over. 'Something else?'

He had big teeth.

'What's happened to the usual mob?'

'Pardon?'

'The people who usually work here?'

'New management,' he said. 'New staff.'

'What?'

'Sold.'

'As of when?'

'Pardon?'

'When did this happen?'

He held up his hands. 'Temp, mate, can't help you there.'

I got up and went to the kitchen door.

'Hey,' said the man at the coffee machine.

I ignored him, looked in. No Enzio. A small fat man was at the stove. He sensed me, turned his head.

'What?' he said.

'Enzio?'

'Who?'

'The cook.'

'Dunno.' He looked away. 'Ask the manager.'

Behind me, the big man said, 'Staff only, mate.'

I didn't look at him, went back to my table, picked up my paper, made for the door. The waiter said loudly, 'Hang on, coffee's not free.'

I turned, he was close. 'That isn't coffee,' I said with venom.

'Lettim go,' said the big man, back behind the counter.

I looked at him.

'Piss off. See ya, buddy. Go somewhere else.'

Walking away, holding a course, the flow of the aimed and the aimless breaking around me, I was compelled to look back. The sign-writer was scraping at the name Meaker's on the window.

A chilling sense of fate's impudence came over me. How could there be no Meaker's in Brunswick Street? How could it simply be taken away?

Hooted at, I crossed the street and went into a place I didn't know, barn-like, atmosphere of a school staffroom.

It had once been a social club. Macedonian? Portuguese? I couldn't remember. The coffee was awful, I was too bemused to care, left most of it, wandered back to the office.

I saw him from a long way off, leaning against the wall next to my door. He saw me too but he looked away, smoked his cigarette, studied the sky, clear today, some high cloud. I was metres away before he turned his head to me.

Enzio, clean-shaven, in a black suit, white shirt, dark-blue tie.

'Jack,' he said.

'What the fuck's going on?'

He took a last drag on his cigarette, ground it savagely underfoot. 'The bastard Willis sold.'

Neil Willis had owned Meaker's for about fifteen years. He also owned two wedding reception caverns out in the suburbs and his stewardship of Meaker's consisted of hiring a succession of untrained managers and scrutinising the takings at night. Enzio was the only constant, and so the cook had always ended up grumpily showing the managers how to run the place.

I unlocked the door and we went in. I took my seat. Enzio stood.

'Sit down,' I said.

He sat, shifted around in the chair, crossed legs, uncrossed.

'What's this suit business?' I'd never seen him in a suit.

He frowned. 'I'm comin to see a lawyer. You dress proper.'

I understood.

'Smoke?'

'Smoke.'

I fetched the ashtray from the sink in the back room. He lit up, exploded smoke.

'Tell me,' I said. 'Tell me.' I closed my eyes.

'Tuesday, Willis come in, business sold, new boss come in tomorrow. No worries about jobs, he says. Bloke wants all staff to stay.'

He took a deep drag, spoke through smoke. 'Yesterday, the cunt come in. I know straight away, I look at the cunt and I know. Before lunch, sacks Helen. Carmel he sack at the door, says she's late. Martina, she's going off, he tells her, customers complain, pick up your pay tomorrow. Closing time, he come in the kitchen, it's me and the boy cleaning up, he says he's looked at the books, there's stealing going on in the kitchen.'

Enzio looked away, looked at my degree certificate on the wall, took a moment to compose himself.

'Fourteen years, Jack,' he said, still studying the wall. 'Steal?' A catch in the voice. 'Like I steal from my mother?'

'I know.' I wanted to give him a pat.

We sat in silence, contemplating ourselves, our histories at Meaker's, perfidy, the callousness of people. But I was coming out of shock, cruising past resentment. Revenge and compensation were now in mind. This was a natural progression and I had some training in it.

'What's the offer?' I said.

'He says, the prick, he's got the money in his hand, he says four weeks pay I give you, lucky you get anything. Don't like it, I get the cops, you can tell them who you sold all the stuff to.'

'Take it?'

Enzio put his head back, looked at me over his cheek-bones, over lines of spiky hairs that survived his shave, a prickly frontier.

'I spit on him,' he said.

Our eyes held for a moment.

'Right. You in the union?'

He shook his head. 'No. Willis wouldn't have the union.'

This wasn't going to be effortless for someone who'd spent most of his legal career in the criminal courts. I might actually have to find out something about employment law. Either that or I farmed this out. Tempting.

But how could I farm out Enzio?

'Okay,' I said. 'We've got no choice but to nail the poor bastard.'

I got out a yellow pad. I'd bought four dozen yellow pads when the stationer in Smith Street went under. 'Now tell me again what happened. Slowly.'

When we'd finished, I went out with him. The day was turning foul, the wind was sharp against the cheek, coming down the street, chasing bits of litter, harrying them like a bully.

'So,' said Enzio. 'You fix it?'

'I'll fix it.'

We shook hands. I watched him go. At the corner, he felt my eyes, turned his head, smiled, raised a hand. I did the same.

Oh, Lord, why hast thou anointed me the fixer of all things? And why hast thou ordained this in a cold season in which too many things need fixing?

There were moments when I wished I could go somewhere quiet and ask sensible questions like these. My office wasn't the place because the phone was ringing. It was Drew.

'What is it with you?' he said. 'You no sooner take an interest in someone and bad things happen to them.'

He didn't have to say the name. I knew.

'Who?'

'Alan Bergh. Found dead in his car at the airport. Execution-style killing, says the paper. Three shots in the head from a .22.' Someone was knocking at the door. I knew who it was. My day for being knowing.

They sat in the client chairs, a soft-looking big man with a moustache, a younger man with a long horse face. Agents Mallia and Bartholomew, Federal Police.

'Let me understand this clearly,' said Mallia. 'You asked this Vietnamese gentleman…'

'I have no idea whether he's a gentleman,' I said. 'Do you?'

'Manner of speech.'

'Offensive manner of speech, if I may say so.'

Mallia coughed, looked at Batholomew, who ran a hand over his head bristles.

'If you say so,' Mallia said. 'You asked him a lot of questions about Bergh?'

'No,' I said. 'I'll say it again. Clearly. I was interested in using the services of Mr Bergh's company. He wasn't in, so I spoke to Mr Ngo. I asked him if he knew when Mr Bergh would be back or where he could be contacted.'

'He says you didn't know what Coresecure did, what its business was.'

'That's a misunderstanding. I asked him how much he knew about Coresecure. At that point, I thought he might have some involvement with the company.'

Equine-faced Batholomew thought he'd chip in. 'You wanted to use Bergh's services. What for?'

'What for?'

'Yes. What for?' He developed a smile, as if he'd been clever.

'Security.'

'Security for?'

'Nothing in particular. Security in general. I wanted a feeling of security. I've always wanted to feel secure. What about you?'

The smile departed.

Mallia stroked his moustache, then, carefully, scratched the arranged hairs on his head. 'You're probably not aware of the powers conferred upon us by—'

I said, 'I'm perfectly aware of them, agent. If you're taking that route, my lawyer can be here in minutes. He's a lawyer's lawyer.'

Mallia shook his head. 'Appreciate your co-operation, that's all, Mr Irish. The man's dead, you were at his office the day before, you'll understand—'

'Why's this a federal matter?'

'I can't disclose that sort of information.' He looked at his large hands, bunches of hair on the first joints. 'How did Coresecure come to your attention?'

'I'd seen the name on the door.'

'In the area a lot?'

'My work takes me everywhere.'

'Yes.' Mallia raised himself from the chair. Batholomew followed his lead.

'You're not unknown to us, Mr Irish,' said Mallia, attempting to give me the narrowed eye.

'Nor your agency to me, agent Mallia,' I said. 'And I can tell you I've derived very little pleasure from the acquaintanceship.'

I didn't rise to see them out.

At the door, Mallia turned. 'Have a good day,' he said. 'Give my regards to His Honour.'

Things were quiet at The Green Hill, no-one braving the elements out front and only one customer in Down the Pub. Dieter the barman wasn't on this morning, in his place a young woman in the establishment's dark-green livery.

'Good morning, sir,' she said. 'What can I serve you?'

'I'm after Xavier Doyle,' I said.

'I'll see if Mr Doyle's in,' she said. 'It's Mr…?'

'Irish. Jack Irish.'

She went to a telephone on the back counter and spoke to someone, came back. 'He'll be along in a moment.'

Doyle appeared from my right, through a door beyond the last booth. He was wearing Donegal tweeds and a yellow shirt.

'Jack,' he said, hand out. He looked like a mildly debauched cherub. 'My oath, you legal fellas are up and about with the sparrers.'

We shook hands. 'Come and have a cup of coffee in the office,' he said. 'Coffee right for you?'

'Perfect.'

'Belinda, lass, lay on a pot of coffee darlin. In me office.'

Doyle took my arm and escorted me back the way he'd come. We went through the door into a flagstoned passage, past two doors to the end. He opened a wide four-panel oak door and waved me in.

It was a big room, as much lounge as office, modern leather armchairs in front of a fireplace, a desk behind them, its top a curved slab of polished redgum holding a squat computer tower, a thin-screened monitor and a keyboard. One wall of the room was a floor-to-ceiling oak cupboard.

We sat in the armchairs, a low table separating us.

'Not a social call, Jack,' Doyle said. 'Am I right?'

'Business,' I said. 'I wanted to ask you a few more things about Robbie. Do you mind?'

'Not at all.' He sat back, laced fingers over a tweed knee. 'But I don't think I know much more to tell.'

'Did you know his real name?'

He ducked his chin. 'Real name? Meanin?'

'His name's Marco Lucia.'

Doyle shook his head. 'That's news to me. What's the reason for another name?'

'I'm not sure. He was involved with some fairly hard people in Queensland, may have been on the run.'

There was a knock at the door. Doyle got up, opened it, took a tray from someone. He put it down on the table, poured coffee dark and fragrant into china cups.

'Sugar?'

I accepted a spoonful.

'Have a bikkie. Bake em ourselves. Almond shortbread.' He chewed. 'Delicious. Well, we certainly didn't do any checkin on Robbie. No-one bothers for casuals. Why would ya?'

The coffee was rich as rum, the biscuit dissolved on the tongue, all butter. I got out the photograph of Alan Bergh. 'Ever seen this man?'

Doyle took it from me, had a good look, frowned. 'Don't think so. Although there's an awful lot of people come through, you'll understand. I can't say he's never bin here, that I can't. But I can't recall the face offhand. No.'

'Good coffee,' I said.

'Our own blend. Fella in Carlton makes it up. So who's the man?' He put the photograph on the table.

I drank some more coffee, not in a hurry. Then I took out my notebook and found the page. 'These numbers.' I read them out, numbers from Alan Bergh's mobile phone bill. 'They're your phones.'

Doyle wiped his lips with a napkin from the tray. His look was of mild amusement. 'Now you're findin out a great deal about us, Jack. Business numbers, those.'

He wasn't amused, not even mildly. The expression was an instinctive one, animal, speaking of wariness, uncertainty.

'The numbers? They're not in any book.'

I pointed at the photograph. 'This man rang those numbers. Thirteen times in a month. Sure you don't know him?'

Doyle was raising his cup to his lips. He didn't complete the movement, replaced the cup on the saucer. 'Now Jack,' he said, 'you won't mind me sayin this is borderin on the impertinent. You'd have to be doin somethin illegal to know enough to ask such questions. Would that be right?'

'You don't know him?'

'I've said that. Can't say it any better.' No Irish charm in the tone now.

'And the thirteen calls?'

He held up his hands. 'I've told you, they're business phones, lots of people use them, a dozen or more.'

'So someone else in the business would know him?'

'Possibly. Or they might be bloody nuisance calls, man might be sellin somethin, who knows? And you haven't answered the question. Who is the fella?'

'Don't know. Friend of Robbie's perhaps.'

'The picture. Where'd you get that?'

'Someone sent it to me,' I said, standing up. 'I won't waste any more of your time. Wonderful coffee. And the biscuits.'

Doyle didn't rise. 'And the calls,' he said. 'Where'd you get that from?'

'They sent me his phone bill with the picture.'

'So you do know his name?'

'It was a photocopy. No name on the pages.'

Doyle stood up. I had the sense that he was composing himself. He smiled the Irish boyo smile. 'Well Jack,' he said, 'it'll be hard for me to find out who he spoke to if I don't know his name. Would y'like to leave the photo? I can show it around?'

'No,' I said. 'I'm pretty much done with this matter.' I took a chance. 'Robbie did more than work in Down the Pub, didn't he?'

A moment's uncertainty, the hint of a smile. 'More?' Pause. 'He had a few shifts in the Snug, if that's what you mean?'

I couldn't show my ignorance, nodded. 'Yes. Who would he serve? In the Snug?'

'It's admittance by invitation. Our special guests, people...' He realised I was fishing. 'Well, if that's all,' he said. 'Always happy to try to help.'

Doyle escorted me to the door into Down the Pub and said goodbye without shaking hands, no more invitations to share in the life of the pub, drink the pinot, cook from the cookbook, no more pats or jovial remarks.

Driving back, I thought about my handling of the interview. Not good. But I was sure of one thing now:

Xavier Doyle could tell me lots more about Robbie/Marco. Perhaps he could even tell me how the Federal Police knew about my dealings with Mr Justice Loder. At the first lights, I got out my list of things to do, found the address and set course.

Alan Bergh had also made five calls to a mobile registered to a Kirstin Deane, whose work address was a women's clothing shop called Anouk in Greville Street, Prahran.

The narrow street was busy, a fashionable crowd on this side of the river, blonded women everywhere, tanned and tucked, fat sucked away and burnt off, eyeing themselves in shop windows, looking at younger specimens with hatred. I lucked on a park in Anouk's block, slid the old Stud in between an Audi and a Mercedes four-wheel drive.

Anouk's was not overstocked with merchandise. The window display was one dress, a mere twirl of fabric, barely enough to clothe six foot of lamp pole. Inside, two more garments were on display, a cloak-like creation of black velvet, and something that resembled a silk apron. Surely this could only be worn over clothing or in the privacy of the home? Against the left-hand wall, box shelves each held one item, shirts perhaps or cashmere sweaters.

A young woman was on the telephone, seated behind a minimalist counter, no more than three pieces of thick plexi-glass on which stood several electronic devices. She was mostly leg, skeletal, high cheekbones, much forehead under much hair, and her eyes and eyebrows and mouth were works of art.

I waited. Her eyes were fixed on a mirror across the room and never moved in my direction. She was talking without pause in a flat, grating monotone, words seemingly joined and undecipherable. After a while, I got between her and the mirror, blocked her view of herself.

Then she looked at me. She said a few words to the phone and put it down.

'Help you,' she said, not a question.

'I'm looking for Kirstin Deane.'

'Yeah.'

She knew I wasn't in the market for a silk apron or anything else she was selling. This was not going to be easy.

'It's about someone you know. Alan Bergh.'

Silence. She looked at the street.

'Alan Bergh. You know him.'

Her head jerked back. 'I don't *know* him.'

'He's dead,' I said. 'Shot dead. In a carpark. Know that?'

Kirstin frowned, pulled her eyebrow creations together, a little untidiness of skin appearing between them, an imperfection on a face as tight as a kite in a high wind.

'I've had it with you lot,' she said.

'He phoned you often,' I said. 'Your dead friend Alan.'

She took a deep breath, she still had lung capacity, her emaciated upper body expanded, she opened her mouth and breathed out like a steam train.

'Not my fucking friend,' she said, some life in the voice now. 'I said I don't know who the fuck Alan is. I'm the messenger girl. And I don't wanna know any more of this cop shit, right? Right? I'm finished with Mick, wish I'd never seen the prick in my life and I'll kill him if he ever—'

I held up my right hand. 'Settle down.'

Kirstin's eyes vanished, became slits. 'Don't you fucking tell me to settle down, I'll—'

'Taking messages can get you into deep trouble,' I said, now a kite myself, out on the winds. 'When someone says he doesn't know about the messages, never got a message from you, you're in trouble. Who'd you give the messages to, Kirstin?'

She closed her eyes, punched the plastic counter top repeatedly with both long-fingered fists, symbolically beating someone. 'Tell Olsen I'll kill him. He's not landing me with his shit. You people, you call yourselves ethics squad or fucking whatever, you're trying to cover something up for the cunt, aren't you. Well, forget that, detective whatever the fuck you are. Whofuckingever. Piss off.'

I did, left without a murmur, like a poor person given too much money by a bank machine.

A name. Mick Olsen. A cop called Mick Olsen.

Alan Bergh left messages for Mick Olsen with the engaging Kirstin Deane, super-salesperson. Who thought I was from ethical standards or whatever name it now had, the old police internal affairs section, the dog investigating its own balls someone once said of it, unkindly.

I would have to ask Senior Sergeant Barry Tregear about Mick Olsen.

At the office, the answering machine held three messages: my sister, curt but with a hint of forgiveness, Cam, equally brief but with no hint of anything, and one that said:

Re your accommodation inquiry, please ring at your convenience.

The D.J. Olivier code.

I went to the window. McCoy was at home, lights on in the alleged studio. I crossed the street and knocked. He came to the door wearing a knitted blanket with a hole for his head. Beneath it, his massive legs were bare save for their covering of beard-like hair and his feet looked like parcels badly wrapped with lengths of horse harness.

'So,' he said. 'Don't think I didn't see you spying on me yesterday.'

'Watching that innocent young thing enter this house of horrors,' I said, 'I considered calling the police. I need your phone.'

'She wanted to learn from a master's hand,' he said, leading the way into the studio.

'No chance of that here.'

I stopped at an unfinished canvas of monumental size and awfulness. 'What an inspired way to recycle fowl manure and horse hair,' I said.

'That'll fetch ten grand,' said McCoy. 'Gissa name for it.'

'Stick some chicken bones on it and call it Century of Bones.'

'Century of Bones,' said the hulking fraud approvingly.

'Gotta ring to that. Century of Bones. You can have the call on the house.'

'Calls plus ten per cent,' I said.

The telephone reposed on a tree stump in the far corner of the former sewing sweatshop. I dialled and got D.J. Olivier himself.

'You're a busy lad,' he said. 'This bloke's ex-army, got two convictions for fraud and he ran a building company that took customers for plenty. Now he's tied up with Geddan Associates. Know them?'

'No.' We were talking about a man called Warren Naismith, someone Alan Bergh had phoned regularly.

'Strategic consultants. That's PR, with violence if required. Do the lot.'

'The lot?'

'Fix. Here, New Zealand, Pacific islands. Office in Canada. Rumour says they blackmailed a cabinet minister in Queensland on behalf of a client. Developer client.'

'I didn't know that was necessary in Queensland,' I said. 'Sounds like overkill. And this person, what would he do for them?'

'Low level, a postman, fetch and carry, that sort of thing. Not welcome around the office, that's for sure.'

I said thanks, rang Cam's latest number. He was a long time answering. I told him about Jean Hale's names.

'This bloke Almeida,' he said. 'I've got him.'

I needed a second to place the name. Too many names. Yes. The dealer on the motorbike Marie pointed out to us in Elizabeth Street was called Glenn Almeida.

'At that address?' My inquiry had provided a vehicle registry address in Coburg for Almeida.

'Long gone. New one from the landlords' revenge file,

my real-estate shonk looked him up. He's out there in the hills.'

A rubbing noise, a towelling sound.

'I found this milk bar lady in Coburg,' said Cam. 'Round the corner from Glenn's old address. She knows the boy, knows Artie too. Her kid, he's naughty, studyin at this new place, the Port Phillip college, new slammer, the boy told her Glenn and Artie had the holiday together.'

I tried to think about this. I was heavy with information, underweight on thought. 'We still don't have Artie.'

Cam said, 'Maybe Artie's just the hammer. Maybe Glenn's the man.'

'I don't think so.' I didn't know that I didn't think so until I said it. 'Jean Hale's trouble. How's that fit?'

'Dunno. Might have a look up there in the foothills tomorrow. Free?'

'No,' I said, 'tomorrow's bad.' I felt guilty.

'Come round on my way back. Sawin or lawin?'

'Lawin,' I said. 'What passes for lawin.'

Receiver replaced, I stood for a moment, no energy in me, no wish to do anything except sleep. Then I sucked in some air and began my exit.

McCoy was staring at his canvas, standing well back, hands on where hips would be if pillar boxes had hips. As I approached, he said, 'Century of Bones. What about a skull in the middle there?'

'I don't think you should kill humans for your art,' I said. 'Unless it's yourself. In which case, just mark the spot and I'll be happy to stick it on for you. For your estate.'

'Animal,' he said, distant, deep in whatever process took place behind the opaque eyes. 'Rabbit. Sheep. Maybe dog.'

217

It was as if I had woken from a dream of toothache to find myself pain free.

'Dog,' I said. 'Dog. I have the perfect dog.'

Outside, the day was at an end, rain had fallen, now a misty yellow light was on the world. The cobblestoned gutter outside my office was painterly, each cobble glistening like the top of a fresh loaf of bread, a top painted with egg and milk.

I set off for home. On the radio, Linda was talking to a man who called himself a life coach.

And what qualifies you to tell other people how to run their lives?

Life coach: *My training. I have a life coach qualification.*

Linda, the amused voice, not insulting, somewhere between curious and dangerous: *Is that from the university of life? School of hard knocks?*

Life coach, serious: *No, from Life Coach College, it's an accredited institution.*

It occurred to me that I needed this man's services or this qualification. And, perhaps, I needed Linda.

No. Well, perhaps. But only on my terms. What would they be? I had no idea, could not think of a single term.

Supper. I could think about supper, the limited range of suppers available. Not so much a range as an item.

I ate pasta and walked around preparing to go to bed early, seek refuge in my bed, take the decision to activate the answering machine and turn the volume down to nought. Incommunicado.

Even to Linda.

And to Lyall.

Perhaps Lyall would ring me one day and say that there

had been a misunderstanding, that Brad had not actually been celibate for all those years and could we take up where we left off?

My shrinking sensible bit said I should not stay awake waiting for this to happen.

The transcript of Mr Justice Loder's trial—I hadn't read it.

I could put on warm and waterproof clothing, leave the apartment and go down to the car, look for the folder, which might be in the office. Or.

I rang Drew at home. 'Are you in a position to talk?' I asked.

'I find myself able to talk in most positions. Is there one I should know about?'

'There's a trial going on before Colin Loder, cocaine smuggling.'

'Ah, the ski jackets debacle.'

'Know about it?'

'As a practitioner of the law, I make a point of knowing about such things. As it happens, I was recently privileged to hear the views of my learned friend Dick Pratchett QC on the subject. Over lunch.'

That was where the Rosa business had begun.

'I remember. Give me the story in as few words as possible.'

'Well,' he said, 'it goes like this. The Feds've got a dog who calls himself Aaron Ross, apparently well known in drug circles. He told them he was asked by someone called Frank Leavis, a mystery man, noone's ever heard of him, to supply six kilos of cocaine. The Feds became dizzy with excitement when they heard this.'

'I get the drift already.'

'Yes, dulled though you are by sniffing wood glue.

Anyway, Ross rounded up Brian Arthur McCallum, a dickhead, and a lad called John Stavros Ionides, an even bigger dunce. I say this as someone who represented him when he was known as John Stephens. Mystery man Leavis hands over a large sum in US and Aussie currency, and the boys take off for South Africa.'

'South Africa? Since when?'

'Apparently it's like Bangkok, Karachi and Beirut all in one. With Russians added. United drugs of the world. But you can bet your last pack of Fitzroy Football Club fundraising condoms that it wasn't McCallum and Johnny Stephens' idea. Couldn't find the place on the map.'

'The Feds' idea?'

'Or someone else's. So off they go with their bag of money, customs instructed not to touch them. In due course, and I have to say this really surprises everyone who knows them, they actually come back with the coke. They're wearing it in matching ski jackets.'

'You can ski in South Africa?'

'Of course not. But would that occur to these dolts? Again, customs usher them through. McCallum rings from the airport. Ross rings mystery man Frank Leavis. Well, he rings a number and leaves a message. In Tullamarine, off Mickleham Road, by arrangement, McCallum and Johnny Stephens meet Mr Ross to hand over. Change of plan, Ross tells them. The client wants you to deliver the stuff to him personally.'

'Feds want to stitch it up tight.'

'Exactly. So Brian and Johnny and Ross and four hundred hyper-excited Feds all end up in the freezing cold at a service station in fucking Brimbank in the middle of the night. But the mystery man is one step ahead of these dunderheads and never shows up.'

221

I remembered what Colin Loder had said:

I don't think it would be unjudicial of me to describe the operation as a massive cock-up.

'Anyway,' said Drew, 'he didn't miss much. The boofheads are found to be carrying less than two kilos and apparently the marching powder is of a quality that doesn't produce quite as much of the wit, confidence and feelings of general wellbeing the punters expect.'

'So what the prosecution's got are two blokes approached to buy drugs by a police informer who says he was acting on behalf of a mystery man.'

'Yup. And the only person the drugs were delivered to is the informer. Needless to say, the judge will have the Appeal Court much on his mind. Pratchett QC is of the opinion Colin Loder will kick the thing into the street next week.'

'The Feds wouldn't be buying their dog a big bone.'

'Only themselves to blame. My mate Terry says the word is McCallum, dumb though he is, knows more than he's saying.'

'Meaning?'

'He may know something about Leavis, the mystery man.'

'Something the dog doesn't know?'

'Possibly. Brian might have been just smart enough to find out who the real client was. Someone the Feds apparently suspect but can't do anything about.'

'Thank you,' I said. 'Your fund of knowledge obviates the need to buy newspapers or watch television. Not to mention read the learned journals.'

'Honoured to be of service. What's your interest?'

'Purely professional. Highly professional. On that subject, how is the high-achieving personally-trained one?'

'Ravishing. A weekend has been proposed. Windswept beaches, just the cries of the seabirds.'

'As they impale themselves on used syringes.'

With a soothing mug of the warm brown fluid to hand, I went to bed with my novel. But I couldn't concentrate, eyes on the page, mind on Marco and Alan Bergh and the judge. If Brian McCallum knew who put up the money for the drug deal, someone would want to be very sure he didn't go down and then decide to bargain with the Feds. And that someone would have made sure Brian knew he had nothing to fear, knew that he was going to walk.

I gave up on the book, doused the light, and lay awake for a long time, soft rain on the old iron roof, liquid whispers in the downpipes, all around the hoot and squeal and wail of the animal city. Oddly comforting sounds tonight.

In the morning, I was at the door, ready to hip-and-shoulder the day, when the phone rang.

'I find you decent?'

Linda.

'I find you jolly nice too,' I said, 'but I'd like to be seen as, well, more raffish than decent. Can you do that?'

'Work needed on my interrogative inflection. No wonder I'm having so much trouble with interviews.'

We met at a place in Rathdowne Street north. Once, this end of Rathdowne Street boasted only the best pizzas in town and Frank and Maria's coffee shop, the best-loved coffee shop in town. I hadn't tried the pizzas in a while but Frank and Maria's was gone and now there was an eating strip two blocks long.

'Toast,' said Linda after we'd ordered. 'Toast is *with* breakfast. Toast is *part* of breakfast. Toast is not *of itself* breakfast. Are you in love?'

I'd forgotten how the morning suited her.

'I didn't want to say I'd had my breakfast.'

'What was it?'

'Porridge, scrambled eggs and a piece of steak. Sausage or two. Three, actually. Bit of bacon.'

'Right,' she said. 'Mouldy muesli with curdling milk.'

'Yes, I am in love,' I said. 'I feel you understand me.'

She gave me several bits of bacon and half a grilled Roma tomato. We were on the coffee when she said, 'Jamie Toxteth. You were asking about him.'

It took a moment to summon up Jamie Toxteth. 'The polo player.'

The unknown woman in the surveillance clip waiting for Robbie/Marco was in a car owned by a Jamie Toxteth company.

'I was talking to someone in Sydney and I remembered your question.' She drank coffee. 'She said Susan Ayliss worked for Jamie and this Blackiston person before she became a media talent.'

Susan Ayliss had for a time been television's favourite economics commentator, a Canberra academic who made Treasury notes sound like love letters. She had long blonde hair and a slightly pointy nose, and when she looked over her rimless glasses you wanted to be in her tutorial and you wanted to be the one who said something intelligent.

'What became of the perfect creature?'

'She's an eco-consultant, she reinvented herself, did another degree. Became the squeakiest and cleanest consultant in the known universe, the flying darling of eco-consultancy. Whatever the fuck that is.'

'Flying?'

'She flies her own plane. Like Amelia Earwig. Sees the world from a great height. And won't be interviewed because it could compromise her. The woman is beyond publicity. Beyond fucking belief, in fact.'

'I forget why we're talking about her.'

'Before her career change, she had an affair with Jamie. More than an affair. She got divorced. Jamie left his wife, some even richer snorting-nostrilled horse-mounter no doubt. They lived together but in the end Jamie would not actually cut the painter.'

She'd lost me. I didn't care much about the affairs of

Sydney people. 'Not since Van Gogh has a painter been properly cut,' I said. 'Why are you telling me this?'

Linda ignored the question, put marmalade on her last quarter of toast. 'Apparently a poisonous break-up. Susan had become a partner in the firm, she was the one bringing in all the business, and she had to be bought out. My friend says Susie's lawyer nailed Jamie.'

'That's interesting. I'm glad I know that. I've always felt there was something missing in my global picture.'

She smiled at me. 'Including a new car every three years for a good while.'

She bit off a piece of toast. I watched her chewing. I'd always admired her eating. She was a very neat eater, no teeth showed, no crumb stuck or fell.

'Susan Ayliss's got long hair,' I said.

'So?'

'The woman driving the car's got short hair.'

'When last did you see Ms Ayliss?'

'Few years ago. Well, five or six, could be more. Ten.'

Linda put her head on one side and looked at me.

'Okay,' I said. 'It's early.'

'She was on the Cannon Ridge tender panel,' said Linda. 'I can't remember why you were interested in the car?'

'It appears in a video. Probably by accident. Why was she on the panel?'

'I'm told the last Premier got prickly feelings around her.'

'If that was the only qualification, panel meetings would have been at the Melbourne Cricket Ground.'

'She's also Ms Integrity.'

'Integrity plus the pricklies, now that's an unbeatable combo. I've got to go. I work in the hours of daylight.'

She leaned forward. 'I sense,' she said, 'that you're withholding. You'll tell me if you chance upon anything of broadcast quality?'

'With what inducement?'

Under the tablecloth, a hand was on my thigh. 'I have inducements to offer.'

'I'm not sure I fully grasp what you mean,' I said.

Her hand moved upwards. The long fingers came into play. I could feel my blood rushing downhill, upper body going pale.

'Grasp?' she said. 'I could fully grasp you right here.'

I looked at her. Her face was impassive, head cocked as if listening to distant sounds. She wasn't wearing lipstick.

'This hasn't happened to me in public for, ah, fifteen years,' I said.

'Is it like Kennedy's death?' she said. 'A whole generation of people know exactly where they were when they heard about it?' She was scratching me, an unbearably erotic feeling.

'It was in a train just outside Birmingham in England. Snow on the ground. Getting dark. I was eating a British Rail sausage roll.'

'Who was the grasper?'

'Let's see now. I think it was someone I knew…'

She removed her hand. 'That's probably the way I'll survive in memory. Just another hand. Oh well, off you go.'

Deep in thought, I drove to Fitzroy.

Finding a phone number for Susan Ayliss wasn't easy. I rang Simone Bendsten. She was back in five minutes.

'Her company's called Ecomenical. She gave a paper at a conference in Canberra last year. Here's the number.'

I rang it. The brisk and pleasant reception person wanted my name and my company and the nature of my business.

'Tell Dr Ayliss my business is Robbie,' I said. 'I'll spell that for you. R-O-B-B-I-E.'

I was early and had no trouble finding parking near the Albert Park Yachting & Angling Club. A cold day, the palms shaking in the wind.

She was early too. A new VW Passat, a trim and potent-looking machine in a Wehrmacht shade of grey, nosed into a space. A woman got out, dark glasses, headscarf. I watched her walk towards the pier, hands in the high pockets of her trench coat.

I sat for a while. Two hardy skateboarders came by, followed by a group of four fit-looking runners, women. I got out and went for a short walk along the esplanade, came back and went out on the pier.

She was looking my way, kept her eyes on me as I approached.

'Mr Irish?'

'Yes.'

'What do you want?' she asked.

'I'd like to ask you about Robbie.'

She made an impatient head movement, the kind of dismissive oh-fuck-off-you-idiot gesture that features in Learn Body Language For Success videos.

'Spit it out,' she said. 'It's cold here.'

'Your choice of venue.'

'I say again, Mr Irish, what do you want?'

'You knew Robbie Colburne?'

'What do you want?'

'You know he's dead?'

'What do you want?'

'You picked him up in your car one evening.'

An exasperated expulsion of air. 'What is this? Can I ask again, for the last time, what do you want?'

'Nothing. Robbie stole something from someone. The owner's disappointed, saddened.'

She fiddled with the scarf, some loss of composure evident.

'What makes you think I picked him up?'

Spots of rain on the pier, felt on my face.

'Someone saw you. That's not important.'

'Who are you?'

'I'm a lawyer acting for the victim.'

She sighed. 'I feel like an absolute prick,' she said. 'No, let me rephrase that before the actress and the bishop are invoked.'

'I could say that never occurred to me.'

She smiled and looked around, took off the dark glasses and the scarf. Her eyes were grey. Susan Ayliss, once the thinking person's academic pin-up, now wore her hair short at the sides and longer on top and she had lines around her mouth and eyes but she could have stepped straight back into that role.

'Christ, I hate scarves,' she said. 'I was once taken at gunpoint to a polo match, and there were all these ghastly nasal women wearing headscarves, like some cult.'

'I blame the Queen,' I said.

'Damn right,' said Susan Ayliss. 'Well, what do you want to know?'

I couldn't read anything in her eyes. She was here because I'd said Robbie's name. Dead Robbie who was Marco, who was not an easy person to understand.

'I hoped you could tell me something about Robbie.'

She turned, put her hands on the railing, no rings, clasped them. 'I know almost nothing about him.'

I leaned on the railing, looked at the view: dishwater sea, seething. In the distance, specks of gulls floated around the Tasmania ferry at Station Pier. 'Robbie Colburne isn't his real name. You know that, of course.'

'No.' Quick.

I kept my eyes away, looked at the ribbed beach.

Two people had appeared on it, a short and a tall, walking close together, heads down like beachcombers. Not quite Gauguin country, Kerferd Road, unless you treasured used Chinese condoms and spent syringes.

'There's only one Robert Colburne on record, but it isn't the dead man.'

'I'm sorry, I—'

'The person in question lifted the identity of Robert Colburne.'

I looked at her. She had a wary expression, as if I had more surprises in store. 'So, who is the person?'

'Marco Lucia is his name.'

Silence, our eyes locked. She looked away. I kept looking.

'Ms Ayliss,' I said, 'Robbie was a blackmailer or he worked for blackmailers. Did you know that?'

Horn player's lines around her mouth, an intake of air. 'Yes.'

'You're right, it is cold out here. My car or yours?'

'No,' she said. 'I'm happier here.'

'Will you tell me how you know he's a blackmailer?'

'I had an affair with him,' she said. 'No, that's nonsense. I had sex with him. On several occasions.'

'And?'

She moved her mouth, another sigh, deeper. 'There was a video.'

It was getting colder, the sky changing colour like a quick-developing bruise.

'Made with your consent?'

'Consent? Well, I didn't object. Not strenuously anyway. Coming after some bottles of Dom.' Pause. 'Are you shocked?'

I looked at her. The wind and the cold had tightened her skin, put colour in her cheeks. She looked a good ten years younger.

'No,' I said. 'Shock went by some time ago. Passed in the night. So you made a video.'

She didn't answer quickly. 'It seemed like harmless fun at the time. Do you know that I was on the Cannon Ridge tender panel?'

'Yes. How did you meet Robbie?'

She raised her hands, long fingers, I hadn't noticed. 'Don't laugh. At the supermarket. I go to the same one almost every night. I'm always late at the office, never anything in the fridge at home. He bumped into me one night. Then I saw him again a day or two later and we said hello and he said something funny. I saw him again another night, we had a few words and he invited me for a drink.'

'It didn't strike you as more than coincidence?'

'No. You go to the same place, you see the same people. And Robbie's got…Robbie had a casual way. Quick and funny, nothing threatening about him. He was also very good looking and he didn't seem to be aware of it.' She looked at me, looked away. 'And I was lonely, Mr Irish. I work all day and then I go home to nothing.'

It hadn't occurred to me that people like Susan Ayliss also knew about loneliness.

'Did he tell you he worked part-time at The Green Hill?'

'Yes. He said he was trying to write a novel, took any job going.'

Silence. I watched the pair inspecting the beach. From time to time, the smaller one would stoop to look at something. Look but not touch. Sensible.

Susan Ayliss put her hands to her ears, rubbed them gently. Her nose wasn't quite as pointy as I remembered. 'Anyway,' she said, 'we ended up at my place and had sex. I hadn't actually had sex like that before. The men of my acquaintance had not prepared me for the experience.'

My thoughts went to Milan Filipovic. I'd asked him what kind of work Marco did.

Marco's all cock. Work it out.

'How was the video made?'

She looked at me, startled. 'By Robbie. Christ, it wasn't a film set.'

'On the first night?'

'Certainly not. I was sober. The third time. He had a tiny camera, a digital thing, you could watch it on a monitor. That's about all there was in this huge apartment. That and the bed.'

In some circumstances, people tell you more than they need to.

'You watched it on a monitor?'

'Yes. Are you enjoying this?'

'And this was where?'

'At a friend's place.'

'Your friend's apartment?'

'No, a friend of his.'

I thought about the surveillance video, the shot of Robbie going into a building.

'Cathexis,' I said.

She was looking away and she jerked her head at me. 'I don't know. I wasn't paying attention at that stage.'

'Who's the friend?'

'No idea.'

'And the blackmail came when?'

Susan tilted her head, smiled a smile with no life in it. 'A man came to my office. He said he had a business proposition. I knew what was coming and I told him to get out. He said wait and he dialled a number on his mobile, said someone wanted to talk to me. It was Robbie. He said he was watching the video.' She was looking down at the rail, shaking her head. 'Shit,' she said. 'Talking about it makes me feel sick.'

'I can understand that. What else did Robbie say?'

'Nothing. I didn't give him a chance. I gave the man the phone back and I said they could give the film to every television station and newspaper in the country, I did not give a damn.'

'That was brave.'

'Brave?'

'You were taking a big risk.'

She shrugged. 'They just picked the wrong person. A film of Susan Ayliss having sex? I don't have family to worry about. All I've got is my professional reputation. Show it. It might improve my social life.'

She was a brave person.

'When the man talked about a business proposition,' I said, 'what did you assume?'

'The Cannon Ridge tender. I wasn't doing anything else worth blackmailing me for.'

'Did the man say which side sent him?'

'No.'

'What did you think?'

'WRG.'

'Who?'

'He asked me if I'd had an offer from Anaxan.'

'Did you tell the panel?'

'No. I'm only stupid once. I hadn't been blackmailed, Cannon Ridge hadn't actually been mentioned.'

'Splitting hairs though.'

Susan Ayliss gave me a look that said something I didn't quite understand. 'Mr Irish, in my life, I've worked very hard for everything. I grew up in foster homes. Fought off men since I was ten, put myself through university cleaning toilets. I can't be blackmailed. But I wasn't going to cut my own throat.'

I found my picture of Alan Bergh. 'Is this the man?'

No hesitation. 'Yes. Who is he?'

'Alan Bergh. The late.'

She sighed and looked away.

'Robbie had a relationship with a man,' I said. 'Does that surprise you?'

'Well,' she said, 'he said he took any work that was going.'

'There's an album of photographs missing.'

'I think we're talking about sex again, not a relationship.'

'Yes. We think the album was passed on to someone. Any idea who that might be?'

A shake of her head. 'No, no idea, not the vaguest.'

'Robbie didn't mention anyone.'

'No. He didn't talk about himself. One of the things I found attractive.'

Rain again, big spots freckling the pier, cold on the face.

'Thanks for talking to me,' I said. 'Did his death surprise you?'

She looked away, at the sea. 'Yes,' she said. 'It made me sad. I was hoping I'd have the chance to kill him myself for making me feel so defiled and so worthless.'

I watched her go, the wind pulling at her trench coat, lifting the shoulder flaps found so useful on the Somme those many years ago, now threatening to levitate Susan Ayliss. She turned her head and looked back, came back.

'I've told you everything I can, Jack,' she said. 'Will you promise me it'll remain confidential?'

'Yes,' I said. 'Susan.'

I liked her even more than I had when she'd been a media star.

I brooded, driving automatically, registering nothing, a danger on the roads. There was nowhere else to go in the matter of Marco/Robbie. I couldn't help the judge. It had all been for nothing, traipsing around the country, the city.

Marco was a blackmailer's bait, bait for all sexual persuasions. The blackmailer could be Alan Bergh, representing other interests. Why else had he been filmed? In any event, both men were dead. The attempt on brave Susan Ayliss had failed, the one on principled Colin Loder would too. Cannon Ridge was a decided matter, another judge would make the finding Colin Loder could not.

This matter was almost at an end.

And yet and yet. Marco was murdered, Alan Bergh was murdered.

I pulled up at lights.

Susan Ayliss had no doubt that the Cannon Ridge tender was the reason for the plot against her. Which side? Anaxan or WRG? The latter would have been eager to add some weight to their side of the seesaw, the other side having a Cundall, son of a man who could walk into the Premier's office and berate him. But they didn't get the weight, their tender failed. That could have left Bergh and Robbie as untidy bits, much too knowing.

Cathexis.

I had been looking at the building, looking at it across the intersection without seeing it. It was austere, all its materials visible, concrete and marble, bronze and glass, steel and copper—rough, smooth, shiny, dull, hard, soft materials. I could see the incised name that Marco was photographed passing.

Cathexis.

The lights changed. I went around the block, found an unlawful park, walked back to the building. A smoked-glass sliding door admitted me to an extravagant, hard-surfaced lobby, a hall that hummed the word Money. Directly ahead were two lift doors, pale timber. Nothing so crass and indiscreet as a list of tenants was in sight. I was glad I was wearing a decent suit. A recent suit, anyway.

A hotel-sized reception counter was at the right, two young women in black on duty behind it. Beyond that was a door marked Security. I couldn't see cameras but they would be on me and the entrance.

'How may I help? She was English, willowy, blonde, nectarine skin.

'Gone blank. I can't remember the agents for the building.'

'Barwick & Murphy,' she said, smiling. 'Is it something I can help you with?'

'Well, you might.' I took out my notebook, thumbed. 'Here it is. The Doyle apartment. For sale.'

'Doyle?' She looked at the other woman, also blonde but more mature oak than willow. 'Do we have a Doyle?'

The woman was looking at a monitor, didn't turn her head. 'No.'

'Sorry,' said the first blonde. 'It's probably in another of their buildings. They handle dozens.'

'Yes,' I said. 'Thanks anyway.'

I walked away. Another hunch that failed to deliver. Near the door, I thought, what the hell, try another one. I turned and went back, notebook open.

'I think I had the wrong page,' I said. 'It's Cundall, the Cundall apartment that's for sale. If I've got the right building.'

The willowy blonde frowned, turned. 'Jean, do we have a Cundall?'

Mature-oak blonde didn't turn. 'What?'

'It's supposed to be on the market. The gentleman's not sure whether he's at the right building.'

Mature blonde looked around, an annoyed face, deep lines between her eyes, spent a millisecond on me, made a judgment. 'Who says it's on the market?'

'B and M told this gentleman.'

Jean sniffed. 'They told you it was Mrs Cundall's apartment?'

'Yes.'

'That is quite irregular. Twelve two is owned by Dalinsor Nominees.'

'I don't really care who owns it,' I said. 'I'm looking for an apartment.'

'They're supposed to inform us,' said Jean. 'And there are no inspections without a B and M agent.'

'I'll be back with one,' I said. 'One of their top agents. Licensed to sell.'

Walking back to the car, I felt smug for a minute. A hunch that paid off. Or had it? What had I learned by finding out that Ros Cundall owned an apartment in a building Marco had gone into? Nothing. Ros Cundall probably owned apartments in every expensive block in the city.

Marco working at The Green Hill, Marco going into Cathexis, Marco from the Umbrian idyll turning up on Colin Loder's doorstep.

I was beginning to like the Umbrian story less and less.

Too romantic for my taste. And, in the light of what I now knew about Marco and Susan, implausible.

From the car, I rang Colin Loder's borrowed mobile. He wouldn't be in court, it was lunchtime.

'Yes.'

'Jack.'

'Jack.'

'Clarification. Umbria, the person arrives on the doorstep, later reappears.'

'Yes?'

'Bullshit, yes?'

A pause, a sigh. 'Well. Yes. A story.'

I waited.

'I didn't want it to sound like…well…'

'A pick-up?'

'Yes. Umbria was a fiction.'

'Where then?'

He hesitated. 'A place I've had a few drinks at. So as not to be completely removed from reality. As are most of my colleagues.'

'The Green Hill?'

Pause. 'How exactly did you work that out?'

'Is that in the Snug?'

'Yes. You know it?'

'No. I know Xavier Doyle.'

'Well, the Snug's like a club, I suppose. You have to be with someone who's persona grata.'

'Who were you with?'

'Ros Cundall, Mike Cundall's wife. I'm on a gallery committee with her. She insisted I join her after a meeting. Introduced me to Xavier.'

'Who introduced you to Marco?'

'Ros. He was behind the bar. She said, meet Marco before he's famous, he's writing the great Australian novel. Words to that effect.'

This was a small city. But in the end all cities are small.

'Any headway, Jack?' Not a confident voice.

'A little. Get back to you.'

'Thanks.'

Little was the word. I drove back to Fitzroy thinking about the versatility of Marco, the number of lives he'd touched.

I was unlocking the office door, wind pulling at my clothes, when a respectable Subaru drew up, double parked.

Cam.

I got in. It was warm and comfortable, things I had been missing.

'Pretty up there in the hills,' he said, no expression. 'Total waste of time. The address's at the top of a dead end, three houses on the road. Dunno how you deal drugs from a place like that, all that commutin.'

'Anyone home?'

'Woman hangin up washin, two kids hangin on her, cattle dog.

'What now?'

'The plumber and the wood man.'

I went inside, found Jean Hale's faxed list, made haste to quit the dusty ice cave for the clean warmth of the vehicle outside.

'Plumber I wouldn't be hopeful about,' said Cam, eyes on the paper. 'Make too much money. Like doctors. Now wood's another matter. Very seasonal, wood.'

'What's his name?' I said.

'Lizard Ellyard.'

'Lizard Ellyard,' I said. 'Used to be a bikie gang called the Lizards.'

Cam turned his head, interest in the dark eyes.

I found the Hales' number in my book, got out the mobile. Jean answered.

'Jean, Jack. Can you ask your husband or Sandy if they know why this man Ellyard is called Lizard?'

She was gone for several minutes. I heard the labrador bark, a door bang.

'There, Jack?'

'Yes.'

'Dave says Lizard wears an old leather jacket with Lizard on the back. Bought it at an op-shop, he reckons.'

I said thanks.

Cam was looking at me. I told him.

'The Coburg milk bar lady said Artie was a bike person, very noisy,' he said. 'What happened to the Lizards?'

I tried to remember. 'They were in the news, fighting with some other mob.'

'Lizards,' said Cam. 'Not a good name for a gang. Too close to the ground, the lizard.'

Something on television: a smouldering building, fire engines.

'Their clubhouse was attacked,' I said. 'Or they torched the other lot's place.'

'They all do that,' said Cam. 'That's what they do on Sunday night. I might ask around. Listen, the big man said to tell you, eight in the seventh at the Valley on Sunday. Not the house at all, each-way. And pray for rain in the mornin.'

'Getting back into it?'

Cam half smiled. 'Kiwi horse, come for the winter pickins. Trainer's dad's a Pom, rode against Harry in England. This nag loves mud. The big man's picked the suitable outin for him.'

In the office, a male on the answering machine said: *Jack, here's a number.*

I wrote it down, walked to the Lebanese shop and

ordered a salad roll. Then I rang the number, a mobile. Senior Sergeant Barry Tregear answered.

'Working days now?' I said.

'Days, nights, on a taskforce, mate. We're all on taskforces, force of taskforces. Listen, go a beer? I'm about five from that place, y'know?'

He was standing with his back against the counter, a depleted beer in his right hand: a big man in a dark rumpled suit watching two stringy young men playing pool.

'Where'd you get the tan?' I said.

'Holidays, mate. Private-school boys wouldn't understand. Life's all play to you.'

'I'm close to played out.' I found my beer behind him and had a deep drink. Cooper's. 'What taskforce did you draw?'

'Street dealers. War on street dealers. Finished our task, mate, it's a fucken indoor activity.'

'That's when you form a taskforce to drive them onto the streets again.'

'Exactly. We're like the tides. Move shit in and out.' He drank half his glass, burped, a full-blooded burp. 'I reckon they should give McDonald's the franchise to sell drugs. Quality control, clean premises, collect fucking GST. Plus the junkies get a burger with every hit, keep em healthy. McSmack.'

'Leaving you and your colleagues free to drive around at high speeds and shoot people.'

'Yeah. That and the relationship counselling, role modelling.' He eyed me. 'Down in the weights. Dying or a new girlfriend?'

'Exercise, strict diet.'

'Dying then. On the subject, this query of yours. Mick Olsen. Why are you always fucking around with dangerous things?'

One of the pool players wore a bandanna, the other a cap backwards. Bandanna man was going for an impossibly acute angle. We watched. It wasn't impossible after all.

'Fuuuck,' said his opponent.

'The person's a cop,' I said. 'Cops are only supposed to be dangerous to wrongdoers.'

Barry turned his head, had no trouble finding the barmaid's eyes where she stood talking to a fat man in a Bombers beanie and scarf. She tossed her head. The light from the west window spangled off the rings and stones in her nose and ears and eyebrows.

'Mick's a cop in history,' Barry said. 'Resigned a while ago. Now a man of leisure. But dangerous still. You don't even want to know his name.'

'Why?'

'Drug squad. Policing where the shit interfaces with the fans, if you get my meaning.'

'Just the melody.'

'Here ya go.' The multi-pierced one put two new beers on the counter. I paid.

'I say again, dangerous is the word,' said Barry. He was intent on the pool players. Bandanna man was sighting down the length of the table, trying to pot one of three balls in a cluster.

'This bloke's fucken ambitious,' said Barry.

Bandanna picked the nominee out of the group, thudded it into the corner pocket.

'Shit,' said Barry, impassive, appreciative. 'Man with the golden stick.'

'This Olsen,' I said. Mick Olsen had picked up messages from Alan Bergh left with the lovely Kirstin Deane at her minimally stocked boutique.

246

'The Commissioner's enema. Just the name's a suppository. And there's blokes in the squad want him dead, they say.' He drank. 'Anyhow, Mick's highly deadly, shouldn't speak ill of him.'

'The name Alan Bergh mean anything?'

Barry looked at me briefly, probed a tooth with his tongue, shook his head, went back to watching the pool.

'Bergh made calls to Olsen's girlfriend. To be passed on, I gather.'

'Jack, Mick's in the drug business. Get lots of messages. It's a message business.'

'What's made him history?'

'Done the Feds like a dinner. Unbelievable fuck-up.'

'Coke jackets?' The case before Mr Justice Loder.

He looked at me, a full look, shook his head in a sad way. 'Jack, I don't know. You had a profession. I looked up to you.'

'Did you really?'

'Fuck off.'

'Tell me about Olsen,' I said.

Barry drank some beer.

I drank some. I was starting to like the taste. I put my glass down, pushed it away. Just a few centimetres away. The symbolic distance between the me who would once have knocked back this beer and then woken up somewhere strange with a full beard, and the me now.

'A bloke called Ross set it up,' said Barry. 'Conned the Feds he's got Mr Big on the line, the man's placed a trial order. A controlled delivery scam. Very stylish, made the Canberra boys look like absolute cunts.'

Bandanna's opponent played a two-cushion shot that sank a ball.

'Jeez, luck,' said Barry. 'These two cunts were supposed to

247

lead to a Mr Big, like you get to the big-time by being such an arsehead that the delivery boys can take the Feds to you.'

'Where's Olsen come in?'

Barry put a hand into his jacket and, without taking out the packet, found a cigarette. He lit it with a plastic lighter, coughed, calmed his throat with a long drink of beer. 'The talk is that Olsen's the brains. He's a smart fella. Nearly finished law at Monash.'

'That's not a sign of smartness,' I said. 'He got what out of this business?'

'Well,' Barry said, looking around the room, 'it appears the Feds helped the boys bring in more stuff than the two k's they find on them, so the extra's what Mick got out. Between the airport and the handover, that vanished.'

'How do they know that?'

Barry shrugged. 'Apparently they heard from the supply end. After. Over here, these Fed dickheads just took it on trust what the boys were carrying. Couldn't have a look in Perth, open their cases. It was on the pricks, in these jackets, world's heaviest fucken ski jackets, must've hung down to their knees.'

'Where'd Olsen's excess go?'

'On sold quick-smart you'd imagine. Same night. But that'd be a contract.'

He finished his beer, wiped his lips with a thumb. 'Got to go, sweep some of Mick's stuff off the fucken streets.'

'There's a small thing,' I said.

'Oh yeah.'

'I need to find out who identified a body.'

'Fuck, Jack, you're a nuisance.'

'Your day will come.'

'I doubt that very fucken much. Shoulda been a crook.

Chose the wrong end of the fucken stick. What body's this?'

I told him, watched him leave. The pool players watched him too. They knew a cop when they saw one. Then they looked at me. I looked back. They found other things to look at.

A new BMW was parked outside my office, illegally. The driver was on the phone, head back on the rest. I recognised the profile, tapped on the window centimetres from his face. His head jerked around.

Gavin Legge, former journalist and master of the contra-deal, now, according to Linda, a spin-physician for an international PR firm. He got out, right hand outstretched.

'Jack, old mate.' Legge exuded warmth. He also exuded prosperity: new pinstriped suit on the chubby body, expensive haircut and a good dye job, rimless glasses to replace the thick-framed, scratched and smeared pair I'd last seen him in.

'Gavin.'

We shook hands.

'I hope you're not looking for legal representation,' I said. 'I've got a new policy of only taking on clients who promise to pay within five years.'

He slapped my arm. 'Man on a mission, I am. Can we talk inside?'

We went in. Legge looked around the unadorned chamber.

'Backstreet law, eh? Down at the level of the people. I admire that.'

'Some slurp champagne from the tainted silver chalice,' I said, 'some choose honour and a stubby.'

Legge laughed, not a convincing effort, and sat down. I went around the desk.

'I won't beat around the bush, Jack, no, that's not our way at all.'

'Our? Have you subdivided yourself? Been cloned? Is there more than one Gavin Legge now? The world may not be ready for that.'

Another feeble attempt at laughter. 'I'm speaking for Ponton's,' he said, crossing his legs, pulling at his trousers. 'I'm with Ponton's now. World's most respected image management consultants. Headhunted.'

'Are you sure they've got the most valuable part? What can I do for you? All of you.'

'Jack, one of our clients is Anaxan. You'll be familiar with Anaxan, they're going to develop Cannon Ridge, multimillion-dollar development, something all Victorians, all Australians, will be proud of, a world-class ski resort and casino, the Aspen of...'

I held up a hand. 'Gavin, I liked you more when you weren't writing the media releases, just sneaking them into the paper.'

He coloured a little. 'Sorry, my enthusiasm carries me away. It's about Alan Bergh. We understand you were interested in Alan Bergh.'

I didn't say anything. I sat back and laced my fingers on the tabletop and looked at him.

'That's correct, isn't it? You were interested in Alan Bergh.'

I didn't reply, kept my eyes on his. He licked his lips, made a smacking noise with them.

'Now, Jack,' he said, hands in action, 'please don't take this amiss, we've known each other a long time and I'd hate to think—'

'Gavin,' I said, 'you have no way of knowing what interests

me unless you've been spying on me. Will you confirm that you're spying on me?'

Hands in the air. 'Jack, Jack, mate, mate, hold on, listen to me for a second, I'll explain. I can explain.'

'Explain. Briefly.'

'Right.' Legge coughed. 'Right. Now, Jack, our client, that's Anaxan, they've been very disturbed, disturbed and disgusted, I might say, by the tactics of WRG, the other tenderer…Are you with me?'

'Yes.'

'Of course you are. Our clients believe that WRG gained information from inside the Cannon Ridge tender panel. Alan Bergh was involved, we're pretty sure of that, an absolute scumbag, Jack, you'll know that.'

'Why are you here, Gavin?' I asked.

A raised hand. 'Out of courtesy, Jack. Courtesy and friendship. Someone told us you were inquiring about Bergh—no, don't get angry, there was no spying involved, pure chance that it came to our ears. And I wanted to tell you to be careful that WRG didn't try to use you, feed you misleading information. That's all there is to it. No more than that. Just an act of friendship. And courtesy.'

'You're saying that Bergh worked for WRG?'

'Absolutely. Dangerous people, Jack.' He looked relieved.

'What's he supposed to have done?'

'Well, I suppose it's pretty much an open secret. Bribed Paul Rykel. Department of Conservation.'

'I thought the story was your clients bribed Rykel? Anaxan.'

Legge nodded sagely. 'That's the story WRG have put out. Total fabrication. Opposite of the truth. Diametric.'

'Forgive my naivety, Gavin, but if WRG had stuff leaked to them, why didn't they win the tender?'

He smiled, eyes narrowing. 'We believe that Rykel told them the panel was sensitive to price. So they thought they could pull it off by just topping us, coming in a few dollars above. Not very smart. The panel put the extra dollars aside, went for an all-Australian company, top-class consortium, broad range of expertise, access to—'

'Quite,' I said. 'Who killed Bergh?'

His look turned conspiratorial. 'I can't speculate on that, Jack. But of course—'

I waited. He smiled, shook his head. 'Let's just say WRG are known for covering their tracks.'

I didn't have anything to lose. 'So WRG went for Rykel. And your mob went for Susan Ayliss.'

Without hesitation, he said, 'Ayliss was WRG's first choice but she gave them the arse. Rykel was second cab and he delivered.'

Legge rose, tugged at his tie. 'Well, Jack, that's all I came to say. WRG are people who will try to use anyone. Use them and spit them out. Take it from an old mate.'

'Thank you for your concern,' I said, 'but I don't know WRG and I don't know that they know me.'

He nodded at me in a way full of meaning. 'They know you, mate. Believe me.'

At the door, I said, 'Good luck in your new career, Gavin. I can't fault Ponton's judgment in hunting your head.'

'Thanks,' he said. 'Next time we'll crack a bottle of the French.'

Rain had beaded on the BMW. I was beginning to hate beading.

At the Prince, the youth club were conducting a panel discussion covering, simultaneously, the certain outcomes of all eight of the weekend's games. I joined in but most of my mind was elsewhere.

'Now, Jack,' said Norm, 'we goin to this bloody Docklands again on Sundee or not?'

Sunday afternoon was St Kilda against Essendon, second from the bottom against the top.

'Going,' I said. 'There'll be a million Bomber fanatics there. They can't get enough blood. The team needs us.'

'Goin then,' said Norm. He turned to the others. 'Sundee's on.'

They raised their glasses.

'We might have a bet on the way,' I said.

All eyes glittered.

'Got the oil?' said Eric. 'Got the oil, Jack?'

I held up my right hand, moved it around in the maybe, maybe not way.

'He's got the oil,' said Wilbur. 'He's got the oil.'

She rang when hope was gone. I was at the freezer, looking at my personal Antarctic, Scott knew no bleaker moment.

'I'm shutting down my week here,' said Linda. 'You'd be on your way out, I suppose. Freshly showered.'

'Well, yes and no. On my way out I have no doubt. Showering I was putting off until later.'

'Yes or no?'

'Yes. Please. There's nothing to eat here.'

Silence.

'Well,' she said, 'we'll cross that little obstacle when we come to it.'

I made the bed, cleaned the toilet, the washbasin, stacked the dirty dishes. For the rest, the place was reasonably clean from my recent manic attack.

The Avoca kindling came to life briskly. I put on Milly Husskind, sad and sexy trailer-park songs, a voice torn at the edges.

A shower, a quick shower.

I was barely in clean denims and an old and faithful shirt when the buzzer went.

Tonight, her hair was drawn back severely and she was dressed for outdoors in a leather jacket, polo-neck sweater and corduroy pants.

'That's a good look,' I said. 'Sort of tough.'

She came in and looked around. 'I am tough. Toughest woman on radio.' She took off her jacket.

'I heard you roughing up that life coach.'

'That was nothing compared with what I did to the woman selling her book on colonic irrigation.'

'Stuck it right up her, I'm sure. I'm opening white wine. I suppose…'

'I'll drink anything.'

Linda followed me into the kitchen and sat on the table while I opened the wine. I brought the glasses over, put them down next to her. She put a hand in my waistband and pulled me over into the fork of her legs.

I looked down at her. 'That's a suggestive thing to do,' I said.

'I'm in a suggestive frame of mind.' She hooked her legs around mine, drew me in tight.

'Nothing wrong with those muscles,' I said, experiencing shortness of breath. I bent down to kiss her neck, her mouth, felt her hands in my hair.

We came apart.

'You're pretty suggestible, aren't you?' she said, moving a long-fingered hand between us. She was flushed, an erotic sight.

'I've got a new mattress,' I said, hoarsely. 'Very hard.'

She took hold of me. 'Hard I like,' she said. 'Harder the better.'

When it was over, Linda lay on her back, her legs over me.

'We never went anywhere,' she said.

'Anywhere? How far away is anywhere?'

'Far. Europe. America.'

'I've been there.'

'Not with me. With the mystery hand on the train, but not with me.'

'How could we go anywhere? I'd barely got a grip on you when you left for Sydney.'

'You encouraged me. I thought you wanted to get rid of me. Not at the time, I didn't think that at the time. It came to me later.'

'I had your interests at heart.' I rolled over, took her chin in my hand. 'What I didn't know,' I said, 'was that once a starfucker, always a starfucker.'

Linda had been married to a doctor, left him for a rock musician.

'Yes,' she said, 'I've fucked the stars. Rock stars, TV personalities. But that's behind me now. I'm going for the lesser lights in the galaxy. Butchers, I want. Newsagents. Seedy suburban solicitors even.'

'As it happens, I can help you there.'

'Yes?' She had her right hand on me.

'Yes, I know an excellent butcher and a...'

In the pre-dawn, misty rain in the streetlights, a much happier person left the boot factory, a rumpled, low-crotched figure fit only to be abroad in darkness. Today, I would vary my route, stumble along…no, the usual route was better. Stick with a known way.

As was always the case, I felt a surge of wellbeing as the recalcitrant muscles and tendons and sinews warmed up and stretched. I prepared myself for the dog ambush, was caught unawares yet again when the calculating beast waited until the last second before launching itself at the fence.

My thoughts turned to gluing the entire dog to a McCoy creation, but my mood was too good to be coloured by the encounter. I stepped up the pace to the point where I could have overtaken one of those scooters for the disabled, the silent machines that carry flags.

Did the drivers ever wish for something more under the pedal, a bit of grunt? Just for emergencies, mark you. An emergency power surge that spun the back wheels, lifted the nose. That would empower the disabled, brighten an entire day.

Thinking these and other innovative thoughts, I cantered in the dark up Napier Street to Freeman, turned left for Brunswick, the sacred ground on my right, the site of the departed Fitzroy Football Club, my sacred ancestral site. Here, Irish men, my antecedents, their founding male genes coming from the Jewish quarter of Hamburg, had on pale and icy afternoons heard the crowd suck the oxygen from the air as they rose to take the screaming mark.

Sucking oxygen myself, I turned right up empty Brunswick, still moving at tram-catching pace, went past the bowling club and turned right for the trip through the gardens. They were in near-darkness, the light from the lamps diffused by the soft rain.

Then the reserves of energy were found to be non-existent. I slowed to a controlled stagger near the lovely tree where a young woman had been found one winter morning, sitting in the comfortable fork. Dead, strangled, dumped.

Where paths met, I was at a walk. Winded.

The walking winded.

Like a real athlete, my head was up, my hands were on my hips. I was always this way by the time I got to this point. Warming down, they called it. How can you warm *down*?

Exhaustion with signs of distress was what it was.

Standing there, panting, I heard something.

The shift of a foot on leaves?

Something out of the corner of my left eye, just a movement of the dark trunk of a tree.

Close, two metres away.

I turned my head, saw the figure take a step towards me, a man, saw light from the high park lamp ahead gleam on something…

Oh Jesus.

At once, a sound like a fist thumping a desk and a flash, a shutter blinking on a white-hot fire, a tug at the tracksuit hood, burning on the back of my head.

Instinctively, I reached for the man, lurched, covered the distance between us, got both hands on an arm as I fell, pulled him down with me.

He hit me on the side of the head with his left hand, lost his footing, fell towards me, half over me. I let go with my right hand, tried to punch him, made contact somewhere, he made a noise, I rolled over, took him with me, I outweighed him, a slim person but strong, I was on top, no face beneath me, a mask, a silk ski mask, mud on it. I tried to hit him in the face with my left hand, then my right, missed both, realised he had no hold on me.

I got to my feet.

He was bringing the weapon up.

I swung a kick at him, connected, turned and ran. Not for home, too far, get out into the open. I ran in the direction of the playground, the barbecue, sliding on the gravel, got off the path, looked back, saw him coming, moving well, I hadn't hurt him.

Why didn't he shoot? Had he lost the weapon?

No, he wanted this to be neat. He'd wanted to shoot me from close range, a clean hit, a professional hit, Alan Bergh had been shot by a professional…

Run, just run.

I could hear him behind me on the path.

He was closing on me. I could hear his running footsteps over the sound of my heart, of the blood in my ears, of my panting.

The children's playground ahead, beyond that the road gleaming wetly in the streetlight, the school, a light on in the school, a cleaner at work…

If I could reach the road.

Just reach the road.

I wasn't going to reach the road before he caught me.

I looked over my shoulder and saw the dark figure close behind, all black, white blurs for eyes. I changed direction to run through the swings, run between the swings, the ground wet and slippery underfoot.

No more breath in my body, slowing down, he was going to run up behind me, shoot me in the back of the head.

Shoot me. Metres from me.

I saw the swings, solid planks suspended on heavy chains.

I was between them, on an isthmus between the troughs worn away by children's swinging feet.

Behind me, I heard his breathing.

He was almost on me.

Going to die.

I grabbed the swing to my left, grabbed the nearest chain, swung the heavy plank, it jumped up awkwardly, twisting.

He was a metre away, in stride, both hands on the pistol.

I brought the swing seat around shoulder-high.

It smashed into his forearms, knocked them sideways, he fired, the flat sound, no muzzle flash seen, the shot way off course.

His momentum brought him up to me, I smelt his breath, sweet, his left hand was off the gun...

His right hand was bringing the gun back towards me, not worried about neatness now, just a desire to kill me.

I had the swing seat in both hands, threw it over his head, grabbed the chains, pulled them together, no thought in any of this, wrapped them around his throat, twisted with all my strength. He had a hand at his throat, both hands, I twisted, twisted, maniacal strength in my arms, in my torso.

He went down on his knees in the swing's depression, making a gargling noise.

I didn't stop twisting, couldn't stop, went on...

When I stopped, I didn't look at him, walked away.

Without a backward glance, I walked home, slowly, little

shudders passing though my arms, my shoulders, more like tiny convulsions, spasms, a great feeling of tiredness upon me.

At home, I was sick for a long time, then I rang the police emergency number, told a woman that there was a body in the north playground of the gardens, at the swings, gave her my name, address and telephone number.

It was twenty minutes before they knocked on my door. I was showered, shaved, dressed. My breathing was normal.

He was a weary-looking uniformed cop, blue-chinned, probably at the end of his shift.

'Jack Irish?'

I nodded.

'Rang about the body?'

'Yes.'

He looked at me for a while. 'Reckon it's a good joke?'

'What?'

'Don't fuck with me. We don't appreciate this kind of crap. I can charge you.'

'At the swings.'

'No body at the swings, there's no body in the whole fucken park.'

'Sorry,' I said. 'Must've been a dero having a nap. Sorry.'

When he'd gone, I went to the kitchen and sat at the table, my elbows on it, my head in my hands.

Someone was sent to kill me. Instead, I killed him.

Had I killed him?

Or had he recovered, crawled away? Perhaps someone had taken him away, dead or alive, because it was less trouble that way? It had been at least fifteen minutes before I'd phoned the police, plenty of time to remove the masked man.

I hadn't seen his face. I had wrapped a chain around his neck and tried my best to strangle the life out of him, thought I'd succeeded, and I had no idea what he looked like.

Just the silk-masked face in the near dark, the smell of his toothpaste.

I walked around the apartment aimlessly, made the bed so recently left. Looked at my watch. It was just after 7 a.m.

Who?

Someone who wanted the matter of Marco to stay closed.

Would they try again? They'd have to find another hit man.

Perhaps they had a supply of hit men. Hardly likely.

Who?

The same people who'd murdered Marco?

It was almost certain that WRG had used Bergh to attempt the blackmail of Susan Ayliss. In that case, he'd hired Marco. But the bid had failed, leaving Bergh and Marco as potential embarrassments. Now they were both dead.

And then I came along, asking questions about both men.

Bergh had held the key to everything. He talked to Doyle, to Mick Olsen, drug scam mastermind…

I needed to look at Bergh's phone bill again.

No.

I needed to do nothing. This wasn't worth dying for. Colin Loder would recuse himself from the cocaine jackets trial and, with luck, never hear anything more about his missing album. As for Marco, his death was of no personal concern to me. I had no interest whatsoever in Marco.

Send a message to WRG that I was no longer interested in Bergh or Marco, that was what I needed to do.

Go away for a while. Go far away. Leave now. That would convey the message that I had disengaged from anything that annoyed them.

Ring Cam, ring Linda, ring Wootton, ring Colin Loder on his borrowed mobile. Ring Stan and tell him to pass the message on to the youth club that I'd gone away, wouldn't be picking them up on Sunday. Ring Gus and leave a message for Charlie. Enzio. I'd have to get hold of him.

A life to run away from.

I could do that. I could spend a few weeks with Claire.

No, I couldn't do that. They might not accept my gesture of submission and send someone to Claire's house to look for me. I couldn't go near anyone I knew.

I couldn't run away from this. There wasn't any way to backtrack, to undo.

Bergh's phone bill. Another look at it.

The city hadn't fully woken yet, only those without a choice were astir: the greengrocer on the corner, the newsagent, dry-eyed shiftworkers going home. I was opening my office door in ten minutes.

There hadn't been any malice in the job they'd done, but they didn't care who knew they'd been there.

My one filing cabinet had been emptied, every file taken from its folder and dropped to the floor.

My old Mac's hard drive was gone.

The in-tray where I'd carelessly tossed Bergh's phone bill was empty. So was the out-tray.

There was the faintest glow of light from the back room.

I went to the doorway. The door of the small fridge was open and a rectangle of pale-yellow light lay on the floor.

I switched on the light.

Everything had been taken out of the small sink cupboard—ancient dishwashing liquid, a tin of drain cleaner, a few scouring pads, a bar of yellow soap I'd never seen before, two rolls of paper towels, a box of tea bags, the jar of sugar.

They'd looked in the old microwave, left the door open. I went to the steel back door. It was open. They'd left that way, down the lane, carrying the hard disk.

I locked the door, looked around, feeling light-headed, queasy in the stomach.

What else had been in here?

Robbie's suitcase. I'd put it between the fridge and the sink.

Gone.

If things had gone to plan, I would be dead now, lying in the park, dragged into the bushes, blood seeped into the tanbark, waiting to be found by some early walker's dog. And there would be nothing in my effects to connect me with Marco or Bergh.

I went to the front room, willed myself to tidy up, failed. What was the point?

Eric the Geek had done the Bergh reverse-directory for me. Would he have kept a copy of his findings? Possibly. There was something distinctly retentive about Eric. I got out my wallet to find the card with his number, searched through the pockets, couldn't find it. In exasperation, I pulled out half-a-dozen cards.

A small dark-blue object. For a moment, it meant nothing. Then I remembered.

The small plastic torch-like device from Robbie's jacket, found in the inside key pocket. The device without hint of function.

I held it between finger and thumb, pressed the button, looked at the red light it emitted for a second or so, turned it over. Something had been scratched into the plastic. I held it to the light. Numbers: 2646.

I thought I knew what this thing did.

The Cathexis carpark was in the basement, entered from a concrete driveway on the eastern side of the building. I found a park two blocks away and walked back, a cold wind opening my jacket, no-one in the streets.

I didn't turn in when I reached the driveway. I walked to the far side, then turned right and stayed close to the wall as I made haste to cover the 50 metres to the carpark entrance. The camera above it was stationary, looking down on where drivers would activate the door-opening machinery by communicating with a steel pillar.

Robbie's device was in my hand as I walked. At the carpark's huge door, I did a right-angle turn, went up to the pillar, saw the eye set into it, pointed the small torch and pressed the button.

The carpark door made a noise and began its rise. I was inside long before it reached my height.

No more than two dozen cars were in the brightly lit chamber. Quality not number, all foreign: Mercedes, BMW, Volvo, Saab, Audi, an Alfa, a yellow born-again VW Beetle in the corner.

I looked around. In the centre of the space, a glowing green arrow on a concrete shaft pointed upwards. I was there in seconds.

Another eye.

I pointed and pressed.

The lift door opened.

A big stainless-steel box, carpet on the floor, deep

plum-coloured carpet. No ordinary lift. No floor buttons to press, just a keyboard, an eye and, above it, a green screen. Beside that, two large red rectangular buttons said ASSISTANCE and EMERGENCY.

The green screen had a message: *Welcome to Cathexis. Please enter your code.*

Point and press.

The screen said: *Thank you. Please enter your password.*

My password?

I hadn't thought about a password. Ah, the numbers scratched on the torch. I managed to read them, typed them in: 2646.

The screen said: *Error. Please re-enter password.*

Time to leave. I was turning when I remembered. The apartment was in a company name. The woman at reception had said it. It had crossed my mind that it was an anagram of Rosalind.

Dalinsor Nominees.

It was worth a try. I typed in Dalinsor.

The screen said: *Thank you.*

The lift was moving. I breathed again. Numbers blipped on the screen, stopped at 12. The door opened.

A foyer with a pale rose carpet. Soft lighting came from wall sconces beside four doors. Number 12 was on my right, a security camera set into the wall above it. Plus another electronic eye, another keyboard. How did the residents put up with this? Better to risk burglary.

There was a button. I pressed it. If anyone was home, I had explaining to do.

No response. I pressed again, waited. Then I gave the eye a beam with the torch.

The keyboard lit up and a voice said: 'Entry code, please.'

If the number scratched on the torch didn't work I was going to be trapped up here on the twelfth floor, waiting for security to arrive.

I tapped in 2646.

The voice said: 'Thank you.'

My shoulders sagged. Bolts slid.

I went into a long hallway, unfurnished, looked around for the alarm system. It was behind the door, a steel box with a green light glowing. The entry code had deactivated the alarm.

An open door from the hall led into a huge sitting room, empty except for two leather chairs and a sofa. Outside, on a balcony, the wind was whipping the bare branches of trees in pots. I walked through into a kitchen, stainless steel and granite, sleek, no visible appliances, no signs of habitation. From the sink, you could look out over the city, blurred by the wet glass.

I went back to the hall, found the main bedroom. The bed was the size of a Housing Commission bedroom, bedding on it, striped sheets stripped back.

Facing the bed, a home-cinema-size screen was built into a wall of cupboards, record and stereo equipment beneath it.

Was this where Susan Ayliss had seen herself on screen? Live in action with Marco.

A dressing-room led off the bedroom. I had a look in the cupboards. Two held women's garments, after-dark wear at a glance, and there were underclothes in drawers and women's shoes in a rack. Ros Cundall obviously used the place occasionally.

Beyond the dressing-room was a bathroom that was also a gym and spa and sauna, an antiseptic Nordic-looking place. In a glass-fronted cabinet, glass shelves held cosmetics—jars and tubes, bottles of all shapes and sizes containing pale liquids and golden vials—three perfumes, atomisers, cologne, cottonwool balls, ear buds, mouthwash, toothpaste.

Nothing. I was wasting my time.

I went back to the kitchen, sighted along the granite countertop, saw the faint trails. It took a while to find the fridge but it was empty except for a bottle of Perrier water.

I opened another door off the hallway. A study, built-in shelves along one wall, a modern desk and a chair, nothing in the desk drawers. Tall and narrow cabinets flanked the doorway. On the way out, I opened the door of the right-hand one. Empty. I tried the other one. Empty.

Time to go, to end this trespass.

But I was reluctant to leave. I went back to the sitting room, looked around, walked around the kitchen again opening doors, checked the other bedroom, the main bedroom again, the dressing-room, the bathroom/gym/sauna.

I was turning to leave, leave the room, the apartment, the building, when I saw, on a shelf behind a chrome-plated exercise bicycle, a bag, a leather-look bag, the size of a small toilet bag.

I went over and picked it up, opened it.

It held a camera. A small digital video camera.

The camera that filmed Susan Ayliss?

Now it was time to go.

Leaving Cathexis didn't require any codes. In a few minutes, I was on the wintry street, curiously elated for someone who only hours before had been running for his life in a public park.

The woman at Vizionbanc in South Melbourne took

the camera away and when she came back her tone was apologetic.

'Only one image on it is retrievable,' she said. 'Sometimes everything isn't completely wiped. A beach. Want to see?'

I followed her into a room lit by the glow from half-a-dozen monitors on one wall. She took me to the end one. It showed a beach, a featureless and windy beach by the look of it, sea to the left, low dunes to the right, scrubby vegetation. There were two sets of marks in the sand, possibly footprints. In the distance, at the right of the frame, on the dunes side, there was something solid, just a dark blob.

'What's that?' I pointed.

'Vehicle,' she said. 'Old Land Rover, Land Cruiser, something like that. The boxy shape.'

'That's good,' I said. 'That's a gift.'

'Trained at huge expense by the Defence Department,' she said. 'We pass the savings on to our clients.'

She went to a work station and fiddled at a console. The dark blob now filled the screen. It was a fuzzy image but it was a vehicle, not quite side-on to the camera, definitely a four-wheel drive, grey.

'Land Cruiser,' she said. 'Short wheelbase.'

'Is that the date the picture was taken? On the bottom.'

'Yes.'

'Can I use a phone? Can someone ring me back here?'

She nodded, took me to the reception area.

I rang Eric the Cybergoth, told him what I wanted. Then I looked at the street, the passers-by, at the rain falling on the Stud where it stood in the loading zone. No beading was taking place on its blue-grey skin. The parking persecutor, the grey ghost who left the message for me around the corner from The Green Hill, he would take better care of the Stud. Love it more. Cherish it. Wax it. It would bead for him. I had his number. I should sell it to him.

On the other hand, if he waited a short time, he could buy it much cheaper from my deceased estate.

The phone on the desk rang.

'Jack?'

Eric the Lawless, master of the cybersteppes.

'Yes.'

'There's one.'

'What is it?'

'Land Cruiser. '82. Want the rego?'

'Yes.'

I walked around the corner to a place I'd noticed called Cafe Bonbon, just two seated customers and a person getting a takeaway. I ordered a short black and a cold croissant from the coffee-maker, a saturnine youth in a chef's white top.

There was a used copy of the *Herald-Sun* on top of the unwanted newspaper dump. I took it to a seat, sat down carefully, the day so violently begun taking its toll on my back, my neck, on everything that supported my unworthy skull.

My eyes had been on the front-page headline for a while before the small active section of my brain registered the big words on the page.

DRUGS BUNGLE
LINK TO KILLING

The opening paragraphs said:

Police sources last night linked the murder of a man at Melbourne Airport to the disappearance of cocaine worth more than $2 million in a bungled Federal Police operation.

The dead man, Alan Bergh, 47, of Toorak, is believed to have been involved in a 'controlled importation' of cocaine from South Africa that went badly wrong and allowed smugglers to get away with cocaine worth more than $2 million.

Victorian Police believe that the Federal Police operation was compromised from within. The Federal Police have declined to comment. Sources say the importation was financed by a Melbourne group looking for new drug sources. 'There are well-known identities involved,' a source said. 'They're trying to break away from their usual suppliers. The

Federal Police had a golden chance to nail some dealers to the big end of town and they stuffed it up.'

The story went on to list other strange goings-on in the local drug squad. Bergh's was the only name given. It was all speculation based on information from unnamed sources, but it had the unmistakable feel of a story planted by the cops and dressed up by a journalist.

I looked at the street for a while, something at the edge of thought, then I got up and asked if I could use the phone next to the coffee machine.

Cam answered at the second ring.

'That pilot with the cap,' I said. Harry and Cam used a pilot who wore a baseball cap backwards.

'Yeah.'

'I've got a name. I need to find out if it filed flight plans recently. Local airports.'

A silence lasting just long enough to express wonder.

'What's the name?'

I gave it to him.

'Call you on what?'

'Hold on.'

I found a $5 note, put it on the counter. 'Can someone ring me here?'

'Sure,' said the coffee-maker pushing the money away. 'Twenty-five cents goin out, comin in's free. What's your name?'

I told him, read the number to Cam and went back to my seat, drank my coffee and ate the croissant without tasting either.

I didn't hear the phone but the coffee-maker shouted my name.

'What's that hissing noise?' said Cam.

274

'Snakes,' I said. 'I'm in the jungle.'

'That'd be right. The name flew from Moorabbin this morning. Filed a flight plan for Sale. One passenger.'

'Any other flights to Sale?' Sale was near the sea. Beaches.

'June 4 there's one. With passenger.'

The picture of the beach was taken on June 5. There was something very wrong here, something I should have considered earlier. I paid my bill and left. As I rounded the corner, cold rain blew into my face and ran down my neck and under my collar.

At the office, a message on the answering machine. Barry Tregear didn't identify himself: *The query. ID was by the bloke we were talking about. The dangerous one.*

I closed my eyes, let my head fall forward.

Mick Olsen had identified Robbie Colburne's body. Mick Olsen, drug cop, the commissioner's suppository, receiver of messages from Alan Bergh, now the late Alan Bergh.

This was even wronger that I'd thought.

I rang inquiries, asked for the Shire of Sale. One last stab. But not in complete darkness.

When I turned off the tarmac, the western sky was the unnatural pink of denture plates. In the east, the light above the lakes was dirty grey and going quickly. I crossed a cattle grid and drove up a dirt road that made its way around boulders and stands of yellow box.

At the top of the hill, I stopped. The road forked and the landscape revealed itself. To the left was a bay, its right shore a narrow heavily-treed peninsula. To the right, the country was open, grazing country, fenced into paddocks, with a belt of trees along the lake shore. The road to the right twisted down a long way to what looked like a cluster of farm buildings surrounded by trees. The left fork went to the peninsula, entered the trees and was lost from sight.

Dead Point, the map called the peninsula.

I was tired, sore everywhere, filled with a feeling of futility, the feeling that I was moving because I was scared to stop. Sharks couldn't stop; they moved or they died. I wasn't a shark. I was an old goldfish in a pond the new owners were filling with rubble, a fish swimming around trying to find water that had oxygen in it. A shaking of the head, a moving of the shoulders, creaks heard in the joining places. Time to move.

I turned left, drove down to the peninsula, in the direction of what I took to be Dead Point. A few hundred metres before the tall trees began, a new fence and a gate between fat posts barred the way. Beyond the fence, hundreds of trees had been planted, gums, waist-high, not planted in lines but in clusters.

I opened the gate, went through, stopped to close it. Door open, leg out, I changed my mind, left the gate ajar, fuck the farming ethic, drove on, down into the trees.

A narrow road, twisting, etched into the land by wheels, dull water in pools, the old gums close and oppressive, blocking the light.

There was a final bend and then a clearing, large, a quarter of a football field, two timber buildings directly ahead, a ramshackle two-storey structure on the right with a set of big doors, one open a metre. The other building, single storey, was weathered but in good condition. A vehicle was parked in front of it.

An old Land Cruiser.

I parked beside it and got out. Clean air. The sea wasn't far away, its chip-salty taste in the nasal passages.

The keys were in the Land Cruiser. No crime out here in the clean air. I followed a worn route, walked down between the buildings, not so much a path as a rut, reached a portico, a new structure, sheltering a door in the single-storey building.

No bell. This wasn't a bell building. No knocker either.

I gave the door a few hits with knuckles, winced in pain.

Nothing.

Used the left hand to do it again.

No sound from within.

Again.

No-one home.

I tried the door handle. The door opened.

A passage. Dark. Doorways ahead, three to the left, one to the right. Outdoor clothes hung on a peg rail beside the righthand door.

I went in, opened the right-hand door.

It was a big room, warm, a combined sitting room and kitchen lined with timber, its age and its history showing in the adzed posts and beams and the oil stains deep in the now-polished floorboards. The eastern side had once had sliding doors and the upper tracks had been left when a wall of glass was installed. In the middle of the room, a fire glowed behind the glass door of a stove.

'Anyone home?' I said loudly.

No sound, then a log spluttered in the firebox.

I walked to the window past a kitchen table with turned legs and through a casual arrangement of old armchairs and a sofa covered with bright rugs. Beyond the sliding glass doors, a new deck and jetty ran to the lake, huge and still and empty, shining like metal in the gloaming.

Look in the other rooms?

At that moment, nothing on earth held less appeal. I went back to the passage, opened the first door.

A tidy room holding four bunks. Empty.

The second door on the left.

I felt my skin tighten, realised my mouth was dry.

For some reason, I knocked and waited. Turned the handle, pushed the door open.

No surprises. Another bedroom, a large bed, made, nothing lying around.

The third door. A bathroom, two toilet bags on the basin cabinet.

I went out the side door, turned left down the path between the buildings. At the end of the dwelling, I stopped and looked around. The two-storey building had been the boat workshop. Out of its yawning front entrance, wide-apart rusty steel trolley tracks ran down to the water's edge and disappeared under water. Boats had been brought up to the tracks and a wheeled cradle run under the keels. Then they had been winched up the incline into the huge shed.

The shed was a half-dark, empty cavern. I went in, feeling the texture of the packed and oily dirt floor underfoot. Now the cradle stood at the end of its track, near the back doors, piled with 44-gallon drums. It was all that remained of the trade plied in this great space, the hard work of repairing boats.

I went back into the house, into the sitting room, looked out of the window.

A sailing boat was coming in to the jetty, sails furled, under power, two people in yellow rainslicks on board, one at the tiller, one leaning on the cabin.

I moved back from the window and watched the person at the tiller take the boat up to the landing at a near right angle, change direction sharply, cut the power, drift the vessel gently side-on to meet the jetty.

The other person stepped off the boat, went to the bow to begin tying up. A man. He was joined on the jetty by his companion, a woman, who secured the stern line, got back on board, closed the cabin, put a cover over the engine. The man waited for her, put out a hand. She took it. On the jetty, they embraced, kissed, I saw her teeth flash as she laughed. They walked towards the house, his right arm around her shoulders, her left arm around his waist.

I sat down in an armchair, the springs compressing unevenly beneath me.

Waited.

I heard them in the passage, laughing. They would be hanging up their yellow rainslicks.

She came into the room first, didn't see me, ruffled her hair with both hands, an attractive sight.

'Warmth, warmth,' she said, turning back, 'I don't understand…'

He was in the doorway and he saw me and she saw it in his eyes.

I stood up.

'Good evening,' I said. 'Susan. Marco.'

'A drink,' said Susan Ayliss. 'We need a drink. Malt, that's what we need. Double single malts.' She went to the long kitchen counter, where bottles stood on a tray.

Marco walked over, tall, slim, colour on his cheekbones from the cold, wearing a polo-neck sweater. He looked a little older in the flesh.

'You've been looking for me,' he said, smiling, putting out his right hand.

I shook it. His handshake made no attempt to impress.

'Not looking for you,' I said. 'It never occurred to me until yesterday that you might not be dead. I've been trying to find out who killed you and who had Colin Loder's album.'

'Drink,' said Susan Ayliss. She had three glasses on a tray, a bottle in her hand. Marco took the bottle and half-filled the glasses.

I took a glass, put it to my lips, welcomed the smell of campfire clothes, the dark taste.

'Let's sit,' said Susan. She put the tray on the coffee table, switched on two table lamps.

We sat, Susan and Marco on the sofa, not people at ease. I drank some more whisky.

'I'd like to know a few things,' I said.

'I don't have the album,' said Marco. 'I'm sorry.'

'Where is it?'

'The person I took it for, he's got it.' He had a gravelly voice, a man with a cold.

I didn't say anything. We sat in silence. A wind was coming up, gusting, rattling the iron roof. Marco put a hand on Susan's knee, a gesture of comfort.

'I don't know what you know,' said Marco. He tasted the whisky. 'Xavier Doyle. At The Green Hill?'

I nodded.

'Doyle's got it. They're in deep with this drug thing the judge's hearing. You know…'

'Yes.'

'The guys who brought the stuff in, they were told they'd walk, some technicality I don't understand. Anyway, the pictures, that's insurance, concentrate the judge's mind.'

'Doyle and who are in deep?'

'And Cundall. They're both in financial shit. Cundall went to South Africa and met this importer. The guy brings it in by the container. So he came back and worked out this wonderful scheme with Doyle.'

'The judge,' I said. 'You knew he had pictures?'

Marco blinked, twice. 'Yes,' he said. 'Doyle knew.' He drank some malt.

'How would he know that?'

'Knows everything, the X.'

'X arranged for Loder to be in the Snug?'

Marco's fingers went over his hair. He looked at Susan, a long look, his eyes came back to me.

'Yes,' he said. 'I let him blow me. Closed my eyes and thought of England.' He smiled, an open smile, careless of anyone's opinions.

'What brought you to Melbourne?' I said. 'The weather?'

Marco didn't hesitate. 'Weather's okay. I like it, very noir. Actually, I came to make a fuckflick with Susan.' He looked at her and smiled, a slow smile. 'Worst gig of my life.'

Susan took his sleeve, punched his arm.

She was in love.

'Who hired you?'

'A bloke called Naismith. In Sydney. And I wouldn't call it hire. I didn't have any choice. People were trying to kill me.'

'Where does Alan Bergh come in?'

'He got on to Naismith, asked him for someone.'

'Who hired Bergh?'

'Doyle. Well, Sam Cundall through Doyle.'

I looked at Susan. She was tense, didn't want to meet my eyes. I said, 'Susan, Cannon Ridge. Can we go over that again?'

She looked into her glass, sniffed it, a delicate indrawing of nostrils, drank. 'I lied to you,' she said in a quiet voice. 'I passed on WRG's tender to Anaxan. I'm not brave. The thought of the video getting out terrified me.'

Between them, Susan and Gavin Legge had convinced me that WRG were the naughty ones. Legge was going to pay a heavy price for his part.

'I don't understand quite how you got from blackmail to this state of affairs,' I said.

Susan put out a hand and touched Marco's hair. He took her hand, kissed her fingers. Victim and blackmailer, now as one.

'Marco came around to apologise,' she said. 'He does that rather well.'

'I fell in love,' said Marco. 'I didn't expect that to happen.'

'Didn't stop the blackmail though.'

He shook his head. 'No, it didn't. I couldn't stop that, Jack. We're all victims some of the time.'

'The dead person? The person with your wallet in your car? He'd be a real victim.'

'He was dead already,' said Marco. 'A druggie. They found him dead. Overdosed in an alley.'

'They? This is Mick Olsen we're talking about?'

Marco blinked. 'Yeah, someone in the cops found him for Mick. One of his mates.'

I thought about the homemade notice in the Lebanese shop, the face of a missing young man. It wasn't hard to find a body in the city. I drank some whisky, remembered I hadn't eaten since the croissant with nothing. When was that? What day?

'Why did Olsen do this?' I said.

'Didn't want anyone looking for Robbie. Robbie does Susan and the judge, then the book's closed on Robbie.' He laughed, cut it short, pained face.

'Someone tried to kill me this morning,' I said.

'Oh shit.' Marco looked down, ran both hands through his hair. 'Fucking Doyle, he's totally paranoid. Mad.'

I stood up. I didn't ask who had murdered Alan Bergh, what the fate of the real Robbie Colburne had been, I didn't want to know. Already I knew more than I wanted to know, much, much more.

'What made you come here?' said Susan. 'How did you find out about us?'

'I didn't. I found the camera in Ros Cundall's apartment. I knew Marco had some connection with the building and you'd told me about a digital camera. So I associated it with the blackmail attempt. When I saw the picture of the beach and the Land Cruiser, I assumed Marco had taken it. But whose vehicle? I had a look under the name of your company and found an '82 Cruiser.'

'And this place? No-one knows I own it.'

'Someone told me you had a plane. I found your flight plans for Sale. With passenger. Then there was the date the picture was taken. It was after Anaxan won the tender. And you'd flown to Sale the day before with a passenger. That's when I began to think that Marco might not be dead. Hearing that Mick Olsen ID'd Robbie's body put the seal on it.'

She was frowning. 'I still don't see how you found this place.'

'The shire council was kind enough to look you up in the rates register.'

'Sounds simple,' said Susan, tight smile.

'Effortless,' I said. 'Thanks for the drink. I've got a long drive.'

Marco didn't look up, didn't get up. 'What now?' he said. 'What happens?'

'I'm going to ask Doyle for the album. And to behave properly. Apart from that, I've lost interest.'

Susan rose, strain on her face, her age showing. 'Jack,' she said, 'I know, I know I can't ask you…'

'I don't care who runs ski resorts and casinos,' I said. 'I don't care who you told what. The matter's closed.'

'Thank you,' she said. She took my left hand in both of hers for a moment. 'Thank you.'

They followed me out, into a clear night, cold, a fast-rising full moon. At the car, I said, 'I wouldn't like Doyle to know I'm coming around for the album.'

Marco had his arm around Susan. He shook his head. 'Never heard of any Doyle. Count on that.'

I didn't say goodbye, swung the Stud in a wide reverse turn, gunned it. I could be home by midnight.

I could be home by midnight.

I was over the crest of the hill, where the road forked, when I heard the helicopter, saw its lights over to my right, heard the menacing chop and whine.

I drove back without lights, the chalky road clear in the early moonlight. At the trees, I turned the car around, faced the way I'd come.

I sat for a moment, put my forehead on the steering wheel. My body had moved a step beyond tiredness and hurt, gone to a stage where I wasn't feeling anything except a strange sort of buzzing in my limbs, an electrical discharge of some kind.

This was not my business. My business was finished. Almost. Soon. Just as soon as I'd put a proposition to Xavier Doyle that would drain the bonhomie from his cherubic, murderous being. Then my life would resume.

Charlie would be back soon.

Libraries. Ros Cundall had phoned. She wanted a library.

We wouldn't be doing a Cundall library.

Good.

A library every now and then was fine but not a diet of libraries. We would be doing other things, sitting in the workshop fragrant with the smell of wood and discussing philosophical matters. His extended stay in Perth would come under examination. The merits of warm weather. Swimming, perhaps.

I lifted my head, rubbed my eyes, got out. Listened.

Far, far away a dog barking, a long strangled sound. The full moon, it stirred dogs in their blood, all their fluids, people too.

It was cold, a wind coming off the lake, off Bass Strait beyond the lake, a cold passage was the strait.

I shut my mind and set off down the track into the trees, into the dark, walking quickly. The wind was animating the gums, rubbing limbs together until they squealed, pushing under loose bark.

Where the road met the clearing, I stopped. Things were as I'd left them minutes before. No sound save the wind in the trees, at work lifting the corrugated iron.

No. A voice.

Someone talking. A low monologue, no individual word distinguishable.

I crossed the space, went down the passage between the buildings, towards the water, the voice getting louder, words becoming distinct.

I knew the voice.

'Horse prick, secret of life, hey? Fuck people, they smile? That's the attitude?'

In the deep shadows, I stopped, leaned forward.

It seemed so close, the dark helicopter, sitting on the water at the end of the rusty cradle tracks, moving in and out on its floats. I thought I could see a pilot.

Two men on the jetty, near the tethered boat, in sub-tropical clothing, long shorts, boat shoes.

Milan Filipovic and Steve, his short-legged employee.

I couldn't see who Milan was talking to.

'Don't fuck around in there,' Milan said. He had his small sub-machine pistol in his right hand. 'Don't fuck with me, cockboy.'

Susan Ayliss was on her knees in front of him, something around her neck. He was holding her close with his left hand, like a dog on a choke-chain.

To my left, a voice said, 'Got the Pole's gun.'

It was a tall man, heavily built, all in black. He'd come out of the house through a sliding door, stood in the light holding a pistol upright.

'Goodonya, Mick,' said Milan.

Mick Olsen, late of the drug squad, identifier of Robbie's body.

Marco came out of the boat's cabin, carrying something. A bag, a sports bag. He put it on the cabin roof.

'It's all here,' he said.

'Come,' said Milan. He moved his head and his hair was like a silver cap in the moonlight. 'Come here you piece of shit.'

Marco climbed onto the jetty, head down.

'Treat you like a son,' said Milan. 'You steal from me, you whore.'

'I'm sorry,' said Marco.

I could barely hear his voice.

'Get on your knees, cockboy. Put the bag down, get on your fucken knees and say you sorry.'

Marco knelt, head down.

Milan gestured to Olsen with the machine pistol. Olsen came over, took the weapon, gave the pistol to Milan. 'I'm sorry, Milan,' said Marco. 'I'm really sorry.'

Milan went right up to him, dragged Susan with him.

'Okay,' said Milan, 'I forgive you. Look at me.'

Marco looked up slowly. Milan shot him in the face. One shot. He went over backwards, not quickly.

Susan made a noise, a terrible noise.

Milan pulled her head back, stuck the pistol in her mouth and pulled the trigger.

'Okay,' he said, handing the pistol to Steve. 'Wipe it, stick it in her hand. Lovers' fucken quarrel, hey.' He laughed. 'Let's go. I'm thirsty.'

I walked backwards, slowly, very scared, turned, went quickly down the alley. Hide. I should find somewhere to hide until the helicopter left. Somewhere dark, somewhere to hide my head in shame.

I could have done something. Anything. Shouted, distracted Milan.

Where to hide?

I came out between the buildings, saw the big door of the workshop slightly ajar.

Dark. It would be dark in there, in the huge space, high as a church.

I was inside in a second. It was dark, but not dark enough for me, moonlight coming in through the front entrance. I could see the old cradle piled with drums, 44-gallon drums.

The helicopter started.

Drawn forward, I moved up until I could see the helicopter below, at the water's edge.

Milan was standing on a pontoon, getting into the cabin. Steve and Mick Olsen were on land, waiting for him to get in. Steve had the sports bag. From ski jackets to sports bag, I thought. Sporty stuff, the South African cocaine.

I could have done something. Anything.

These men were going to fly away, fly to warm climes, refuel somewhere, Sydney perhaps. They'd be in Milan's sitting room long before midnight, lounging in the white leather chairs and sofas, drinks on the glass-topped tables, having a good laugh. I thought of the huge picture above the fireplace, a picture of a red rose lying on stone steps, its decaying petals holding drops of dew.

I could have done something.

I went to the back of the shed, went behind the cradle, put both hands on the base of the frame, tested.

Too heavy, probably rusted into the tracks.

I pushed again, put some effort into it.

The cradle moved. Moved a few centimetres.

I changed my grip, put my shoulder against a drum, felt the cold metal on my cheek. Put everything I had into my push.

Moving, the cradle was moving. I found more strength, this was pointless, they would come up here and kill me, put the pistol in my hand.

I could have done something.

Push.

The cradle was running, running freely, rumbling along, picking up speed, getting away from me. I stumbled, went to a knee, got up, gave it a final shove…

Steve was the only one outside the helicopter. He was standing on the pontoon, looking up, he'd heard the rumbling sound.

'Go!' he screamed. 'Jesus Christ, go!'

A drum dislodged from the top of the pile, fell forward, hit the concrete, bounced high.

I could see the pilot's face through the open door. He'd seen the cradle.

One pontoon lifted, the helicopter moved.

The drum bounced again, hit Steve, smashed him into the cabin. I heard his scream over the whup of the rotor blades.

The whole cradle slammed into the helicopter, tonnes of metal travelling at speed, a screeching, crushing sound, a string of sparks as the rotors hit metal, drums hitting the top of the cabin, flying into the air.

Sound like a car backfire, another, a flash of orange in the chaos below.

The blast pushed me backwards, took my sight away, took away my hearing. Instinctively, I turned my head away, turned my body, almost fell over. I didn't look again, willed myself to leave the shed, go across to the jetty, to the bodies.

Susan was dead, no pulse in her neck.

I went to Marco, put my hand to his throat, thought I felt something.

No, my own hammering pulse.

I leant down closer, trying to detect breathing.

From his mouth a sweet, clean smell. His toothpaste. French toothpaste.

The second time I'd smelled it today.

I pushed down the neck of the sweater, saw where the swing chain had bruised him.

Then I ran, down the path between the buildings, across the moonpale clearing into the trees, down the dark road, not stopping until I reached the car, got in, couldn't get my breath, fumbled the key.

The engine started.

On the hill crest, I looked back. There was a yellow glow at the end of the peninsula. Dead Point was burning. Mick Olsen's enemies in the drug squad would be pleased. All they'd had to do was slip me some surveillance clips and I did all their dirty work.

Surrounded by the silent faithful, some with tears in their eyes, we were watching a slaughter at the Docklands stadium when the starter at the Valley sent them off: eighteen hundred metres, class six for four-year-olds and upwards, apprentices claiming, going heavy.

I'd said I'd take the youth club to the football. I'd done it.

Four men with small radios held to their heads.

Number eight, the Kiwi horse, was called The Return. We'd stopped at the TAB on the way to invest our money.

'This thing doesn't come with a guarantee,' I said. 'Could run stone motherless last. Be warned.'

Norm O'Neill laughed. The others laughed.

'I don't think I'm getting through to you,' I said. 'I don't want your families coming around to see me.'

They all laughed.

Now, we all heard the caller say: *They've strung out at the thousand, Pelecanos leads by two lengths from Armageddon, Caveat's poking up on the inside, unruly mob following, bit of push and shove, going's terrible…*

He named seven or eight other horses before he got to The Return.

We all looked ahead, mouths downturned, eyes on the game. An Essendon player, bandaged like a burn victim, was about to kick another goal. Some people don't know when to stop.

I closed my eyes, opened them quickly. If I closed

my eyes for long, I would have to be slapped awake by a paramedic, encouraged to breathe.

On the bend, Caveat's gone up to Pelecanos, Armageddon's struggling, Portobelle's edging into it now and coming very wide is The Return.

Four sets of eyes flicked at one another. Too soon to hope.

Hird kicked the goal. A dog could have kicked it. His teammates came up and patted him. Just another career statistic, what did it matter that it broke hearts?

At the four hundred, Caveat and Portobelle, and coming at them in the centre of the track is The Return, the Kiwi, could be a surprise packet here at big odds, very ordinary recent form…

Heads down, no interest in the scene before us.

The Return's coming at them, Portobelle stopping under the big weight, Caveat's a fighter, won't give in, it's The Return and Caveat, it's going to be The Return, she's clear, the Kiwi raider's going away…

Four men stood up, hands in the air, making animal sounds of satisfaction in the midst of the grieving St Kilda faithful, who looked at us, murder in their eyes.

We sat down.

'No surprise, Jack, me boy,' said Norm O'Neill. 'Had the pencil on the animal this mornin. Put me in mind of a certain Kiwi horse…'

'Say the bloody name Dunedin Star and I'll kill you,' said Eric Tanner.

We made the collect on the way back to the Prince. It frightened me to see how much money was handed over to the youth club, fifties dispensed, repeatedly.

In the car, after crossing the city and listening to a great deal of hilarity, I said, primly, 'I'd never have mentioned it if I'd thought you were going to put that kind of money on.'

Silence. Rain on the windscreen. The Stud had had a long day. The Stud and the Stud's owner, who couldn't remember when the day had begun, remembered, and tried to shut it out.

'Jack,' said Wilbur, low voice.

'Yes.'

'It's our bloody money.'

The wipers needed replacing. So did the door seals. The clutch had that certain feeling too.

'Point taken,' I said.

'You bastard,' said Eric. 'Had the oil.'

'Well,' I said, 'the study of class, sectionals, draw, going, trainer, jock, track, barrier, weight, these things help inform a decision.'

'The oil,' said Eric.

I pulled up outside the Prince, a space waiting for us.

'And then there's the oil,' I said.

The men in the back seat attacked me, beat me around the head with rolled-up copies of the *AFL Record*.

We went in, had a few beers, no e-people in, didn't talk about the Saints' failings, too numerous to count, concentrated on the positives. All two of them. From Stan's office, I rang Linda's home number. Answering machine.

'Jack,' I said. 'I'll be home by six. Do with that information what you will.'

I said goodbye. The lads were in the process of shouting the bar, not an expensive exercise this Sunday evening. In the street, thoughts of sausages and mash and bed uppermost, my mobile rang.

'Listen, I could use a hand.' Cam.

'Now?'

'Yeah. Can't wait.'

I wanted to groan. 'What?'

He told me where he was. I did groan.

'Bring a torch,' he said.

In the unlovable depths of Coolaroo, Cam was waiting for me at the gate of a car wrecker's yard. In the dark, in spotting rain, we walked down an avenue of car bodies. Hundreds of them, piled two and three high.

'Artie lives down the back,' said Cam. He was in biker gear: leather jacket, jeans, boots.

'Where is he?'

'Handcuffed to a Lada Niva. Hasn't been helpful.'

We went around a large shed that served as an office and set off down another passage between wrecked vehicles.

'Don't they have dogs guarding these places?' I said.

'Should be halfway to Albury by now, the dog.'

I didn't ask what he meant.

'How'd you find Artie?'

'Lizard. Big help, Lizard. Given up the wood business. Just today. Gone home to New Zealand. Wouldn't know this shack was here.' He went through a gap in the wall of old twisted metal. In a clearing stood an ancient weatherboard cottage, sagging everywhere as if dropped from the air onto the site. On its verandah stood two bench seats from cars. Pieces of motorcycle covered the rest of the space.

'In the Lizards together, Artie and Almeida and Lizard,' said Cam. 'Lizard reckons Artie's topped three people. Gets carried away.'

'That Lada strong enough?'

'Artie's tired. Engine block fell on his leg.'

'Don't tell me any more. I'm a respected suburban solicitor.'

Cam led the way through the front door of the house. We were assailed by the smell of burnt cooking oil and cat urine with a strong underlay of blocked toilet.

'Well,' said Cam, 'where'd you reckon he'd keep it? Tried all the usual places.'

'Appliances?'

'Only got a beer fridge.'

'With money, they're scared of fire.'

I went from room to disgusting room, shining my new truckstop torch over everything, unwilling to touch anything. The kitchen was the worst, cats lived there, dozens of them.

We went out the back door. Off the porch was a washhouse, the bottom of its door rotted away leaving jagged wooden teeth.

'Looked in there?' I said.

'Yup.'

The door was jammed. Cam opened it with a kick.

It was the cleanest room in the place, just an old concrete laundry sink, a boiler the size of a 400-pound bomb, and grey dust and cobwebs.

I shone the torch on the boiler, tentatively tried the fire door. It opened with a screech, ashes spilling out.

'Course it could be out there somewhere in a wreck,' said Cam. 'Probably is. Boot of some scrap iron.'

I was looking at the boiler's fluepipe. The ceiling collar had come loose, tilted.

'Hold this.' I gave Cam the torch.

The top of the boiler was at shoulder height. I put both hands around the fluepipe just above where it entered the boiler and twisted.

It turned easily.

I lifted.

The fluepipe went up into the roof, its bottom end came out of the boiler.

I pushed it to one side, let it hang from the ceiling, stuck a hand into the hole in the boiler, found something to grip with my fingers, lifted.

The top of the boiler came off.

I dropped it into the sink, put my arm down the boiler, touched something wet, recoiled.

'What?' said Cam.

'Don't know.'

I reached in again, touched the thing.

Plastic, something plastic. Rain had come down the pipe.

I took hold, pulled. It was heavy. I got some of it out. Cam put the torch down, helped pull the rest out.

A heavy-duty garbage bag, grey, closed with a plastic tie.

Cam opened it. I held the torch.

'Sweet Jesus,' said Cam. 'My sweet lord.'

On the way out, down the dark avenue of dead machine bodies, Cam carrying the bag, he said, 'Artie's storin chemicals down the back. Thought I came for em.'

'As in?'

'Amphie cook.'

'That's punishable by law.'

'Law doesn't know. The big man says drop in for a drink. Good day's racin.'

We passed through the gate. Cam put the bag in the boot of the streetslut. I read my notebook by torchlight, found the number.

Cam lounged against his vehicle, looking at me.

A woman answered, no name. I gave her mine. Barry Tregear came on.

'What now?' he said.

'Arranging your promotion,' I said. I gave him the directions. 'The shed on the back boundary,' I said. 'That's where the fun stuff is.'

'Never thought you'd end up my dog.'

'Also there's a bloke chained to a Lada Niva.'

'Cruel and unusual,' said Barry. 'Chained to an old Ford Prefect's bad enough.'

'Help's on the way,' I said to Cam.

I drove to Harry Strang's house in Parkville, got there just after Cam. Lyn Strang let us in, robustly sexy as always, flesh an alluring shade of pink. She left us in the study, standing by the fire. Only the table lamps were on and I could see the flames reflected in the glass doors of the lower bookshelves. Charlie Taub bookshelves, made long before my time.

Harry came in, freshly shaved, hair oiled, brushed, a herringbone sports coat over a fine-checked shirt.

'Jack, Cam,' he said. 'On the little mudeater, Jack?'

'Handsomely,' I said. 'My creditors send their thanks.'

'Pleasure. Element of risk there. Bollie's in order, I reckon.'

Harry was looking at the canvas bag on the floor next to Cam.

'Brought your swag, I see,' he said. 'Always welcome to stay. Plenty of room.'

Cam picked up the bag and put it on the desk. He gestured to me to open it, long fingers, puffy tonight, the knuckles puffy.

I shook my head.

Cam unzipped the bag, opened it.

'Stuff,' he said.

Harry stepped over, looked. He put his hand in and took out a bundle of notes, fifties, put it back, eyes on Cam.

'Ours,' said Cam. 'And the Hales'.'

A smile grew on Harry's face. He looked like a teenager, a naughty teenager, discoverer of sex.

'Well, bugger me,' he said, eyes going back and forth. 'Chance maybe I thought, coupla bright fellas like yerselves.'

He went to the door, opened it, turned back to look at us, left the room.

'Darlin,' we heard him shout, 'forget the Bollie, coupla bottles of the Krug.'

An inaudible response.

'And an emergency one,' shouted Harry. 'No knowin.'

He came back, closed the door. 'Violence,' he said. 'That wouldn't be involved.'

Cam looked at me, looked at Harry, brushed fingers across his lips. 'Not that you'd notice,' he said.

Krug singing in the veins, all fatigue and guilt banished by the tiny silver bubbles, I parked outside the boot factory.

Lights on upstairs. A moment of fright.

Linda's car parked in the shadows. She had a key. As my breath went out, my carefree mood returned.

She was on the sofa, lengthwise, watching television, drinking what was probably Campari and soda.

'This is what it comes to,' she said. 'The little woman at home, washing socks and waiting for the man to come home from drinking pots and pots of beer with the blokes at the pub.'

I took off my coat. 'Did that for a while. Went on to drinking Krug with a sexy woman in a little black dress.'

'You bastard. Come closer.'

I came closer, stood over her.

She put out a hand, ran it over me. 'Just as I thought,' she said. 'You're still excited.'

I leaned down and undid the top button of her shirt. 'No,' I said. 'This is a new excitement. I am capable of several excitements in the same evening.'

'Better damn be,' she said as she pulled me down. 'I've got a newsagent waiting.'

'Butchers are meatier,' I said as I sank.

When the lust was spent, we warmed the duck pies Linda had brought, sent them down with a Mill Hill shiraz. Mid-pie, Linda looked at her watch, found the remote control.

'News, got to have the news,' she said. 'News is my life.'

I said, 'I was taught it was rude to have sex wearing your watch.'

'Not if it's on your wrist.' She blipped through channels, found what she wanted, a dollwoman speaking.

Six people have been found dead at a remote house on the Gippsland lakes. One of them is Susan Ayliss, a member of the panel that decided the multi-million dollar Cannon Ridge ski resort and casino tender.

I saw Dead Point from above. Then the television helicopter went in low. I didn't want to watch.

The item went on for a long time. At the end, dollwoman said: *The Premier has announced a full-scale inquiry into the Cannon Ridge tender process.*

Linda cut the power. She didn't look at me, snuggled down on the sofa, looked at me.

'What would a seedy suburban solicitor know about that?' she said, suspicion in voice and eyes.

'No more than a newsagent. What he hears on the news, reads in the paper.'

She sat up. 'Shit, I forgot. A courier came. It's next to the front door.'

It was a square package, stoutly wrapped, taped like an injured footballer. I took it to the kitchen, performed surgery on it.

An album. An album with a red leather cover. I opened it, paged through it.

Mr Justice Colin Loder was a person of much greater versatility than I'd imagined, a man of wide-ranging interests and exotic tastes. The problem was he didn't photograph well. He had a tendency to slit his eyes.

'What exactly are you doing in there?' said Linda.

'Opening a bottle.'

I closed the album Xavier Doyle had decided he didn't

need, put it in the cupboard with the dud French frying pan that had a hot spot, opened a bottle of Seven Hills.

'I'm not finished with you,' said Linda.

'And nor am I complete.'

I took the bottle and went next door.

'You'll tell me,' she said, athlete's legs on the arm of the sofa, bare. She opened my old dressing gown, revealing more flesh.

'I've taken an oath,' I said. 'You must respect that.'

'Put that down and come here.'

'It's late. I run in the mornings.'

'Come here, sunshine.'

All bad things come to an end. Almost. Now all I had to do was get justice for Enzio and the Meaker's gang. I put this out of my mind for the moment. A long moment, but not long enough.

BAD DEBTS
Peter Temple

WINNER OF THE NED KELLY AWARD FOR CRIME FICTION.
THE CLASSIC FIRST JACK IRISH THRILLER

Melbourne in winter. Rain. Wind. Pubs. Beer. Sex.
Corruption. Murder.

A phone message from ex-client Danny Mckillop doesn't
ring any bells for Jack Irish. Life is hard enough without
having to dredge up old problems: his beloved football
team continues to lose, the odds on his latest plunge at the
track seem far too long and he's still cooking for one.

But then Danny turns up dead and Jack has to take a walk
back into the dark and dangerous past.

'Temple can be as tough as nails, but also displays a
wickedly droll sense of humour which…frequently
has the reader holding his sides with laughter even
while immersed in some particularly unpleasant
scenario.' *Sydney Morning Herald*

'Someone should make a film of Jack Irish.' *Age*

'The genuine article...an absolute pearler of a read.'
Australian Book Review

PAPERBACK, RRP $22.00, ISBN 1 877008 72 9

BLACK TIDE
Peter Temple

Jack Irish has no shortage of friends. Jockeys and journos, lawyers and standover men, people in nameless occupations who aren't in the phonebook. These days, though, the only family he sees are Irish men in faded football team photographs on the pub wall.

So when Des Connors, the last link to his father, calls to ask for help in the matter of a missing son, Jack is happy to lend a hand.

But sometimes prodigal sons go missing for a reason. As Jack begins to dig, he discovers Gary Connors was a man with something to hide.

And his friends are people with darker, more deadly secrets.

'Rips, crackles and snorts with a delicious pace.' *Age*

'Temple's prose is polished and slick, his dialogue spot-on and his sense of place entrenched firmly in contemporary Australia.' *Sun-Herald*

'A must for thrill-seekers.' *Who Weekly*

'Puts Temple at the forefront of contemporary Australian crime fiction.' *Sydney Morning Herald*

PAPERBACK, RRP $22.00, ISBN 1 920885 13 7

WHITE DOG
Peter Temple

WINNER OF PETER TEMPLE'S FOURTH
NED KELLY AWARD FOR CRIME FICTION

Mickey frances was funny and clever, but there was always something dangerous about him. Now he's been shot five times and his old girlfriend has been charged with murder.

Jack irish, lawyer, gambler, cabinetmaker and finder of people who want to stay lost, has to try and save her. He soon realises he has entered a world where evidence can be bought and sold and violent death is a commodity. And just as he's wondering whether to walk away from the whole thing, someone takes the decision out of his hands…

'Peter Temple's fourth Jack Irish thriller is like slipping into deliciously dangerous quicksand—edgy and thrilling…a clever, fast-moving and multi-faceted yarn that demands to be read in one sitting.'
Herald Sun

'Pumps more muscle in one paragraph than lesser writers muster in a page.' *January Magazine*

'One of those rare books I wanted not to end…A haunting, poetic novel that certainly raises the bar for crime fiction in this country.' *West Australian*

PAPERBACK, RRP $22.95, ISBN 1 920885 29 3

AN IRON ROSE
Peter Temple

When Mac Faraday's best friend is found hanging, the assumption is suicide. But Mac is far from convinced, and he's a man who knows not to accept things at face value.

A regular at the local pub, a mainstay of the footy team, mac is living the quiet life of a country blacksmith—a life connected to a place, connected to its people.

But Mac carries a burden of fear and vigilance from his old life. And as this past of secrets, corruption, abuse and murder begins to close in, he must turn to long-forgotten resources to hang on to everything he holds dear. Including his own life.

'Fast, funny and assured.' *Australian Book Review*

'The coolest and most elegant of Australian crime writers.' *Age*

'A must for thriller seekers' *Who Weekly*

PAPERBACK, RRP $23.00, ISBN 1 920885 50 1

THE BROKEN SHORE
Peter Temple

Before Rai Sarris, Cashin was different. He moved more quickly then, he was less thoughtful, less easily spooked. But there are consequences when you've come that close to dying. For Cashin, they include a posting away from the world of murderers, of Homicide, to the quiet place on the coast where he grew up. Here all he has to do is play the country cop and walk the dogs. And sometimes think about how he was before Sarris.

Then rich Charles Bourgoyne, the local benefactor, is bashed and everything seems to point to three boys from the nearby Aboriginal community. Cashin is unconvinced and as tragedy unfolds relentlessly into tragedy, he finds himself holding onto something that might be better let go.

'Calling Temple a crime writer only reveals part of the truth...Every word in *The Broken Shore* contains meaning. It's all killer, no filler.' *Courier-Mail*

'Might well be the best crime novel published in this country.' *Australian*

'If you only read one crime novel this year, read *The Broken Shore*...This book is the best yet from a writer who has already won a well-deserved reputation as one of our finest crime writers.' *Age*

PAPERBACK, RRP $29.95, ISBN 1 920885 77 3